BAD BLOOD

ACID VANILLA BOOK 8

MATTHEW HATTERSLEY

BOOM BOOM PRESS

GET YOUR FREE BOOK

Discover how Acid Vanilla transformed from a typical London teenager into the world's deadliest female assassin.

Get the Acid Vanilla Prequel Novel:
Making a Killer available FREE at:

www.matthewhattersley.com/mak

CHAPTER 1

Perched atop one of Rome's seven ancient hills, the Parco Savello is an ancient sight of beauty and grandeur. Known by locals as the Orange Garden, it is home to a plethora of fragrant bitter orange trees that fill the air with the smell of ripe citrus during spring. Constructed in 1932 by architect Raffaele De Vico, the public park offers breathtaking views across the city. Below lies St Peter's dome; on either side, the domes, basilicas and pinnacles of San Carlo alle Quattro Fontane and Santa Maria degli Angeli e dei Martiri. The area is said to have been favoured by Roman aristocrats who had their mansions built here so they could watch over the city, though now it is enjoyed by visitors from all over the world. Flowers and fountains criss-cross like a spider's web across lawns dotted with sculptures and benches for relaxed contemplation. Steep terraces lined with cypress trees slope down from the hilltop to meet intertwining paths. Legend has it that Saint Dominic himself planted the first orange tree here in the thirteenth century, and his tree, now eight hundred years old and bearing fruit to this day, stands humbly on the grounds of Saint Sabina Basilica.

The pinnacle of the garden, however, is the ornately designed viewing terrace located at the very top of the hillside. Flanked by rows of the most impressive orange and pine trees, the symmetrical terrace looks out over the expansive cityscape and offers picture-perfect views of the Eternal City. If you are lucky enough to be standing at the end of the terrace at sunset, you will see the sky turn a magnificent burnt-orange colour. Surrounded by such natural beauty and with the spires and domes of Rome at your feet, it's hard not to feel like a king. Or, indeed, an emperor.

A man stood alone on the stone border that ran around the edge of the terrace, gazing out on the city beneath him and embracing his new world. With eyes closed, he rocked back onto his heels and took a deep breath, filling his lungs with the warm late-April air. He felt good. He felt powerful. A passing onlooker might have described the man as thin and of average height, but this estimation would not take into account the layers of sinewy muscle and single-digit body fat underneath his clothes. Many months of a strict gym regime, along with a fastidiously followed plant-based diet, had made him lean and strong, lithe and athletic – ready for whatever his new life might throw at him. He was wearing black jeans that hugged his thighs and gripped at his ankles above his Cuban-heeled Chelsea boots. The boots had been recently commissioned from a local artisan shoemaker and were made of the best Tuscan leather money could buy. Despite the warm evening, he wore a long black overcoat with the collar raised, casting a shadow over his strong jawline, fine nose and dark, intense eyes.

He dropped his arms and allowed himself a solitary moment to appreciate all he had achieved over the last month. He was now not only physically standing on the precipice of greatness, but also metaphorically. Soon the last pieces of his operation would be put into place and his goal would be complete. It felt good. It felt right. He did this. All of it.

Because the Orange Gardens and the terrace were located within a gated complex closed to the public after dusk, the man was the only person there at this time of day. The old groundskeeper had let him in and, as long as he kept his mouth shut about what happened here tonight, he would be safe from harm and remunerated for his troubles. He was another pawn, bought and paid for and ready to look the other way when the guest of honour arrived shortly. The man knew there would be many others over the years who would look the other way. There would be even more who'd be paid for their silence and for what they could offer him. He flicked out his arm to reveal his new Bulgari Octo timepiece. He'd bought the watch just last week after the final payment from his first big assignment had landed in his Cayman Islands bank account. Seeing it was already a few minutes after seven and time to meet his guest, he tore himself away from the view and stepped down onto the terrace.

The area in front of him, a delightful expanse of rich green space, was arguably one of the most romantic settings the already romantic city of Rome had to offer. Suitors looking for a suitable location to propose to their loved ones placed the Orange Gardens high on their list of places to pop the question. Tonight, however, these glorious gardens would be the setting for a different kind of proposal. And a different kind of union.

The man allowed a smile to spread across his face as he saw a stout figure ambling down the central avenue towards him. He had come alone, as instructed, and as he got closer he squinted up at him, illuminated in the orange glow from the last sliver of the day's sun before it disappeared below the horizon. He was a rotund man, who appeared uncomfortable in his own body. His dyed black hair was plastered back with pomade, but failed to cover entirely a tanned cranium that was almost a perfect half-sphere. A thick black moustache that was possibly the result of more dye hung down over his thin lips and danced as he spoke.

"*Ciao, Signor Duke.*" His eyes flitted up and down the taller man's frame. "So... I am here."

Darius Duke raised his head. "You're also late, Mr Bosco."

The smaller man's arm flinched, but he resisted looking down at his watch. "By only a few minutes. It is quite a walk up here from the gates."

"But a beautiful spot, all the same." Darius threw his arms wide, gazing around him at the impressive vista. "Don't you agree?"

Bosco sniffed. "Of course. But I know you didn't invite me up here to discuss the scenery."

"No. You are correct." Darius smirked and wagged a finger at Bosco. "I like a man who wants to get straight down to business. No point in all that boring foreplay, is there? Let's jump into the good stuff."

Bosco didn't laugh, but he didn't look away or blink either. The fact that someone with such high-level security clearance at the Agenzia Informazioni e Sicurezza Esterna – Italy's foreign intelligence service – was so guarded in his presence, pleased Darius Duke a great deal. His reputation for being a ruthless and savvy operator was growing stronger all the time.

"I spoke to... umm... the relevant parties, like you asked me to," Bosco continued. "They have concerns about working with unknown contractors, but I was able to convince them your organisation was legitimate and that we should utilise your services. It will have to be on a trial basis at first. I hope this is acceptable and that—"

"Wonderful news," Darius cut in. "I knew you could do it. It just goes to show you, my friend, anything is possible with the right leverage and persuasion." He tilted his neck to one side. He had a tight muscle in his left shoulder that had been bothering him for the past few days. "Don't look so worried, Bosco. I'll make the call as soon as we're finished here. Your daughter will be transported safely back to your home within the hour."

The relief on the older man's face was palpable. "Thank you, Mr Duke." But a dark shadow quickly replaced the reprieve, tightening the man's jaw. Darius knew Bosco despised him, but that wasn't too much of a concern. As long as he feared and respected him more than he hated him, their arrangement would work.

He rolled his shoulders back. "Please, call me Darius. We should start off on friendly terms, don't you think, *Andreas*? Now, I believe you have something else for me?"

Andreas Bosco swallowed and it looked like it hurt him. He was, perhaps, wondering if he really should part company with the document he was carrying in the inside pocket of his jacket. But what else could he do? In persuading both his team and his superiors that it would be in their best interests to work with Darius Duke, he'd put his job and his reputation on the line.

"Here you go," he said, glancing around him as he removed the paper file from his coat and handed it to his new ally. "Piero Manzo. An ex-government agent who has gone rogue. We need him brought down before he shares what he knows with our enemies. He was last sighted in Slovenia and we believe he's working his way up to Russia."

Darius narrowed his eyes as he opened the file and scanned the document. There was a photo of Manzo in there. He was notable for having the same thick dark hair as Darius. Manzo even wore it in the same style, long and swept back in a slight pompadour. "He's a good-looking chap, isn't he?" he said, flashing his eyes at Bosco. "But if he's been a naughty boy, then rest assured we'll get him for you. The price will be an even fifty-K for starters. Half to be paid now and the other half once we provide evidence the hit was successful. That's how it will work going forward, although once this trial period is over and we've proven ourselves, the fee will rise. *Capito?*"

Bosco gave a curt nod. "It needs to be done quickly before he can make contact with—"

"Yes, yes." He shut up as Darius waved his hand in his face. "I've got one of my best men already on his way through Eastern Europe in hot pursuit. If he's not onto him yet, he will be by midnight tonight. Once I give the word, Mr Manzo will rue the day he ever got saucy with your secrets. So, consider it done. Tonight, or tomorrow. You have my word." He widened his eyes at Bosco, conveying to him that this wasn't a flippant statement. His word was his bond, and if he said the work would be completed, it would be. Respect and fear. That's how you ran an organisation like the one he was building.

"Thank you, Mr Duke. One moment, please." Bosco took a phone out of his pocket and dialled a number. Not taking his eyes off Darius, he spoke briefly in Italian to whoever was on the other end. Darius picked out the words *invia pagamento* – send payment. He hung up and sighed. "The money will be with you soon."

"Then we have a deal. Wonderful." Darius puffed out his chest and rose to his full height. At five feet ten and a quarter, he wasn't the tallest of men, but he made up for any lost inches in bravado and ego. Plus, in his Cuban heels he towered over the stocky Bosco. As he stretched, he noticed a shadowy figure hanging back behind a row of orange trees on the far side of the terrace. He recognised them immediately as Stig Saga, the svelte but deadly assassin from Sweden who was fast becoming his number two at the agency. Darius gave him a nod of recognition before turning back to Bosco and slapping him playfully on the upper arm.

"Okay, my friend. That's it for now. You should leave."

"But I... What will I say..." he spluttered, before Darius leaned down and fixed him with a hard stare.

"I've told you. The work will be carried out and your daughter is safe. You and I do not need to speak any more on these matters. I thank you for your discretion and look forward to working with the Italian secret service going forward. In the future, it will be one of my associates that you will deal with." He turned from Bosco and peered out across the landscape. Rome. It certainly was an inspiring and remarkable city. The perfect place to start what he hoped (no, what he knew) would be the greatest and most untouchable assassin organisation the world had ever known. If, indeed, the world was ever privy to such organisations. Which it wasn't and would never be. But those in the know – shadowy government departments, South American cartels, leaders of industry and technology, even kings and queens – would soon know his name and that of his organisation, *Kancel Kulture*.

Darius had come up with the name a few months earlier, but had initially believed it to be too silly or blasé for what he was trying to create. Yet, as he'd mulled it over, the name had grown on him and today he could not think of a better moniker for his deadly network of hand-selected assassins. The name was modern and dynamic and provided them with the perfect online cover – a web forum that promoted free speech, anti-censorship, and innovative thought. The fact that on the surface the website was being utilised primarily by puss-mottled young men who spent their days raging at a woke world they saw as unfair and unjust, was delightful in its irony. The site had drawn some unwelcome attention at first, but nothing he couldn't handle and now a robust algorithm ensured any incendiary or defamatory posts were immediately deleted. Anyone viewing the public-facing side of the website would quickly dismiss it as a mere playground for the pathetic and wilfully ostracised. Once they made that judgement, they wouldn't again look too deeply. Yet those people with special logins – such as Andreas Bosco and his associates – were able to access an encrypted part of the forum, where they could post jobs and ask for help in the 'cancelling' of those who had become more than just a nuisance.

Speaking of Bosco, why the hell was he still here?

Darius let out a long sigh full of bristly subtext as he waited for the older man to get the message. Finally, Bosco mumbled something under his breath in Italian and scurried away into the night, the leather soles of his shoes slapping against the stone terrace as he exited the area. A moment later, steadier, stealthier footsteps could be heard prowling down the avenue. Darius didn't turn from the view as he sensed the new presence beside him.

"I trust everything is good?" he asked, raising his chin.

"Indeed. Everything all going to plan," Stig Saga replied, in his deep Scandinavian accent.

"Excellent. And how are the new headquarters coming along? Do we have the lease?"

When Saga didn't reply, he turned to look at him. The Swede's ice-blond hair was cut short and gelled forward, creating a perfectly straight line above his equally striking white brows and eyelashes. If not for his pale blue eyes, he could be mistaken for an albino.

Saga had worked as an off-the-books assassin for SÄPO, the Swedish secret service, for the past ten years, but recent events – the death of his former mentor, his dislike of the way the Swedish government were running things – meant he was already looking around for something new when Darius approached him. Saga had seized the opportunity to join his new organisation with both hands and was already proving to be a worthy asset. He was fierce and deadly at work but reserved and humble at other times. He was also incredibly loyal – a vital trait that Darius required in all his operatives.

"What is it, my friend?" Darius asked. "Is there a problem?"

"Not a problem. Just a slight setback. It seems the owner of the building in San Giovanni that we hoped to purchase is now dragging his heels. But don't worry, I will persuade him that we are the buyers he should sell to."

Darius grinned. Another trait he enjoyed about the Swedish assassin was his creativity and the often bizarre ways he took out his prey if given free rein. Darius knew most of their future clients would want a mark taken out a certain way – their deaths to appear the result of an accident or a suicide – but when no specific death was requested or, better still, they wanted to send someone a message, then the Swede's 'blue-sky killing' would be something to behold. Like the time he took out a German gunrunner by reversing into him in a Maserati with an open passenger door, at the last minute spinning the car around and having the door flip the helpless mark into the path of an oncoming tram. These were the sort of hits that got you noticed and meant your organisation was talked about amongst those that mattered. Soon Kancel Kulture would be the only murder-for-hire company anyone would ever need.

"We need that building," Darius added. "I want us to be set up and ready for action within the next month."

"I understand. I'm on it."

"Is there anything else?"

Stig Saga cleared his throat. "There was a call before. On the secure line. *The* call. The one you told me to inform you of as soon as it came through."

Darius jerked his head up as a shiver of excitement ran down his back. "The head scientist?"

"Yes. He apologised profusely for the delay, but he has

amassed each of the separate DNA analyses and has the results."

Darius stiffened. "And? Is she...?"

"He said you should call him back right away. He said he only wanted to speak to you about it."

"Fair enough." It was an anti-climax, but expected.

"What do you want to do?" Saga asked.

"What do I want to do, Saga?" Darius repeated, bellowing the words into the night sky. "I want to get back to the house! Pronto! I need to find out whether I've got a sister or not."

CHAPTER 2

Spook tensed as Acid Vanilla dabbed at her bottom lip with the base of her thumb. She'd caught her with a lucky blow, but it felt good. As Acid lowered her hand, she saw the blood and raised her eyebrows at Spook as if to say *Good job*.

"Are you okay?" she asked, still with her fists raised, still bouncing from foot to foot.

"Yeah. I think so. I don't know," Acid replied. She lowered her hands and straightened her stance. "I feel a bit woozy all of a sudden."

"Ah, shit, really?"

Spook dropped her guard and went towards her. As soon as she did, Acid stepped around the side of her and grabbed her wrist. In the same motion, she twisted it around Spook's back and pushed it up between her shoulder blades. As Spook yelled in pain, Acid shoved her forward, growling in her ear.

"Come on, kid, you should be wise to this by now. What

do I always say? Trust no one. When you're in fight mode you stay in fight mode until you're the last person standing. Every time. No matter what."

"Get off me," Spook hissed. "That was uncool. That was sly."

"Yes and that's how most people are," Acid bit back, grinding Spook's arm against the joint before releasing it. "Especially people who want to kill you. They don't play fair. Neither should you."

Spook spun around, shaking her arm as Acid stepped back. "Piss off. This was supposed to be a sparring session. You were supposed to be showing me some moves, not trying to break my damn spirit." She glared at Acid, the skin across her chest and neck burning. She wasn't playing fair. But then, why was Spook surprised? Acid had been trying to toughen her up since the day they met. It seemed at every opportunity she would say something cynical and upsetting, designed to unsettle Spook and make her appreciate the extent of evil in the world.

Well, if that was her goal, she'd achieved her aim. Spook was there now. She got it.

Boy, did she get it.

"Can we stop now, please?" She let her head drop along with her shoulders. "I don't feel like it right now."

"We've barely started," Acid replied. "Come on, you'll never learn if we don't keep going." She stepped towards Spook with her hands out, a supercilious smile twitching the corners of her mouth.

"Yeah, but I'm tired," Spook told her, leaning her weight onto the balls of her feet. "But maybe you should... I don't know... practice what you preach." Hunkering down, Spook launched herself at Acid, grabbing her around the middle and forcing her backwards. She slammed her against the wall with a dull thud, sandwiching her between the plasterboard and the sharp bone of Spook's shoulder.

"Shit!" Acid gasped, as Spook leapt back and into a fighting stance, ready for what came next.

Acid recovered from the attack quickly. Pushing off from the wall, she ran at Spook, rising up at the last second and driving a knee into her stomach. Spook cried out as she lost all sense of who or where she was. Gasping for air, she staggered over to the side of the room before an open-handed blow to the face snapped her back to the present moment.

"Fuck you!" Spook snarled. "What the hell!" But she was more irate than injured. She lunged at Acid, her fingers hooked into claws. Acid blocked her attack and shoved her away.

"Calm yourself, kid. You're going to get hurt if you come at me like that."

"Try me."

Spook spun around, driven by rage for a change, rather than reason. Her muscles throbbed with effort and her jaw ached where she'd been grinding her teeth. It was a novel way of being for the usually self-conscious and meek American. But there was nothing like almost getting your throat sliced open to shift your mindset.

"You're a pain in the ass," she yelled, swinging her fist at Acid's head. "Do you know that?"

"Yeah?" Acid retorted, slapping her hands away. "Why don't you do something about it?"

Spook swung wildly but her attacks were evaded or

blocked each time. She was certainly angry these days, angrier than she'd ever felt. But anger didn't make you a good fighter. "All right, stop!" she called out. "Time out." She walked over to the other side of the room to prove she meant it.

"Had enough?"

I've had enough of you, Spook thought. But she didn't say that. Instead, she grabbed her towel from the chair in the corner of the room and wiped the sweat from her face.

"I thought you were going to teach me some attack moves," she muttered, before chucking the towel onto the chair and turning around. Acid was standing with her hands on her hips, her chest rising and falling heavily. She had that same maddening smirk on her face she always had.

"You need to learn to defend yourself first," she said.

"I know how to defend myself."

"Do you?"

"Yes. I think I do."

For a long time it had been Acid leading the charge, pushing Spook to train with her. But then Darius Duke had pressed the cold blade of a knife against her throat and something inside of her had changed. It had been a profound moment for Spook, and in the subsequent weeks it had dawned on her that she could no longer shy away from violence the way she had been doing. Darius Duke was still out there somewhere and he wasn't going to leave them be. When he returned, she had to be ready.

So now it was her pushing Acid for more training. She wanted to learn how to fight. She was sick and tired of feeling scared and timid all the time.

"Getting too cocky and taking on someone when you

aren't ready is a sure-fire way of getting hurt," Acid told her. "I should know, kid. I was that over-confident young girl once."

"But I'm not a young girl, am I? I'm not a *kid*. I'm a grown woman and I've spent too long with my head in the sand. I have to face up to the facts. That, through no fault of my own, I now inhabit a world of killers. I have to be able to look after myself in that world. If Darius Duke or another of his cronies comes after us, I want to be able to not only defend myself but be the aggressor."

Acid frowned. "What are you saying?"

"I want you to teach me how to kill. From short range to long range. With weapons or just my body. Whatever it takes and however you know. I want to feel safe. I want to feel strong."

Acid shook her head. "No, Spook. You're not a killer. Stick to what you're good at. Leave the blood and guts to me. We're a good team."

"Are we? Since when?"

Acid glared at her then dropped her gaze, scoffing as she did. "You're a nightmare, do you know that?"

"*I'm* the nightmare?" Spook leaned back and folded her arms across her chest.

"Whatever. I'm not training you to kill. You'd end up killing yourself, more than likely." She sneered at her own joke. It made Spook want to grab the chair and fling it across the room at her.

She knew Acid had a lot on her mind and for the last few days had been in a darker mood than usual, but it wasn't fair to only take her so far. Self-defence was all very well, but Spook could learn self-defence at the local youth centre. In that cold warehouse, as she watched The Dullahan bleeding out in front of her, she'd had a kind of epiphany moment. She realised the only way she was going to survive in this world was to fight fire with fire. An insight like that fundamentally changes a person. When you see something like that, you can't unsee it.

And Acid was wrong. Spook had killed. And she was prepared to do it again.

What had begun in London with Banjo Shawshank, and then on that terrible island when she'd pulled the trigger and blasted Raaz Terabyte to hell, had been filtered through the last few years of people trying to kill them and led Spook to this moment. She was now prepared to kill to protect herself. But she needed more training. She needed confidence in her abilities. After taking out Banjo from across the other side of the heliport, she'd bragged to Acid it was her years playing online shooting games that had helped train her eye. But she knew even then that her words were the result of nothing but bravado buoyed by adrenaline. The truth was, both of the times she'd administered fatal shots had been total flukes. She'd even screwed her eyes up as she'd pulled the trigger to kill Raaz. Even if by some miracle she'd been born an innate crack shot, she still had limited real-world experience of shooting a gun. She wanted to improve her aim.

She *had* to improve her aim.

But whenever she brought this up with Acid, she got the same response. That typical eye-rolling dismissal. Her telling Spook it's she who's the killer. That Spook should stick to her own wheelhouse.

"I need to know how to protect myself," she muttered, walking over to Acid. "You wanted to train me before. What's changed?"

Acid saw her coming and met her in the middle of the room. "Everything. Okay? Everything has changed." They stood face to face and glared at each other. Neither one of them blinked. After ten, twenty seconds, it became clear to Spook this had become some kind of staring contest. A battle of wills. Well, fine. Bring it on.

"I know you're hurting. I know you've got a lot on your mind," she said, keeping her voice low despite the adrenaline in her system urging it to rise a couple of octaves. "But you need to understand, Acid, I've been through what you've been through. And I'm still here. I still want to help you. I want to help us. But to do that I need to know how to react to danger. I'm ready now. You keep saying I'm not ready, but I am."

"You're not." Acid's face was hard and unflinching. Spook noticed the pain in her brittle features that was always there. Yet there was something else, too, in those intense eyes of hers. One blue. One brown. Was it... disgust? Hatred, even? Spook knew they hadn't been getting on well for some time, but is this where they were now? The thought had her relax her shoulders a touch. She blinked. Looked away.

"I don't get what your problem is," she mumbled to the floor. "You want to teach me to defend myself – it's not a big leap from there to show me how to attack, to take someone down who I see as a threat."

Acid blew out a long, deliberate sigh. When Spook raised her head, she saw Acid hadn't moved. She was still staring at her. "It's very different," she whispered. "When you step into that world you change who you are. That's not you, Spook. That world is dark and evil and full of monsters. It's too dangerous. When I was training you before, you were pulling the other way. That was good. The fact that you now want to be some sort of killing machine worries me. It worries me a lot."

Spook snorted. "Killing machine? That's not what I said. All I want is to be trained in how to attack someone if needed. To make sure that if they're hell-bent on killing me, I can stop them. For good. All I want is to—"

"No, Spook!" Acid yelled. "You leave me to do the dirty work. That's how it works. That's how we work."

"How *we* work? We don't fucking work! Not anymore!"

Acid's eyes widened. Spook tensed. Maybe she'd taken it too far saying that, but she was only articulating what they were both thinking. Up to this point, their partnership had been based on a shared desire to survive. But if Acid wasn't going to help her do this, what was the point of staying together? They weren't friends. Not really. Spook couldn't remember the last time they'd had a laugh together or even shared a light moment.

"Fine," Acid said, jutting out her chin. "I agree. So let's stop this nonsense. After we get through today, we'll talk about what we do with the apartment. And our future."

Spook opened her mouth but couldn't get any words past the knot in her throat. All she could do was nod and splutter and try to remain cool. Not easy with those intense eyes boring into her. She understood that Acid was more troubled than usual right now. Not only had her old friend been brutally murdered in front of her, but she'd also found out the killer might also be her half-brother. A half-brother who had been prepared to kill Spook and Acid herself. Spook had a lot she wanted to talk to her about on these matters: how she was feeling about her discovery; whether she believed she and Darius Duke really were related. But she'd been waiting until their own relationship was on more stable ground.

Yeah, right.

It didn't appear like their relationship was ever getting back on stable ground.

None of this gave Acid free rein to be such a bitch, though. Spook had been on the receiving end of her cold shoulder and icy stare many times over the years, but she knew now that Acid being that way said more about her than it did Spook.

Spook might have been sick and tired of feeling scared and timid. But she was sick and tired of being made to feel like a foolish child, too.

She sniffed and raised her head, meeting Acid's stare. "Okay," she said. "If that's what you want, that's fine with me. I can't do this anymore."

The tiny muscles at the side of Acid's jaw pulsed. For a moment Spook thought she was going to strike her, but she didn't move. They remained facing each other, neither one wanting to give any ground. Five years of death, pain and anguish fizzed in the air between them. Finally, Acid shook her head.

"Whatever," she said on an out breath. "I need a shower. And then we need to get ready. Our flight is in two hours." With that, she flicked her hair over her shoulder and barged past Spook on her way to the door.

Ever the petulant teenager.

Spook turned to watch her go. At the door Acid stopped and looked to one side, as if she was about to say something else. But she must have thought better of it. She shook her head again, then disappeared into the hallway beyond.

"Selfish bitch," Spook whispered to herself under her breath. "But you do you, Acid Vanilla, and I'll do me. I don't know why I ever thought you could change." She grabbed her towel and headed for her room.

CHAPTER 3

Manchester's Southern Cemetery is a sprawling expanse of grass and marble, spread out over one hundred and twenty acres and bordering the infamous Moss Side region of the city. The graves date back to the 1600s and include masons, royalists, local gangsters and non-conformist ministers. Sir Matt Busby, the legendary Manchester United manager, is buried there, as is the artist L.S. Lowry and the sculptor John Cassidy. And today, the cemetery was the setting for the burial of another legend. Although this person's fame – or, rather, infamy – would never be known to the general public.

Acid adjusted her footing on the wet grass, not looking up as the priest finished off the ceremony. A handful of dirt was scattered over the top of the dark mahogany coffin as it was lowered into the grave. She lifted her hand to wipe at her eyes, not removing her Ray Ban Aviator sunglasses as she did.

"So long, old friend," she whispered at the box. "I'm sorry. For everything."

It was silly, talking this way. Especially as The Dullahan's remains weren't even in the coffin. It had been four weeks since Darius Duke had lured her to that warehouse and executed The Dullahan in front of her. In the subsequent weeks, a clean-up crew had arrived and taken the body to an underground facility where they'd disposed of it respectfully and quietly. The funeral today was to appease the authorities and to avoid any awkward questions from his nephew Danny and any other next of kin. The ornate wooden coffin currently being laid to rest would have been weighted with bags of sand or a John Doe of similar stature that one of The Dullahan's acquaintances had 'acquired' from the local morgue. It was the way they did things in the industry. But whilst The Dullahan had no physical body here, his presence still loomed large over Acid.

Four weeks.

She could still see the scene playing out in front of her like it was happening today. She recalled the old man's face right before it happened. He'd had such a resigned expression. He'd known what was coming. He'd maybe even accepted his fate.

But that didn't make it any easier.

The Dullahan had once been Acid's rival. An adversary. The first time they'd met was a vicious and bloody affair – she still had the scar to prove it – but it left them both with a healthy respect for one another. When The Dullahan had retired, it was he who'd helped Acid track down her ex-colleagues and finally Caesar, her old mentor. Disclosing the whereabouts of operatives wasn't the done thing in this industry, especially when you suspected their lives were at risk, but The Dullahan had understood why Acid needed her revenge. He understood her. He was maybe one of the only people who ever did. He was certainly one of the only people she could truly trust. And now he was dead. Another casualty of the chaos that came with being close to Acid Vanilla.

She lifted her head as the priest finished off the ceremony, intoning those immortal words. Ones she knew so well, despite this being her first proper funeral.

"...earth to earth, ashes to ashes, dust to dust: in sure and certain hope of the resurrection to eternal life. Through our Lord Jesus Christ..."

She couldn't help but sneer at the sentiment. It was a nice idea. But not one she shared. Over the years she'd looked many people in the eyes as the life faded from them. They never looked at peace. They never looked as if they were going to a better place. But maybe that was just those particular people. It was also up for debate whether or not any of the people she'd killed had a soul to begin with.

Across the other side of the grave, Danny was looking at her. He smiled and she allowed him the measliest of grins in reply. He looked good, tanned. His hair was tied back in a tight ponytail and his blue eyes sparkled in the late afternoon sun. She remembered the last time they'd spoken, how he'd professed his love for her and asked her to be with him. It felt like a lifetime ago now. Would she have been happy in that life? She didn't think so. But that didn't mean she was happy with the one she'd chosen.

Bloody buggering shit.

Why was life so pissing complicated?

There had been a time – long ago now – when it felt as if she had everything sussed out. She was young, fiery, motivated. She had more money than she could spend and a career that, albeit unconventional, was one she'd made peace

24

with and found rewarding. She killed people, but they were bad people. People who didn't deserve to carry on living. In any one year she'd rid the world of devilish drug dealers, human traffickers, mad despots hell-bent on wiping out their own people. In general, evil-doers and total utter bastards. She'd loved her life. She'd found her calling.

So why the hell did she screw it all up?

In that one moment atop the Eiffel Tower when she'd chosen to spare Spook Horowitz's life, her entire world had shifted on its axis. She glanced at Spook now, who was standing beside her. She didn't want to blame her, and she didn't, not really. But when things were as strained between them as they had been, she couldn't help but wonder – what if? Her life would be very different now if the two of them had never met.

Acid pushed her sunglasses up her nose and tightened her pout. All around her were the good, the bad and the ugly of the assassin world. In situations such as this – funerals, weddings, parties (mostly funerals) – the deal was that any rivalries were put aside for a twenty-four-hour period and no hits were to take place. But that didn't stop Acid from feeling somewhat wary surrounded by so many thugs and killers. A lot of them she recognised, and she could tell by the way they returned her glances they knew who she was also. The crazy woman who went rogue and wiped out her entire organisation.

She'd found herself thinking about Caesar a lot lately. She wished she could talk to him, ask his advice. He'd meant so much to her, too. Given her so much. Regardless of what had transpired between the two of them, she missed the cocky old bastard. What would he tell her to do regarding

Darius Duke? She closed her eyes, hearing her old mentor's voice bellowing in her head.

Screw that pathetic rubber-legged cock-scoffer. Brother or not, he needs to be eradicated. After what he put you through, you should chop his pissing head off, sweetie. There's no such thing as blood relatives in this world. You don't need family. I'm your family.

And he was. He had been. Why had she only realised that when it was too late? Yes, things had got ugly between them, and Caesar had done something terrible in retaliation, but she didn't blame him for that. She knew the life she'd taken on. All was fair in love, war, and the killing business.

Except it wasn't fair. Was it? Caesar was dead and now The Dullahan, too. Both her mentors, both her father figures, gone. She was alone in the world.

"Acid? What do we do now?" Spook's voice, accompanied by a gentle nudge on the arm, brought her out of her thoughts. She looked around to see the crowd of mourners was now dispersing and splintering off into smaller groups.

"I've no idea," she replied. "There's a wake at his local pub, I think."

Spook sniffed. "Right. Yeah, I know what Irish wakes are like. A lot of drinking is going to take place. I take it you want to go?"

Acid curled her lip. "I'm not sure I feel like it." Which was true. She wanted a drink, of course she did, but she'd rather get back to London and hole up in her room with a bottle of something strong than have to make small talk with any of these miscreants.

"Fine with me," Spook said. "I'm going to go find a

restroom and take a pee and I'll see you by the cemetery gates."

Acid nodded and turned back to The Dullahan's grave. As she did, she noticed a man standing beneath the low branches of a large oak tree across the other side of the graveyard. He was tall and broad-shouldered, and had a shaven head with a line spiralling around the crown that was either the result of a hip barber or was scar tissue where the hair no longer grew. Judging from his overall demeanour, Acid deduced it was the latter. He was wearing an ill-fitting grey suit with a black shirt and black tie. If he was part of the funeral party it would make sense, but she'd never seen him before and the way he was staring at her – not looking away even when she raised her sunglasses to meet his gaze – concerned her.

She was wondering if she should march over there and confront him when she felt a hand on her shoulder. She had her fists up, ready for an attack as she spun around.

"Whoa there, hotshot," Danny gasped, stepping back and holding his palms up in defence. "It's only me."

Acid dropped her hands. "Sorry," she said, shaking her head. "I'm a bit jumpy at the moment."

"Aye. I can see." Danny leaned back some more and squinted as he looked her up and down, trying to get a read on her, perhaps. She stiffened her mouth back into a sharp pout.

"What do you want, Danny?"

"Oh, and it's grand to see you as well. Feck me. We're at my uncle's funeral, my last living relative. I've just flown over here from Dublin. I thought I might be owed a little compassion?"

"I don't owe you anything." She glanced past him over to the oak tree. The man hadn't moved. Not a muscle. He was like a statue and still staring right at her. It didn't make her feel any less uneasy.

"All right, bad choice of words. But come on..." He tapped her arm with the back of his fist. "You can't blame a guy for saying hello. It's good to see ya again. Even if it is in these shitty circumstances."

Acid nodded. "I'm sorry about your uncle."

"I'm sorry about your friend."

"So you're still living back in Ireland?" she asked.

"Aye."

"Still in the antiques business?"

"That's right." He frowned and leaned forward, lowering his voice as he spoke again. "I heard you were with the old fella. When he was... when it happened."

"Who told you that? What did they say?"

Danny held his hands up again. "Hey, don't shoot the messenger. I just overheard from some guy earlier that it was you who was with him. I've no idea of the details and I don't want them. You and Uncle Jimmy did things I still can't get my head around, and I certainly don't want to get involved in another dangerous adventure with ya. All I want to know is... can ya... will ya make it right?"

Acid remained still. She knew what he meant but didn't want to react. Mainly because she didn't know how to. In the hours following The Dullahan's demise, she'd been baying for Darius Duke's blood. Revenge had been all she could think about. Yet as the weeks had gone on, her desire for retribution had faded, to be replaced by more troubling and complicated emotions. The bats didn't help. Nor did the emails...

No!

Stop that!

She shook the thoughts away and rolled her shoulders back. Today was about remembering her old friend. That was all.

"Acid?" Danny cowered down to try to make eye contact with her. Not easy through her Ray-Bans. "I'm asking you outright. Will you go after whoever did this and make them pay? Will you avenge my uncle's death?"

She tilted her head back. Out of the corner of her eye she could see the shaven-headed man over by the trees. He was still staring at her. "Is that what you want?"

"Of course it's what I fecking well want."

"Your uncle understood the world he was a part of."

"Jesus. That's pretty cold, even from you. So is that a no?"

Acid chewed on the inside of her cheek as she considered the question. Danny was right, she was being cold, but that's how she had to be. It was how she survived. People like Danny and Spook viewed her as flippant and cynical, and maybe there was some truth in that estimation, yet for her it was more about self-preservation. Being cold was the only way you stayed sane in this world. The Dullahan knew that. Caesar, too.

"I'll see what I can do," she said. "But I've no idea where your uncle's killer is. He could be anywhere."

"But you'll try?"

She looked away. "I said I'll see what I can do."

"Great. Thank you." He tapped her on the arm again. He

was starting to piss her off. "You going to come for a drink? Say goodbye properly."

"Ah, I don't think so. I—"

"What? No? Come on. One drink. We need to pour out a shot for Uncle Jimmy."

She looked at the man under the tree. Then back to Danny. "Fine. One drink."

"Lovely. I've got a car waiting. Come on." He placed his arm around her shoulders and gave her a squeeze. Normally she'd have shrugged him off, but she let it go. Danny wasn't a bad guy, and him being a six-foot-two ex-boxer wasn't a bad thing either. She could still sense the shaven-headed man watching her as they walked up the path to the main gate. The bats were nibbling at her nerve endings. They told her he wasn't here to say goodbye to The Dullahan. They told her he was trouble.

CHAPTER 4

Danny insisted Acid and Spook travel with him in one of the black funeral cars to The Dullahan's wake. Acid hadn't wanted to accept, but before she could tell him thanks but no thanks, Spook had jumped in the car, grumbling to her that if they were now attending the wake she'd rather travel there in comfort. For the journey, Acid kept her sunglasses on and peered out the window in silence. Probably the other people in the car thought her to be in quiet reflection over the loss of her friend – and this was true, in part – but she had a lot of other things on her mind also.

The shaven-headed man hadn't taken his eyes off her as she'd walked through the graveyard. She knew this because she'd turned back at intervals to check he was still there and had even waved at him at one point. He hadn't responded. He'd just kept on staring. His stillness was disconcerting. As was his size. But screw him. There was still the possibility he was someone on the fringes of the industry she was unaware of and simply there to pay his respects. If so, he needed to have a word with himself in terms of how much he was gawking at her, but some men were like that.

The wake was being held in The Green Devil, the Irish pub in Levenshulme, around the corner from where The Dullahan had set up home with his wife, Sheila, after he retired from the industry. As soon as Acid was through the door, she left Spook and Danny and pushed through the crowds to make a beeline for the bar. If she was here, she needed a damn drink.

"Two double Jamesons," she told the barman. "No ice."

The old man behind the bar had a thick neck and red cheeks mottled with acne scars. He mumbled something under his breath in a strong Irish accent before shuffling away to get her drinks. Acid turned around and leaned her back against the bar top. The main room was already filling up with people, faces and egos from all corners of the murder-for-hire industry. At the other end of the bar was Johnny Blades, over from the US. He saw her and raised his pint of Guinness as a greeting. Acid nodded back, noticing Zalaph over his shoulder, an Israeli hit man with a glass eye who she'd run into a few times over the years. People had come from all over the world to pay their respects to The Dullahan. But why wouldn't they? He'd worked as a freelancer his entire career and had always conducted himself honourably and fairly. In an industry that was so (literally) cut-throat, he was someone genuinely liked by most of his peers. Indeed, the fact that he had been able to retire in peace, without a hit being put out on him, spoke volumes. Not many people got to retire in this industry. Unless they wiped out their entire organisation first.

But had Acid retired? She didn't think so. The late-night

killing sprees she'd been engaged in at the start of the year (taking out a vicious drug dealer and a doctor with a fondness for murdering his elderly patients) had now stopped. She didn't know why. She still had the urges, and her bloodlust was still strong, but without structure or any sense of purpose, her undertaking had begun to feel rather futile. She wasn't a vigilante; she wasn't some do-gooding superhero. She was... well, she knew what she was.

"Acid Vanilla! I thought you were dead."

She spun around to see a man leaning on the bar beside her. He was tall, with thick dirty-blond hair that would have been curly if it wasn't cropped so short. As she looked up at him he stepped back so she could take him in. He was wearing a sharp black suit and a tight white shirt that highlighted his chiselled torso and broad shoulders. The build of an Olympic swimmer.

"Sorry? Do I...?"

He laughed, or rather smirked, but not in an annoying way. In fact, in a rather attractive way. "Winters. Nate Winters." He grimaced. "But back when I started in the industry I used to call myself Nate Nitro. That's probably how you know me."

Acid leaned back. "No fucking way. You're Nate Nitro! Jesus." She waved her hand over him. "You've certainly... filled out, haven't you?"

He grinned. "I was only twenty-three when I was pitched against you on that job in Mexico. I'm thirty-five now. People change a lot in twelve years." He gestured at the bar. "Can I get you a drink?"

"No. Thanks. I..." She turned back to see the two glasses of Jamesons waiting for her and the barman on the other side of the bar. She had no idea how long he'd been standing there. She pulled a twenty out of her pocket and handed it to him. "Here. Keep the change."

She picked up the glasses and raised them at Nate.

"I see," he said. "Drinking for two?"

"Always." She closed one eye, pointing her finger at him as she did. "I remember that job in Mexico. A group of corrupt police who were hiring themselves out as hit men."

"That's the one. The local gangsters needed rid of them, so clubbed together to get them taken out. They floated the job on the old Currency Xchange forum, and it was won by Annihilation Pest Control and The Sons of Sam who I used to work for. I'm freelance now. Or rather, I'm actually trying to—"

"That's right!" Acid cut in. "Shit. Were we pitched against each other?"

"Not really. But it always seemed to be a competition with you. I think you took four of them out and I got two."

"Doesn't sound like me, sweetie." She downed the first glass of Jameson and winked at him as she placed the glass on the bar. Nate bloody Winters. Nate Nitro. He'd certainly grown into his looks over the last twelve years, and on another day, in another time, she'd have enjoyed seeing where this chance encounter might take the two of them. But she wasn't in the mood. She hadn't been in the mood for some time. She raised her second glass. "Well, cheers, Winters, it was good to see you again. I'd best go find my friends."

She walked away, sipping her drink as she scoured the room for Spook. It would be in her best interest to clear the air. After their argument this morning they'd not said a word to one another on the flight up to Manchester, and she didn't fancy sitting amidst an additional stinky mood on the flight back to London that evening. Especially if she was going to have a few more glasses of Jameson. Which she absolutely bloody well was!

"Acid, wait!" She stopped and turned around to see Winters following her. She didn't need this. Not now. "I actually came over to talk to you for a reason," he said, raising his eyebrows expectantly. "I have a proposition for you."

Acid twisted her mouth to one side. The obvious saucy retorts arose inside of her, but all died on her tongue before she could give them life. "What is it?"

"Can we sit down?" He moved over to the nearest free table and pulled out a chair for her. "Please?"

She gave him a hard stare, but sat. Across the room she saw Danny leaning over the bar and whispering something into the ear of a pretty blonde barmaid. At least some things didn't change. "What is it?" she asked.

Winters sat down beside her and the charming swagger he'd displayed moments earlier dropped away. His smile was gone and his eyelids appeared to grow heavier as he leaned in to speak.

"Does the name Kancel Kulture mean anything to you?"

CHAPTER 5

"Cancel culture?" Acid scoffed. "It's hard to not have heard of it. It's all people seem to be talking about lately." She didn't follow the news, or politics, or have any social media accounts, but even someone as wilfully blinkered to modern culture as Acid couldn't avoid the current discourse. But Winters laughed.

"No, Kancel Kulture. With two K's. They're a new organisation. An assassin network. It's only early days and no one has much intel on them yet, but word on the street is the man behind it is the man who killed our mutual friend." He gestured over to the large gold-framed painting of The Dullahan that was standing near the entrance of the pub, welcoming the mourners. Whoever the artist was, they'd captured him perfectly. In the painting he was wearing an emerald-green suit with a purple and gold smoking jacket over the top. His expression was distinct and perfect, halfway between charm and malevolence. It was the sort of painting where the eyes didn't just follow you around the room but bored into your soul.

Acid raised her head, searching Winters' face for a tell. Her heart was beating fast and she held her breath to slow it down.

"I see," she said. "I wasn't aware that the details of The Dullahan's death were common knowledge. You have to appreciate that I did all I could but was unable to stop it from happening. I was—"

"Hey, it's cool." Winters raised his hand. "No one is blaming you for what happened. But this new organisation, they're growing in numbers. A guy that I know, who's not here today, was approached by someone in Pamplona a few weeks back and asked to apply. It sounds like the top guy knows what he's doing. He's recruiting the best operatives in the world right now, all hand-selected."

Acid stiffened. She didn't like where this was going and wished Nate would cut to the damn chase. "Do you have a name? For the top guy?"

"No. I thought you might. Seeing as you were there. When... you know."

She bit her lip. Shook her head. "A lot was going on. I could maybe pick the main players out of a line-up, but it's kind of hazy." This was a lie. If she closed her eyes, the entire scene played out in her mind. The Dullahan and Spook sitting in the middle of the warehouse. Darius Duke standing behind them brandishing a large hunting knife. Then him grabbing The Dullahan by the hair and forcing his head back, exposing his slender throat... When she tried to sleep at night, it was all she could see.

She should have done more.

"I understand," Winters said. "But that's a shame, because a name would be a start. To date, no one I've spoken with has any clue who's behind Kancel Kulture. All the operatives have been approached via highly encrypted online communications. Whoever it is, they're good."

"I see." Acid forced herself to take a deep breath. She was glad when she picked up her drink that her hand wasn't shaking. She drank it down in one gulp.

"If you ask me, the main guy is setting himself up as the new Beowulf Caesar," Winters continued. "With an army of elite operatives situated around the globe. Only, he's not playing by the rules. He's not adhering to the code. That's angered and concerned a lot of people in the industry in equal measure."

"I bet it has. Not playing by the rules. Tut tut."

Acid placed her empty glass on the table. She'd always had an issue with some of the archaic rules and limitations of the assassin's code. But Winters was correct to be concerned. Darius had said he was going to take over the industry and, to give him his credit, that was what he seemed to be doing. But the new Caesar?

No way.

Not going to happen.

"I was talking with Danny, The Dullahan's nephew, earlier," she said. "He wants me to go after the people who killed his uncle." The words were out of her mouth before she could stop them. The two whiskies on top of her already fractured emotions had lowered her guard.

"And will you?"

She pursed her lips. There was the question. She knew she should. And for the first few weeks after The Dullahan had been killed, it was all she could think about. But now, today? She wasn't sure. Things had taken a turn. She was used to feeling tortured and conflicted about who she was, but now these feelings were like nothing else.

Who was she?

Who was Darius Duke?

"If you are planning on going after these people, you'll need help," Winters went on. "I'd like to be involved if you were interested in joining forces. In fact, this is why I approached you. I'm setting something up myself. A new organisation."

Acid leaned back. "I see. This is the reason you're so interested in going after these Kancel Kulture people. You see them as competition."

"It's not like that. I swear." He jabbed his finger on the table as if to emphasise his point. "The ball was already rolling before I ever heard of Kancel Kulture. But they killed a great man, someone well-respected and loved in this industry. They need to pay, don't you think?"

"Yes. Maybe." Winters' brow creased into a scowl. She'd sounded too dismissive. She blew out a long breath. "This is our industry though, sweetie. People die. A lot. Every day. Hardly anyone in this room is going to be drawing a pension. The Dullahan understood the way it worked. He was ready."

"Was he? You sound as if you're excusing what these bastards did. They went against the code, Acid."

"Yes! I know!" She shook her head. "The Dullahan was a friend of mine. It's awful that he died in the way he did. But... I don't know... The truth is I'm not sure I have it in me to go after these people."

"Wow. This coming from the great Acid Vanilla. The deadliest female assassin in the world. What happened to you?"

She puffed out her cheeks.

Where to start?

"I haven't said I wouldn't go after them," she told Nate, giving him a wicked smile. "Why don't you tell me more about your organisation?"

He held her gaze a moment. "I've been planning it for a while. There's still a big hole in the industry ever since Annihilation Pest Control was... disbanded. And I've grown tired of being a freelancer. I want to build a co-operative, where everyone is equal but has access to a vast range of skillsets. I've got a property in Wales, down in the southwest of the country. An old farm. It's huge and completely isolated. The nearest village is a place called Tregaron, more than five miles away. It's the perfect place. My dream is to set it up as a headquarters, plus a training camp for a team of elite assassins. I'd love you to be involved. We could even talk about a partnership if you'd be interested. I know you've been out of the industry a while and word on the street is you're done, but I reckon you've got a lot you can bring to the table."

"Who said I'm done?"

He shrugged. "People. They say you've lost your edge. That your killer instinct is gone."

"Well, they're bloody wrong. You tell them that from me!" No doubt he was trying to rile her, to force her hand. It was working. She looked away. "I can't commit to anything right now. I have too much going on."

"Fair enough. But how about we stay in touch, regardless?" He produced a card from out of his suit pocket and slid it across the table to her. "All my details are on there. If you do decide to go after these people, I'm on board. We can't let them disrupt the industry this way. It's not cool. I'll keep my ear to the ground and let you know if I hear anything, but apart from the name of the organisation, there's little to go off. No one I've spoken with can give me any names or even a vague location."

"Bugger!" Acid slammed her hand on the table a little too forcefully. Her empty glass fell over and rolled onto the floor as she jumped to her feet. "Well, it was good seeing you again, Winters. You take care now."

She was done talking. The only thing occupying her thoughts presently was what she should do about Darius bleeding Duke. She didn't need it shoving in her face here.

No one I've spoken with can give me any names or even a vague location.

Maybe it depended on who you asked.

She picked up Winters' card as she made to walk away, but he called after her. "Acid?"

She stopped. Didn't turn around. "What?"

"Don't you miss it? The thrill of the chase. The excitement of not knowing where you'll be from one week to the next. The power."

She lowered her head. Damn right she missed all those things. But she couldn't go back to that world. She'd come too far. Besides, a change of career – plus all the upheaval that would cause – seemed preposterous whilst Darius was still out there. She had to get him out of her head. One way or another. She had to face him.

"I'll see you around, Nitro," she called over her shoulder, as she headed for the exit.

CHAPTER 6

The flight back to London was neither as tense nor as awkward as Spook had feared, but it wasn't due to any renewed amicability between the two women. The taxi ride to the airport was made in silence, the atmosphere in the back of the cab brittle and heavy with subtext the entire trip. Then on finding their plane had been delayed for two hours, Acid had headed straight for the executive lounge and downed the best part of two bottles of prosecco. She'd passed out as soon as they'd boarded and slept for the rest of the journey home.

Spook had tried to sleep but couldn't. Instead, she'd kept watch over Acid as she snored and mumbled nonsensically in the seat beside her. Every so often her eyebrows would twitch into a deep scowl and she'd curl her lip, sucking in a sharp breath as if dreaming about something horrific.

There had been a time when Spook had believed Acid Vanilla to be one of the most enigmatic and intriguing people she'd ever met. Not only was she a highly skilled assassin, but she was sharp-witted, super-intelligent, and seemed to be finding her heart again, beneath the ice cage she'd constructed around it in her time working for Caesar. Spook was aware her friend had struggles with her mental health, including a rare form of bipolar she anthropomorphised as 'the bats'. But over the past year something had changed. Acid was always going to find it hard to adjust to civilian life, but for a while she'd tried. Then, suddenly, she just seemed to stop. Spook had tried to ignore her midnight jaunts initially. But when she'd discovered her returning home covered in blood, she had to say something.

I am a killer, Spook. That's what I do.

She could still hear Acid's voice in her head and remember the way she'd looked at her with cold, dead eyes when admitting how she'd succumbed to her old ways. The excuse she gave was that the people she'd killed deserved to die, and this may have been true, but it hurt Spook that everything they'd been working towards together – the Avenging Angels Agency, their friendship, Acid's road to recovery – had been trashed.

And then Darius Duke came along and everything changed again.

By the time their plane landed at Heathrow, it was almost midnight. After being woken up, Acid's mood was even darker than usual as they made their way through the airport and jumped in a black cab. Spook tried to engage her in light conversation, but after a few minutes Acid put her sunglasses on and that was the end of that.

Once back at their apartment in Soho, Spook tried again, hoping that Acid might open up a little. "Do you want a cup of tea?" she asked, heading for the kitchen as Acid locked the door behind them.

It was an easy enough question, but was met with a grunt and a sneer. Spook watched open-mouthed as Acid flung her jacket on the back of one of the chairs and disappeared down the corridor towards her room.

"Hey," Spook called after her. "Let's stay up for a while. We need to talk."

Acid paused at the door to her room. "Talk about what?"

Spook ran her tongue across her lips, wishing it was just the plane's overzealous air conditioning that had made her mouth dry.

How did she broach this subject?

She stepped towards Acid. "Don't *you* think we have a lot to talk about? The Dullahan. You. Me. Darius Duke…"

Acid visibly stiffened at the name, but then her shoulders sagged.

What was going on with her?

Spook had expected Acid to be gunning for Duke. Ready to do whatever it took to destroy the evil bastard. He'd tricked her. He'd tricked them all. But worse than that, he'd killed The Dullahan. He'd been ready to kill Spook next.

So what she'd told Acid this morning was true. She was ready to kill if it came to it. Darius Duke had to be taken out. Because if they didn't kill him first, he was going to come for them. And soon, she feared. But wasn't it just damn typical that the second Spook changed her point of view on this matter, Acid seemed to back down? It was as if the two of them were part of some weird universal construct where there was only so much bloodlust to go around.

Spook needed the old Acid back. She needed her fired up, eager to find Duke and avenge The Dullahan. Instead, all she got was a woman troubled and introspective, not willing to talk to her about anything. She hadn't heard a catty aside or witty put-down for weeks. It was worrying. Very worrying. Spook couldn't tell if Acid's head was stuck in the sand or up her own arse. Probably it was a bit of both.

"Have you heard anything, about Darius Duke?" Spook asked.

"Like what?"

"Oh, I don't know. Like where he is? What his plans are? Whether we should be concerned about him finishing what he started?"

Acid turned around. Her eyes were like black holes. "No."

"I see." Spook swallowed. The voice in her head was screaming at her to ask the question. She needed to know. It had been bothering her for days. "Are you worried you are related? Is that it?"

Acid stared at her, but it felt to Spook as if she were looking straight through her. "We aren't. We can't be."

"Are you sure of that?"

"Yes."

Spook wanted to say more, but Acid's glare froze the words in her throat. "Fine. But don't you think we should talk about what we're going to do about this threat hanging over our heads?" Acid opened her mouth to respond, but Spook hadn't finished. Waving a finger in the air, she went on. "This is why I need you to train me. I need to learn how to finish a fight. Running away is no longer a viable solution, Acid. I've been around you long enough. I've seen terrible things happen to both awful people and decent people alike. I get it. I'm not some little kid. Please. Teach me. I want to be a badass like you. I need to be."

Acid rolled her eyes. "For heaven's sake! This again? You're like a broken bloody record, do you know that?"

"I'm focused. That's all. Like you should be. I almost had my throat sliced open a month ago. And afterwards I found myself at a crossroads. I knew I could let that experience turn into trauma and break me – that's what would have happened to the old Spook Horowitz – or I could use it to strengthen my resolve. So I chose the second option. Because I'm not the same woman you met. You've changed me. Life has changed me. I chose to let the experience form me into a stronger person. I took the power back. And now I want to do everything I can to stop that evil bastard from hurting anyone else. I'll do whatever it takes."

Acid stuck out her bottom lip. "That's quite the speech, sweetie."

"Piss off. Don't be so damned condescending. Don't you want Duke to pay for what he did?"

"Yes!" She yelled it in Spook's face, but there was something in her eyes that was unsettling.

Spook stepped back and folded her arms "Okay, then. So let's talk about what we're going to do about him."

"Not now."

"Then when? Come on, I—" She stopped short as Acid barged past her. "Where are you going?"

"Away from you," she yelled, as she walked into the kitchen. "I'm sick of hearing about Darius bloody Duke. He's all anyone wants to talk about today."

"Well, we have just attended the funeral of the man he killed. Your friend." Spook followed Acid into the kitchen, to find her pulling open up cupboards and drawers, leaving each one open as she went. "What are you looking for?"

"Alcohol."

Now it was Spook's turn to roll her eyes. "What a fucking surprise."

"Is there any?" Acid asked, yanking open the fridge and wrinkling her nose at the contents. "Why isn't there any?"

"Because you've drunk it all."

And this was another of Spook's concerns. Acid had been drinking a lot lately. A hell of a lot. A lot more than usual. What's more, it seemed to be affecting her ability to focus. By 10 p.m. on most nights over the past few weeks her speech had become slurred and her movements sloppy. It wasn't like Acid. None of this was.

"Fine," she said, slamming the fridge door shut. "I guess I'll go out then."

"Where to?" Spook asked.

"A bar. Somewhere where I can hear myself think without some annoying woman pecking at my head."

"Oh, right. Is that what I'm doing? What a thing to say. Do you know for the past five years you've been desperate to toughen me up and have me appreciate how much danger there is in the world? Well, now I'm ready to do the work. I want to toughen up. Yet suddenly you're not interested. What the hell is going on with you?"

Acid grabbed her jacket from off the chair and Spook moved in front of the doorway to block her exit.

"Move!"

"No. Talk to me, Acid."

"I've nothing to say. I'm fine. Everything's fine."

Spook folded her arms to stop them from shaking. It felt as if she was vibrating, from all the adrenaline in her system. "I want to help you find Darius Duke and take him out.

That's what we need to talk about. That's what we need to do."

Acid actually snarled at her. "Move!"

"No!"

"Wow. Someone grew a spine recently."

"Fuck you."

Acid laughed. "No. Fuck you." She lunged forward, banging Spook's arm with her shoulder and shoving past her. "You stupid bloody child!"

Spook spun around and watched as Acid marched down the hallway. She got to the front door of the apartment and jerked it open, letting it slam against the internal wall with a crash. She looked back, glancing at Spook up and down with a nasty grin, then stepped out into the stairwell. As the door swung shut behind her, Spook gave her the finger. It made her feel only a little bit better.

CHAPTER 7

Outside, the air was cool, but without the wind chill that had been present the past few weeks. Spring was around the corner, and Acid decided to walk for a while rather than jump in the first taxi she saw. It would take her ninety minutes on foot to get to Chelsea. But The Bitter Marxist, her drinking den of choice, was open until well into the early hours. Also, she'd been sitting for most of the day and the exercise would do her good. Or so she hoped. There didn't seem to be much that was 'doing her good' at the moment.

Acid hated feeling this way. Even at her most manic and chaotic she usually had some semblance of control. She'd taken time to understand how her condition affected her, and how her heightened senses and emotions could be properly utilised, and for most of her life it had felt like a superpower. But lately the bats had grown unruly and an almost oppressive uncertainty had descended upon her. She was restless, unsure how to climb out of her mental quagmire. Or maybe she did know what was needed but she wouldn't accept it. Her whole life felt like an itch she was unable to scratch.

As she walked down Piccadilly, past Green Park, her thoughts drifted once more to her old life; to Caesar and the sixteen years she'd spent as one of his top operatives at Annihilation Pest Control.

And, shit.

She missed it.

All of it.

She missed the camaraderie of being part of a team, the work itself, the money, the sense of purpose it gave her. She missed Davros. She even missed Spitfire. And she missed Caesar most of all.

Damn him.

Damn them all.

Why did it have to turn out this way? After her unceremonious exit from the organisation, she'd convinced herself Caesar was evil and that he'd ruined her life. Even today, Spook was adamant that was the case. The way she saw it, Beowulf Caesar had discovered Alice Vandella when she was young, broken and impressionable, and had groomed her into a cynical killing machine. This was indeed true, to some degree, but their relationship had been a lot more than that. Caesar was Acid's mentor, a father figure. He'd taught her so much. He was her family.

Shitting piss.

These thoughts of family were followed by a flood of much darker thoughts, each one more uncomfortable and confusing than the last. She felt in her pockets for her earbuds. If she listened to something loud, fast and heavy, it might stop these unhelpful ideas about Darius from fully forming. But she didn't have the earbuds on her.

Buggering balls.

As she reached Hyde Park Corner, she stopped. It felt as if she'd been walking forever, and coupled with the fresh air it had all but sobered her up. She glanced down the street ahead. Her destination was still another forty-five minutes away.

Screw this.

She needed a drink. Fast. She walked to the kerbside and hailed a passing cab.

"The corner of Old Brompton and Queen's Gate, please," she told the driver as she climbed in the back.

"Right you are." He met her gaze in the rear-view mirror as he pulled away and headed down Knightsbridge. "Going out clubbing, are ya?"

Acid sighed. Why did she always get the talkers? "No, just a late-night drink," she replied, as brusquely as she possibly could.

The driver didn't let it bother him. "The only bar I know near Old Brompton that's open at this time of night is that seedy little joint down the back of the church. What's it called? The Moody Socialist?"

Acid leaned her temple against the window. "Something like that. The Bitter Marxist."

"That's the one. I've never been in myself, but I hear it's a bit dubious. A lot of terrible sorts hang out there. You sure you want to be going somewhere like that on ya own?"

"Oh, I'm sure."

He chuckled to himself. "Fair enough."

That was the last she heard from him, thankfully. Five

minutes later he pulled the car up on the corner and she stuffed a twenty through the hole in the Perspex screen. "Keep the change."

It took her another five minutes to walk the labyrinth of back streets towards the late-night bar. As she approached the street-level entrance, she could already hear the bridge refrain of *Sweet Jane*, and as she made her way down the rickety metal stairwell, she began to relax. A thick, airless heat hit her in the face as she opened the door, followed by a heady smell of body odour and stale liquor. It felt like coming home; even if her memories of the bar were now tainted by the duplicitous Freddie Pearce, who she now knew as Darius Duke. It was her first visit to The Bitter Marxist since being here with him and it felt weirder than she'd expected it to. It was also risky. But if he was coming for her, if he was as resourceful and committed as Nate Winters presumed, then everywhere she went was risky. And not everywhere served whisky until the early hours.

She walked down to the bar, scoping out the room as she went. The place was dead, which for a Thursday was unusual. At the far end, a man sat alone nursing a bottle of beer. He had his back to her and was wearing a dark beanie hat. Along the side wall in front of the bar, two old boys with faces like fists shared a bottle of absinthe. She watched as one of them poured out a set of shots and they knocked them back before slapping the edge of the table with gusto. Turning, she saw the barman was also watching them.

He raised one eyebrow at her. "That's their second bottle. I did try to talk them out of it." He smiled as Acid sauntered over to lean on the counter. "What can I get you?" He was tall and slender with dark skin and a confident expression. His pink satin shirt sagged open as he leant down for a tumbler, revealing shiny pectoral muscles. Acid averted her eyes.

"I think I'll have an Old Fashioned. Wild Turkey, if you have it."

"Good choice." He gave her a thumbs up. "Give me a few minutes."

He grabbed an orange from a bowl on the back counter and went to work as Acid took a seat on the nearest bar stool. Once settled, she rotated around so she could take in the rest of the dingy bar. Despite the Marxist being a home away from home to her for many years, she felt detached from its usual sleazy charms this evening. The buzz from the speaker system whenever a heavy bass line played was annoying rather than distinctive; in the area under the stairs, the upturned barrels used for tables seemed more a lazy workaround than characterful; the sticky floors and tabletops repulsed her. But then, everything looked shitty when you were looking at the world through a shitty frame of mind. The problem was, she didn't know how to stop.

As her attention focused on the gloom, she saw the man sitting alone in the back had finished his beer and turned around to look right at her. He was thick-set, with a smear of salt-and-pepper stubble on his chin, and a bulbous pink scar on his cheek that was accentuated by the low lighting. Acid raised her chin and met his gaze, hoping he'd look away when she did so. Often they did. This one didn't.

Now she had to ascertain whether he was a threat or merely a creep. In The Bitter Marxist it was harder to tell than in most places. The taxi driver had been correct. It was a dodgy place with a nefarious clientele. But that's why she liked it. Usually.

"Here you go. One Wild Turkey Old Fashioned." The barman stole her attention, placing a heavy-bottomed tumbler in front of her and twisting it around so the sliver of orange peel was hooked over the glass pointing away from her. "Do you want to pay now or start a tab?"

"I'd best pay now," she told him, pulling the roll of twenties she always carried out of her pocket and peeling one off. She handed it over. "I don't think I'm going to stay long."

That hadn't been her intention, but she wasn't feeling it tonight. She'd take her time drinking the Old Fashioned then get off home. But, shit. The prick in the beanie hat was still staring at her. She could see him out of the corner of her eye. How was she supposed to enjoy her drink with him ogling her?

She adjusted her position on the bar stool as a shiver of manic energy bristled down her back. The bats were awake, screeching their annoyance across her psyche. They told her to act. Regardless, she sipped at her drink, trying to ignore her base urges. But when she glanced over again, he was still staring.

Fine.

Let's force the bastard's hand.

If he was here for her, if he was a threat rather than a creep, then she needed to know. Pushing her drink away, she slipped off the stool and strutted down the length of the bar without looking around, then stepped through the single door on the back wall that led to the bathrooms. A stench of urine ammonia mixed with a chemical fragrance burned her nasal canal as she walked over to the sinks and twisted on the cold tap. She cupped her hand and brought a palmful of water to her mouth. It was ice cold. Refreshing. She didn't know how clean it was. She didn't care. As she straightened up, her reflection stared back at her in the mirror. The light in the bathroom was stark and bright and made her look pallid and dog-tired. But maybe it wasn't the light.

The bats were still chattering in her head, desperate for a distraction from the niggling confusion and uncertainty that had fogged up their flight path for weeks. They wanted a simple life – for Acid to follow her base instincts.

They wanted blood.

She moved into the centre of the room and slipped her trusty push dagger out of the concealed compartment on her belt.

Then she faced the door.

Then she waited.

CHAPTER 8

Acid gripped the push dagger in her fist, her body tense, her mind quiet. She waited. A minute went by. And another. By the third minute, she knew the man wasn't coming. Either he wasn't the threat she'd assumed him to be or he'd thought better of it.

Well, bugger me.

It had been weeks since she'd been in a state of mind for action and now here she was, all worked up with no dance partner. She slipped the dagger back inside its sheath in her belt and exited the bathroom. The jukebox was playing a track she didn't recognise. It sounded like it could have been Springsteen, but she wasn't much of a fan. As she returned to her drink, she noticed the empty seat where the man in the beanie hat had been sitting. Not only had he taken away her chance of some release tonight, but now the bar looked even more barren and pathetic. The two old boys were still tucking into their bottle of green aniseed-tasting lighter fluid, but that was it. A total washout.

She downed her drink, thanked the barman, and headed

back up the stairwell to the street. Sometimes you needed to know when to call it. At least when she'd believed danger was in the air, her system had reacted the way she'd expected it to. She'd been more than ready to face that guy if he'd followed her into the bathroom. That pleased her. She might have had a lot on her mind, but she wasn't washed up or washed out just yet. The fire in her belly remained; it just needed a little stoking. Chaos was still her driver.

And now she was outside, sober and with nothing to do but head home. It didn't seem fair. It didn't seem right. As she stood, wondering what to do now, she was overcome by a rush of manic bat energy. Too much to hold on to. She needed a release. The bats needed blood.

Turning a full circle, Acid cast her attention up and down the long street, and as she did she almost cried out. Swallowing her surprise, she turned in the other direction, feigning that she hadn't seen the figure standing on the corner at the far end. Silhouetted as they were by a streetlight on the opposite corner, she was unable to make out what they looked like, but from their overall gait and build, she'd have put money on it being the man from the bar.

What was he waiting for?

She rolled her head back and twisted her mouth from side to side, pretending to be uncertain what to do. The expectation of what might happen next gave her butterflies. She felt like a teenager about to be asked to the high school dance by their dream crush. Only this guy was no leading man and she was no prom queen.

Setting off down the street in the opposite direction, she walked steadily but with purpose. And as she crossed the road, she put all her attention into her hearing, picking out the footsteps that fell in time with her own.

That's it, sweetie.

Come to momma.

A side street brought her out on Queen's Gate and she took a left. She didn't know this area well, but vaguely remembered there was a public garden around here somewhere. Down the next street and she found what she was looking for. A large, gated patch of greenery that spanned two blocks and with pedestrian walkways intersecting from all sides. At this time of night, and with the canopy of tall sycamore trees running around the perimeter, the central part of the garden was almost completely hidden from view. The perfect spot.

On reaching the entrance to the garden, she paused and bent down to pretend to tie the laces of her Dr Martens boots. As she went through the pantomime, she heard the heavy footsteps reach the end of the street and then stop. She stood and walked slowly under the cover of the trees.

Once inside the garden, she quickened her pace, moving into the central area where a black metal Victorian lamppost cast the space in a magical orange glow. If it was snowing, it could have been Mr Tumnus' lamppost in Narnia.

And now here was the White Witch, ready for her prey.

She hurried over to the far side of the gardens and concealed herself behind a thick tree trunk as the footsteps got closer. Kneeling, she was able to keep watch without any light hitting her or giving her away. She held her breath, one hand on the push dagger in her belt as a large man in a long overcoat stepped into the light.

It was him. The man from the bar. Clearly he'd been

waiting for her to leave so he could follow her. But the big question was, had he been there waiting for her in the first place?

Darius knew The Bitter Marxist was Acid's favourite bar and he'd also know it was The Dullahan's funeral today. From there, it wouldn't be a far stretch of the imagination to assume she would return to London straight from the wake and head to Chelsea for a late-night drink. In fact, you could probably stake your reputation on it.

But it didn't make sense.

If this goon was here for her specifically, then it had to be a hit. And if that was the case, then Darius had to be behind it. But why? After everything he'd said in his messages...

She shook the thought away. It was too confusing and right now she had to get into a different mindset. One of action and instinct rather than logic or reason. She relaxed her muscles, slipping effortlessly into kill-mode as she assessed the situation.

The man was now standing underneath the lamppost and peering into the gloom. In the light she could get a better look at him.

Well, shit.

He'd taken his hat off and she could now see the spiral scar running around the top of his head. It was the same man who'd been watching her at the cemetery. This had to be a hit. Up close, he was a lot younger than she'd first realised. As he spun around, she caught his expression and detected a hint of uncertainty in his eyes. Good. That's what she wanted. He'd got cocky. Probably figured she was an easy hit. But he hadn't factored in her past, who she'd been and who she could still be when her complicated chemical make-up aligned correctly. Poor bastard. It had just dawned on him that he was the one being stalked.

Acid tightened her stomach muscles and raised her tongue onto her soft palate. Once her airways were constricted, she emptied her lungs, calling out as she did. "Hey!"

The technique made her voice sound as if it were coming from some distance away. The man glanced around, confused.

"Hey you," she called out, this time betraying her position. Before he turned back, she got up and leapt to the cover of a tree a few metres away. Now, suitably disorientated and even more unsure of himself, the man pulled a large blade out from under his coat. Acid smiled to herself. Showing his hand this early was a rookie move. She could take this prick, no problem.

"Hey, fuck you!" he growled in a heavy accent. "Show yourself, miserable bitch!"

Acid sucked air back through her teeth. He was going to regret saying that. Crouching, she ran a quick evaluation of her opponent and the area. The goon might have been younger and more experienced than she'd first believed, but he had at least a foot on her and was broad with it. His gait, however, was ungainly and he looked top-heavy. Before he could ground himself, she leapt out from the cover of the trees and ran towards him, brandishing the push dagger in her fist. The man spun around and she widened her trajectory, running past him and slashing the blade across his abdomen. She heard the rip of cotton, felt the tug of flesh. As she twisted back on herself, jumping away from any counterattack, she saw the blood leaking through his grey shirt and spreading across his belly.

Bullseye!

As soon as the man became aware of his injury, he yelled out and lurched towards her, slashing wildly with his knife. But the fear on his face was palpable. Acid backed away, prowling a circle around the wounded man as he followed her with his beady, unblinking eyes. She wondered how this job had been sold to him. Her being a woman meant she often had the advantage in fights such as this. People had underestimated Alice Vandella her entire life, and even now, as Acid Vanilla, they still did. But usually only once. Someone had lied to this man. They'd told him this was a simple hit. Now she was watching reality hit home to him in real-time.

Bouncing from foot to foot, she lunged to her right before dummying back and going left. As she did, she dipped low, ducking under the swing of his knife while burying her own blade up to the hilt into her opponent's thigh. With a pained grunt, the man stumbled over on his side, and as he lowered his weapon, Acid ran around the back of him and kicked the blade out of his hand. With the long knife clattering onto the paved pathway, she leapt at him. Grabbing onto his jacket and using the knife handle still sticking out of his leg as footing, she clambered up his back until she had one arm around his neck, under his chin. Tightening her muscles, she grabbed her wrist with her other hand and squeezed the hard bone of her forearm against his carotid artery. She was well versed in this kind of sleeper hold. It had once been her speciality. Get it right, depriving the brain of the blood it needs, and the result is a loss of consciousness within a few seconds.

The man lunged onto one knee, and she felt his muscular frame relax. She gripped her legs around his waist in a pincer grip, riding him down before pushing off him and staying upright as he crumpled onto the grass. Once there, she didn't waste any time rolling the big man onto his back and straddling his chest. A quick check through his pockets gave her nothing. Positioning her legs so she had a knee pressed down hard onto each of his biceps, she leaned forward and grabbed his ears.

"Hey, wake up!" she snarled, lifting his head towards her as his now unobstructed blood flow revived him.

His eyelids flickered and his pupils spiralled as he regained consciousness. But he didn't have time to wake completely before Acid smashed his head onto the firm ground.

"Who sent you?"

The man groaned.

"Who sent you? Was it Darius Duke?"

He groaned some more. He curled his lip. He bared his pink, blood-stained teeth. But said nothing.

Acid's grip tightened around his ears, desperately seeking leverage through the sweat and filth. With a forceful shove she slammed his head back, eliciting a sickening thud.

The man's teeth clattered, and the light in his eyes flickered out. Acid knew she couldn't pry answers from a corpse, but his silence seemed inevitable. Even the most novice assassins grasped this crucial aspect of their profession – never reveal your identity or your employer. It was an outdated part of the code, but with the right resources an ID could still be obtained. Especially if you had a tech wizard waiting for you back home.

Seething with rage, Acid yanked his head towards her and slammed it into the unforgiving ground. "Who sent you!? Who sent you?" Her objective was to incapacitate him just long enough to extract what she needed, but the escalating cacophony of bat screeches frayed her nerves. Teeth clenched, she continued to batter his skull into the earth, her frenzied fury all-consuming. Rationality and training abandoned her as she became solely focused on annihilating this prick who had dared to come at her. She wanted to destroy him. And the world.

"Tell me," she hissed. "Was it Darius? Was it Darius? Was it Darius?!" With each question she smashed his head into the earth, and delivering the final blow, she felt an unsettling crack and heard the nauseating splintering of bone.

Shit.

She carefully tilted his head to one side, peering beneath his massive cranium. A jagged rock, previously unnoticed, protruded from the battered ground. It had caved in the back of the man's skull. Releasing her grip, she stood, gasping for air and wiping her hands, sticky with blood and brain matter, on her black jeans.

"Bloody hell, sweetie," she muttered to herself. "This was a bit much, even for you."

Anger had got the better of her. That wasn't cool. And it wasn't professional. But it was happening more and more frequently these days. It was one reason why she'd ceased her righteous killing sprees. There were still evil people out there in the world. People who deserved to have their lives taken away from them. Yet in her current state of mind, Acid worried she might make a mistake that could prove fatal. Or worse, a mistake that could land her behind bars. Anger was a treacherous emotion, more lethal in the field than inexperience. She needed discipline; her emotions were gaining the upper hand.

That bastard Darius.

This was his fault. He'd got in her head, made her question absolutely bloody everything. The worst thing was she knew he was manipulating her, intent on keeping her off-balance and uncertain. That's how you got to people.

If Darius was behind this attempt on her life, it would be no coincidence he'd sent such an inexperienced thug. This was his way of taunting her, a calculated move to provoke her into striking back.

She shook her head. It wasn't going to happen. She wasn't playing his game.

Off in the distance was the faint drone of a police siren. It wasn't coming for her, but was a reminder she was vulnerable and alone out here. Moving swiftly now, she removed her phone from her jacket pocket and swiped open the camera app. Kneeling next to the dead man, she tapped out five or six photos, zooming in as close to his face as possible whilst ensuring she captured the biometric signifiers needed. The fact that this was how she used to operate after a hit wasn't lost on her. Once camera phones were widely available, it was Annihilation Pest Control's policy that an operative would take photos of the mark once the job was complete. This was to allow Raaz Terabyte's facial recognition software to create a positive ID and for her to then send proof of completion to the client.

More than ever before, Acid found herself pining for the old days. Life seemed so much easier when she was working for Caesar. Everything was more black and white, less messy.

She knew where she stood; and if she got out of line, she had the big man there to give her a strict talking-to and slap her back into shape. She missed the routine and the discipline just as much as she missed Caesar.

But there was no point thinking that way. Caesar was dead. Annihilation Pest Control was over. All thanks to her.

Stupid bloody fool.

Her mind swirled with conflicting thoughts, and she forcefully shook her head in a desperate attempt to regain focus. She had to concentrate on the task at hand. Scrolling through her phone's camera roll, she confirmed she had captured the necessary evidence and stowed the device securely in her pocket. The wail of the police siren was growing steadily louder. It was time to get out of there. Casting a final glance at the man's lifeless body, she zipped up her leather jacket and disappeared into the night.

CHAPTER 9

Over in Soho, Spook couldn't sleep. But rather than try to drink herself into a better state of mind, or submit to her baser instincts, she was using her time to better herself. Or at least, that was the plan. She still had a long way to go.

"Eighteen... Nineteen... Twen—" She crumpled to the floor as her triceps betrayed her mid push-up. "Damn it."

But *almost* twenty in a row. That was a new personal best and Spook was proud of herself, regardless. Indeed, just a month earlier she'd never even attempted a push-up, being one of those people who viewed any form of exercise as a hideous and unnecessary way to spend one's time. Being naturally slim and petite in frame, she'd always thought of herself as a thinker, not a fighter. Her skills lay in being a white-hat hacker, a tech wizard who could find her way around any mainframe she'd ever come across and who had hacked into the Pentagon when she was still a teenager. Just to look around. Because she could.

But her outlook on life had now changed. She'd been

fighting the inevitable for too long. She owed it to herself to grow stronger and fitter and more resilient. Ready for whatever came next.

Yet, while it would be easy to attribute this transformation to Darius Duke's influence, Spook knew it was more than that. The reality of a knife held at her throat, the horror of witnessing an execution and the cold realisation that she could be next, had all left their mark on her. But Spook knew her metamorphosis had begun much earlier. The day she met Acid Vanilla.

It reminded Spook of a story her high school history teacher, Mr Miller, had once told her class. About how, if you put a frog into a pan of boiling water, it would scold itself and immediately leap out to safety. But if you put the same frog into a pan of cold water and then slowly heated the water to boiling point, the frog would stay in the pan and be slowly boiled alive. The story was supposed to be an analogy for the rise of the Nazis in 1930s Germany and political reform – highlighting how power, and especially evil, triumphed not by big elaborate actions but small incremental changes that people didn't notice until it was too late. But it was also how Spook felt her life had been for the past five years, exposed to Acid's sordid underworld of killers and crime. Slowly, over time, she'd been introduced to new concepts and ideas that shocked and repulsed her in equal measures. But as the weeks and months went on, she'd grown used to this new world. Blood and death and fear were now a part of life and she often found herself calmly accepting situations she would never have done five or ten years earlier. Back then she was still a hacker in her spare time, so she couldn't have ever called herself law-abiding, but she was moral and just and hated to see anyone in pain. Today, however, she'd happily kill Darius Duke and any of his cronies if it meant she'd be safe. She was a different person. But how could she not be? She'd committed numerous crimes. She'd killed people. She'd been through too much and she'd seen too much. It wasn't her fault. She was a frog in a pan.

But she had to keep going. Pushing herself every day to be tougher and faster and more brutal than she ever thought possible. It was why she did fifty sit-ups every night, followed by as many push-ups as she could handle. The prospect of joining a gym, as well as joining Acid on her daily runs, was next on the horizon for her. Spook knew it was early days, but these initial steps marked the dawn of her transformation and were a testament to her resolve. She still grappled with reconciling her past self with the warrior she aspired to become, but this was a good start.

Breathless, but not stopping, she turned over and flattened out the corner of her yoga mat before lying back and preparing herself for more sit-ups. Another fifty and she'd call it a night. It had been a long day and she hoped now the added exertion would mean she'd fall asleep readily. If not, she had a book on special forces combat, which she'd recently bought from a local thrift store. If sleep still evaded her, she'd read that for a while.

Pulling in a deep breath, she was about to start when she heard the lock turn on the front door of the apartment. Lying as she was, in a supine position, she could see the clock on the wall behind her. It was almost 1 a.m. Acid had been gone for over two hours. Spook sat up and listened, hearing footsteps approaching down the hallway.

The old Spook might have grown terrified at this point,

letting her imagination run riot over reason, fearing this was someone come to kill her. But not anymore. She now understood the importance of staying calm – and of trusting your instincts. Clearly, this was Acid arriving home rather than anyone dangerous (although that in itself was debatable these days). Her footsteps and gait, like everyone's, were distinct. When she was walking with purpose, in stealth mode, she'd shift her weight onto her back foot and go up on the balls of her feet with each step.

"You're back late," Spook called out. The footsteps stopped outside her door. "Are you drunk?"

She heard a deep sigh outside the door and it creaked open to reveal Acid standing on the threshold. Her face was dirty, and she had a strange look in her eyes that suggested an internal battle raging within her. It might have given Spook cause for concern if she hadn't noticed it every day since The Dullahan died and Darius Duke revealed he and Acid might be related. As it was, she was merely frustrated her friend wouldn't share her problems with her. But that was nothing new.

"Are you hurt?" Spook asked.

"No. I'm not bloody hurt." Acid marched into the room and shut the door behind her. She walked over to Spook and knelt in front of her. "I thought you'd be asleep. I was trying to be quiet."

"But you wanted something?" Acid's bedroom was down the other end of the corridor, near the front door. She had no reason to be at this end of the apartment. Spook straightened her back. "Or were you hoping to freak me out by creeping around in the middle of the night?"

"No. Of course not. Don't be so bloody paranoid. I am

glad you're awake, though." She pulled her phone out of her pocket and, after swiping it open, shoved it at Spook. "Do you think you can find out who this is?"

Spook took the phone and examined the screen. It showed the face of a man. He had a shaved head, the start of a scruffy beard, and a vicious scar running down the left-hand side of his face. "Who is he?"

"I don't bloody know. That's why I just asked if you could find out for me."

Spook stared at her without smiling. "I *mean*, why have you got a photo of him on your phone?" She peered closer at the screen. "Is that blood? Is he dead?"

Acid nodded. "He followed me from The Bitter Marxist, but was no match. An amateur, really."

"Do you think Darius sent him?"

"I don't know," Acid replied, but the look in her eyes said differently. "That's why I want you to ID him." When Spook didn't respond, she dropped her shoulders and sighed. "All right, I know I'm being a bitch. But I'm confused. If Darius is behind the hit, it doesn't make sense. Why send someone so lame and inexperienced? Why send anyone at all?"

"What do you mean?"

Acid looked away. "Forget it. I'm still a bit all over the place. It's been a long day." She nodded at the phone. "But can you ID him?"

"If there's a photo of him online linked to a profile, then sure. I've been working on a new AI program that can search the entire web, both mainstream and dark, in under three minutes. Except for a few bugs I can iron out later, it's almost ready."

"That's amazing," Acid said, lowering herself into a sitting position. "This is what I mean though, Spook. We could use this technology. If we were to go pro, then we'd have a real advantage in the industry and—"

"Jesus, Acid!" Spook cut in. "This again? It's like you've got a one-track mind. You've just buried one of your friends." She pushed off the mat and got to her feet. "I knew you'd do this. I knew this was coming. I knew it!"

Acid jumped up also. "It's a good idea. It's what I know. It's what I'm good at. It's all I'm good at. It doesn't have to be as sinister as you think. We'd still be doing good. In a way."

"*In a way*. Shit." Spook walked over to the wardrobe, pulling her t-shirt off over her head as she went. She flung it at the laundry basket in the corner and selected a fresh white shirt from the wardrobe. She put it on, using the time to reflect on what Acid was saying. But once dressed and feeling calmer, she was no less open to the idea. "Is it always going to come back to this with you? That you want to be a hit... person. A killer for hire. And you won't be happy doing anything else?"

"It's all I know."

"Learn something else. People do. All the time."

Spook tensed as Acid strode across the room towards her. "What makes you so bloody high and mighty? You're the one pestering me to train you how to kill."

Despite the rush of adrenaline urging her otherwise, Spook stood her ground. "It's not the same," she replied. "I want you to train me so that I can stop someone from killing me. I want to learn how to keep myself alive in this seedy underworld in which I've found myself. It's not about monetary gain, or because I'm bored, or because I've told myself a story that this is the way I am. If it is the way you are – change. It is possible."

"Fuck you!" Acid barked. "You have no idea what you're damn well talking about."

"Haven't I? Come on, I've been around you long enough, Acid. I get it. And I also appreciate we've not had any new cases come in for the Avenging Angels agency, so we're at a bit of a loss what to do with ourselves. I don't want to kill people as a career, but that doesn't mean I think we should take up crocheting, and it doesn't mean I won't kill if I have to, to protect myself. That's why I want you to train me. I want to be prepared if I have to face Darius or someone like this guy on your phone."

Spook looked down, noticing her hands were balled into tight fists. She released them and raised her head to meet Acid's gaze. Who looked terrifying. Her eyes were wide and stary and her full lips twisted to one side in a callous smirk.

"You can't run from who you are, Spooky. I've learnt that to my cost these last few years. I'm a killer. You're a computer nerd. Best we stick to our lanes."

Spook swallowed. She had so much she wanted to say in response to that statement – that it was bullshit, that Acid was wrong about her, that she should show her more respect – but she kept quiet. When Acid was in this sort of mood, there was no reasoning with her. The only problem was, this *sort of mood* was Acid's default setting these days.

"I'm not a computer nerd and you need to be careful," she said. "I understand what you're saying. In some ways. But you have so much good inside of you, Acid. You're not the person you were before I met you. I've seen how you care for others and how you risk your life to help people. You can tell yourself that everything you do is in your own self-interest, but I see you. And I get it – right now you feel lost and at a crossroads. I do, as well. But we can get through this together. You don't have to go back to who you were. To *what* you were. That life is gone, and if you regress I'm worried you'll end up in a worse place than you were before. You don't have Caesar and the rest of them to lean on and it's not the same world anymore. Please, don't turn to the dark side."

Shit.

Even as the words left her mouth she regretted them. She knew what she'd wanted to say, but this clumsy terminology was only going to dilute her message.

Right on cue, Acid snorted derisively and shook her head. "There you go again with your stupid Star Wars analogies. Tell me again, Spooks, how you're not a computer nerd?"

Spook held her gaze. "I don't have to be. Not anymore. You can train me to be something else."

"You're not ready."

"When is anyone ready? You know, I don't get you, Acid. When you left Annihilation Pest Control, and Caesar... did what he did, you were chomping at the bit to get out there and take your revenge. Nothing would have stopped you. And I got that. And I helped you. I did all I could so you could make peace with your past. But now Darius kills The Dullahan and you press pause. What's going on? I thought you'd be desperate to find him and take him out. Don't you want to?"

Acid's jaw stiffened. "Yes. I do. But..."

"But what? What aren't you saying? Tell me. I need to know. I need you to say it."

"There's nothing to say. Leave it. I've had a lot on my mind lately, that's all. I will go after him. When the time is right. Okay?" She shot her a grin and Spook had to fight an intense urge not to slap her across the face. Yet there was something different about her tonight. Normally when Acid got up in her face like this, she was practically bristling with cocksure energy and manic resilience. But Spook didn't pick up on that from her. She was off-kilter. Playing the role of Acid Vanilla – not living it.

"Are you sure everything is okay?" she asked.

"I wouldn't go that far, Spooky. When is anything ever okay?"

"Fine. Whatever. Just text me the photo of that guy," she muttered, lowering her head. There was no point talking about this tonight. "I'll run the image through my software first thing in the morning and let you know if I get a positive ID."

Acid's grin widened, but there was still little joy or even mischief behind it. It was all surface. "There we go, sweetie," she replied, as she strutted out of the room. "It didn't need to be that hard, did it?"

Spook didn't reply. She was seething and unsure what to do with the ball of frenzy knotting her stomach. Once Acid had left, she relaxed enough to slip out of her leggings and flung them at the door. It made her feel a little better. As did giving her pillow a few good punches as she climbed into bed. But this wasn't over. Not by a long shot. That infuriating woman was being cagey and uncharacteristically cautious, and she needed to know why.

CHAPTER 10

On leaving Spook's room, Acid marched all the way into the kitchen before she remembered there was no alcohol in the apartment.

"Bugger."

But maybe it was a good thing. She needed a clear head if she was to fight her way through the fog of troubling thoughts currently clouding her reasoning.

Moving into her bedroom, she shut the door and locked it before walking across the room to her bureau and sliding open the middle drawer. She lifted the pile of faded black band t-shirts sitting on top of her old laptop and carried the ancient machine over to her bed. Sitting cross-legged, leaning her back against the headboard, she creaked open the lid. As usual, she hadn't shut the machine down the last time she'd used it, meaning she was still logged into The Onion Router and the VPN she used to access the Crypto Jones One Thousand website. To the casual browser, the site was a cryptocurrency trading forum, but behind the scenes, and if you had the right passkey, it was also a highly secure forum used by the assassin industry for passing on information and posting jobs. This forum had been industry standard for the past ten years, and before this they'd used a similar one but with a cover of real estate. It was a clever system and one that had worked without hitch or interference for as long as Acid could remember. Everyone who was anyone in the world of elite assassins used the forum, and a collective of very well-paid and highly skilled techies over in the US ensured the site was secure and would never be detected by the authorities.

Acid typed in her username and password, and cracked her knuckles as she waited for the welcome screen and the secure message portal to open up. The site was running slower than usual. She closed her eyes and released a long breath. The altercation with Spook just now had left her nerves frayed and she needed to calm herself.

Who the hell did Spook think she was, to talk to her that way?

She didn't know what she was going through.

Beneath the surface of her consciousness, Acid felt the bats stirring, their frenzied wings signalling the approach of a full-blown manic episode. She needed to get a handle on the situation before that happened. Her heart pounded with the weight of her inner conflict, the battle between controlling the chaos and succumbing to its destructive allure. She'd long ago learned to channel her bipolar disorder's manic energy into a formidable asset, an invaluable resource in her dangerous line of work. Yet the disquieting uncertainty now plaguing her, threatened to tip the balance and catapult her into too heightened a state, where her volatile nature could betray her.

She opened her eyes. The screen had loaded but there was no red dot on the message box icon. No new messages.

Bugger.

Where are you?

She leaned over and grabbed a lead from underneath her bedside table and plugged her phone into the laptop. A finder window opened automatically. Locating the photos of the man she'd killed, she dragged them onto the desktop. Then she highlighted the two most in focus and emailed them to Spook, before returning to the Crypto Jones One Thousand site.

She wondered, in passing, if she should message Nate Winters and ask him to send more details about the organisation he was setting up, but dismissed the idea almost immediately. The prospect of joining a new organisation was alluring, but Winters' venture seemed far from ready and its uncertain nature left her wary. Besides, she had more pressing matters. With a decisive click, she opened the top message thread and uploaded one of the photos. Her fingers hovered over the keyboard, a brief moment of respite, before she typed the subject line:

One of yours?

As she waited for the photo file to be processed, she clicked inside the message box and typed out some more:

He's dead. I killed him without breaking a sweat.

You need to do better.

She leaned back and, as the photo upload finished, was about to hit send when she stopped herself and added another line.

The answer is still NO.

She hit send before she could change her mind.

One of yours? The question was, of course, rhetorical. Who else would have sent that pathetic goon after her? But knowing the answer didn't make it any easier to understand.

Narrowing her eyes at the screen, she scrolled back through the message thread that had developed over the last two weeks. This here was the reason why she'd been so troubled and confused lately and why she was hiding her laptop from Spook.

She got to the top of the thread and reread Darius' first missive, sent just a week after she'd last seen him. It was a short message, just two words.

Join me.

Then, two days later.

Think of how powerful we could be. Brother and sister working together. A true family business. I know you miss it!

That one had knocked Acid for six, and even weeks later she was still on wobbly ground. It was all she could think about. Yet, she had no clue how to respond. Mainly because she had no clue what her answer was. The self-loathing that accompanied her consideration of his offer ate away at her, as did the undeniable appeal of his proposition.

But her hatred for him ran deeper.

Didn't it?

Then, two days ago a new message from Darius had thrown her world into further disarray. It was another short one. A chilling ultimatum in four words:

Join me or die.

CHAPTER 11

Darius Duke was in his new office, standing in front of the large circular window overlooking the stunning Piazza San Giovanni in Laterano, when there was a knock on the door.

"Come in. It's open." Darius turned to see Stig Saga framed in the doorway. Dressed in form-fitting pale trousers and a flowing beige shirt, he looked as if he'd just stepped out of a weathered sepia photograph. He made his way across the room, clutching a tablet to his chest, and stopped in front of Darius. "I hope you have some good news for me," Darius told him.

Saga bowed his head. "I believe so. Our guest has arrived and they are waiting downstairs."

"Oh, goodie," Darius bellowed. "And what's he like?"

"Brash, rude, rather unhinged. I like him. He's just as we'd hoped and seems keen to meet with you and get started."

"Wonderful. And has he completed the task we set him?"

"I didn't ask, but I assume if he's here he's carried out our wishes and has done what was asked of him. Otherwise, it would be foolish of him to bother us."

"Very good point," Darius replied. "Will you bring him up?"

"I will. But there is one other thing first." Darius raised an eyebrow in response and Saga stepped forward, swiping open the tablet and handing it to him. "She has replied."

Darius let his mouth drop open in mock disbelief. "No shit. Well, that is a turn-up for the books. All good, I expect. Let's have a look." He swiped open the screen and tapped on the message thread, his eyes darting to the bottom. "Oh, drat. Did she kill Alexis? That is a blow." His tongue clicked against his teeth in mild disappointment.

His intention for the newly recruited Alexis had been to serve as a warning, that was all. The man was to deliver to Acid a clear message. The fact she'd so easily seen him off was a good omen, however. It meant she was back on form. That pleased him a great deal. This would be no fun without a challenge.

"Would you like me to reply?" Saga asked.

Darius tilted his head back, his gaze drawn to the magnificent chandelier suspended from the ceiling above. As he pondered how to respond, he admired the opulent three-hundred-year-old centrepiece. It had been constructed out of bronze and French crystal and was testament to his refined taste. It had cost almost the same amount in euros as the down payment on the property, but was a small price to pay for the impression it left. It was crucial that his headquarters – and particularly his office – exuded an aura of power and prestige, signalling to the world that Darius Duke was a force to be reckoned with. The chandelier served as a gleaming symbol of his ambition and influence.

But what to say to Acid?

Her last message was curt and could be construed as her mocking him. He didn't like that. Yet he found solace in the knowledge that he too could be rather cutting when the mood took him. Their shared traits were a testament to their blood ties, an undeniable connection. Acid Vanilla was, after all, his sister.

My big sister!

He hadn't quite believed it himself at first, but three eminent biologists had confirmed it. Their DNA profiles were a match. That changed everything. Through this new frame, he couldn't help but smile as he returned his attention to the tablet and reread her last message.

That little minx.

When Darius had first discovered that Alice Vandella – the girl who'd killed his father – was still alive, he'd been consumed by an insatiable desire to track her down and subject her to the most excruciating and gruesome death imaginable. But then he'd met her, talked to her, witnessed first-hand her prowess, even when outnumbered and outgunned. This woman was a force of nature, and even after all these years was still highly respected within the industry. She would be a valuable asset to his fledgling organisation.

But his change of heart wasn't solely driven by pragmatism. As the days passed, Darius had contemplated the possibility that Acid Vanilla was his sister more and more. His once-seething hatred and thirst for her demise gradually transformed into a fixation bordering on obsession.

Having been raised as an only child, Darius was a rather awkward and nervy kid for most of his youth. In contrast, Acid exuded confidence and rebellion and appeared to take the world in her stride. He yearned to know her better, to be closer to her. To work alongside her.

Hell, a part of him even aspired to be her.

He knew she'd suspect his messages were nothing but a ploy. Him trying to get in her head so she'd freak out and make a mistake. However, his intentions were genuine. He wanted her to join Kancel Kulture, for them to stand united as siblings within his organisation. He had always longed for a sister – an older one, at that – and, deep down, he suspected his preoccupation with Acid had never truly been about destroying her, but rather about finding her, knowing her. Even during their encounter in the warehouse, he'd realised this. He wouldn't have killed her. In fact, he was ready to offer her a place at his table there and then. If only she hadn't got so enraged and spoilt the moment. All he did was kill some crusty old Irishman. Did it really matter?

Yet now she'd killed one of his operatives, and he couldn't just let that ride. He met Saga's gaze, who was waiting patiently for his response.

"Leave it for now," he told him. "I'm starting to think this sort of messaging isn't having the desired results."

The start of a smile teased at the Swede's thin lips. At least, Darius assumed it to be a smile. It could have been a sneer or a smirk; it was hard to tell with his new second-in-command. "What do you have in mind?" Saga asked.

Darius closed one eye and countered with a huge grin that would leave nothing to interpretation. "I'm going to let an idea percolate for a few days. I'll let you know when I've made a decision." He puffed out his chest and released a loud sigh. God, he felt good. Everything was falling into place. He gestured at the room around him. "Do you like the new décor?"

Saga appeared momentarily stunned by the enquiry, yet he allowed his gaze to sweep across the room, taking in the ornate flock wallpaper in midnight black and the large black-and-white prints prominently displayed on three of the walls: one of a shirtless Iggy Pop balancing atop the outstretched arms of his adoring audience; one of Ozzy Osbourne screaming cross-eyed into a microphone; and one of Bowie in his Thin White Duke persona, cocaine-skinny and encased in a cloud of cigarette smoke.

Saga spluttered. "Yes. It is good."

"Do you think she'll like it?" He glared at his number two. "Hmm?"

"Oh... yes... I'm sure."

Darius nodded. "Me too. She loves all this stuff." He waved his hand over the photo prints. "And I've seen photos of the original Annihilation Pest Control headquarters in Soho. This black wallpaper is almost identical."

Saga cleared his throat. "Are we sure, Darius, that Acid Vanilla is right for this organisation? I do not want to speak out of turn, but I have my concerns. You killed her friend. She killed Alexis. Why would she join us? How could we trust her?"

Darius rolled his eyes at Saga's incessant questions, striding towards the window to take in the scene below. The piazza was quiet except for a few people. A young couple strolled along the avenue on the far side, their arms intertwined, enjoying each other's company. Near the centre of the piazza, a woman and her two children perched on the metal railings encircling the base of the towering obelisk that commanded attention. The imposing monument stood as the focal point of the square, a symbol of grandeur and history.

As Darius observed the peaceful tableau unfolding before him, the contrast between the bustling world outside and the intense conversation within the room became all the more apparent.

"I hear your concerns," he told Saga. "But you don't have to worry. I know her. I can tell she's weakening. This is her world. It's all she knows. She's lost and lonely without an organisation around her. And Kancel Kulture will soon be the only organisation worth caring about. Am I angry that she killed Alexis? Yes. Sure. That was not how it was supposed to go. But it proves once again that she hasn't lost her gift. This is why we need her. She is one of the best. And so are we. We will be a perfect union. You see, Saga, my sister is selfish, but she is also very clever. Once she realises that being a part of Kancel Kulture is in her best interests, her joining us will be a foregone conclusion. Just wait and see."

The smile he gave Saga was genuine, reflecting the sincerity behind his words. But he'd also meant what he'd written to Acid in his last message to her. He wanted her by his side. But if she refused to join him, he was damned if she should be allowed to carry on living. She might still be a force of nature, but she wasn't invincible.

Saga appeared to be considering the matter, eventually nodding in agreement. "Very good. If you are happy with this plan, so am I."

"Don't be such a worrywart, my dear friend. She'll join us. I'm sure of it." Darius clapped his hands together. "Now, why don't you fetch our new recruit and bring him to my office? I'm eager to make his acquaintance."

CHAPTER 12

The man under consideration as Darius Duke's potential new recruit had been waiting patiently in the building's main hall since his arrival twenty minutes earlier. He didn't like being made to wait for things, but patience was a virtue he had honed over time. He had often endured hours, even days, lying in wait for the perfect moment to take out his mark. Remaining silent and motionless, he had concealed himself on rooftops, under beds, behind doors, and within shadows, foregoing even basic necessities such as bathroom breaks to ensure he was in the right place when his quarry showed up.

To date, his assignments typically involved high-profile targets – individuals who were elusive and well aware of the dangers they faced. However, there were other instances when the hits were messy and brutal, full of noise and pandemonium. Those were the assignments he enjoyed the most. The ones where it didn't matter if they saw him coming. That meant they usually fought back. He loved it when they fought back, the pathetic wretches. Seeing the fear blossoming in people's eyes as they realised they were about to die was like receiving a shot of dopamine direct to his brain.

Yet, here he was, still waiting. He glanced at his watch. He'd been sitting here now for almost thirty minutes.

What was going on?

To better pass the time, he stood up off the wooden bench and walked the length of the room. The old wooden floorboards creaked beneath his sizeable bulk with each step. He was almost six-five and weighed in at three hundred and ten pounds the last time he checked. He could even be heavier now, he'd been working out a lot recently (focusing mainly on bench presses, squats and deadlifts) and his already thick body was firm with muscle. Muscle weighed more than fat. And a fist driven by healthy muscle could deliver a lot more pain.

The room was long, with old paintings in gold frames hanging on the walls on either side. He recognised a Giorgione and a Caravaggio and maybe even a Titian over on the far side. They could have been good reproductions, but he didn't think so. He had an eye for art and wasn't easily fooled. To look at, he was a devilish brute that struck fear into the hearts of his prey, but his huge cranium also held a huge brain that was cultured, refined, and even sensitive. When he wanted to be, at least.

"Mr Grimaldi. Thank you for waiting."

The blond-haired man who'd welcomed him into the building had returned. He marched across the room towards him, his shiny boots clattering against the wooden floor like gunshots.

"It's just Grimaldi," he told him. "Forget the Mr."

The man nodded and gave him a thin-lipped smile. "My apologies."

"You'll remember from now on. People don't make the mistake twice. What did you say your name was again?"

"Stig Saga." He smiled once more, wider, his lips practically disappearing as he did. "Now that we are properly acquainted, would you please follow me? Darius Duke is eager to meet with you."

Grimaldi picked the large canvas bag he'd brought with him up off the bench and followed Saga out of the main hall and down a long stone corridor with windows looking out onto the piazza. It was getting late. The sky was a harmonious wash of crimson and periwinkle. Halfway along the corridor they reached an elevator, the metallic doors and illuminated keypad incongruous with the rest of the ostentatious décor. Saga tapped in a six-digit code, 8-1-0-3-3-7 (Grimaldi always noticed these sorts of things; it paid to be observant), and they waited in silence as the doors slid silently open. Saga moved aside to let Grimaldi enter first, before stepping in behind him and hitting the button for the first floor.

The elevator was made of brushed aluminium and looked to be a new addition to the building. Grimaldi knew Duke had only recently taken on the lease for the glorious sixteenth-century building (it also paid to read up on local history), and he imagined, given time, most of the fixtures and fittings would be updated and the outer and inner structures reinforced. It was a pity, to mess with such a wonderful example of Italian architecture, but he understood the need.

The elevator came to a stop and the doors slid open. Saga stepped out first.

"If you'd like to follow me."

They walked in silence down another long corridor, this one mahogany panelled and windowless. The air was stuffy, but Grimaldi's perceptive nose detected notes of wood smoke and frankincense. They reached a large metal door with no lock or handle and a biometric scanner two-thirds of the way up on one side. Saga stepped in front of it and presented his iris. There was a beep and a click and the door slid open.

"Here we are."

Once more, he stepped aside to let the bigger man enter in front of him. Grimaldi stepped into a vast rectangular room with a high ceiling and an elaborate modern chandelier illuminating the monochrome décor. A large round window at the far end, with iridescent stained-glass panels, was the only testament to the room's history. In front of the window stood an enormous black desk, and sitting on the other side in a black leather chair was a man. As Grimaldi entered the room and walked towards him, the man leaned forward and clutched his hands together in front of him.

"Mr Grimaldi. Welcome."

Grimaldi waited until he got up to the desk before he spoke. "As I told your man just now, I am not Mr. It is just Grimaldi. But you are Mr Duke, yes?"

"Darius is fine."

"As you wish." Grimaldi took in the man on the other side of the desk. His prospective new boss. He wasn't much to look at. Under six foot and slim, with thick hair slicked back from his face that seemed too black to be natural. There was something enchanting about him, however; he had a certain glimmer in his eye that spoke of confidence and pride. "It is good to meet you. I have heard many good things about you recently. You are indeed the talk of the industry."

"Am I?" Darius sat back and fanned his face with his open hand. It was supposed to be amusing, but Grimaldi found camp displays of faux modesty off-putting; even if done in jest. "Things do seem to be going well for us. We are settled in our new central headquarters, as you can see, and my handpicked team of elite operatives is almost complete. Which, of course, is why you're here. I take it Saga filled you in on the details."

Grimaldi nodded. "Ten thousand per job and a retainer of one hundred thousand euros a year. What about expenses?"

Darius raised an eyebrow. "Expenses, too? Well, I'm sure we can work out a reasonable per diem for you when out in the field. You'll also be able to stay at HQ when you're in town. We're converting the basement into self-contained apartments that can house up to six operatives at any one time. And don't worry, this isn't some dingy barracks-style set-up. I want only the best for my operatives. You will stay in luxury when you are here."

"This sounds very agreeable. I like your style. So, what now?"

Darius stuck out his bottom lip and shrugged. "I suppose I need to know that you're committed to the role and to Kancel Kulture entirely. If you join us, there will be no more off-the-books or freelance work. I assign the jobs. You carry out the hits. No negotiation. Are we clear?"

Grimaldi nodded. "This I can do. I've been ready to be part of something bigger for a while now. There is, how you say, safety in numbers?" He laughed at the very thought of this being an issue for him. Darius wasn't the only one who could do the jokes. His new boss, however, only pulled a confused expression. "Yes, Darius, I am more than prepared to work for you. You alone. I believe you are the disrupting force this fatigued industry needs and I am prepared to work to your exacting standards."

"Wonderful." Darius got to his feet. "There is one other matter we need to discuss. The assignment I set for you. The practical aspect of the job interview, as it were. You have completed it?"

"I have," Grimaldi replied, his voice low and steady. This 'practical aspect', as Darius blithely put it, was to take out a man called Cruz Moreno, a Spanish gangster who had seriously pissed off Gael Ruiz, head of the Ruiz crime family over in the Basque region of the country. Grimaldi had been tasked with making the hit as brutal and bloody as possible, to send a strong message to the rest of the Moreno family that they were to back off or face similar fates.

And Grimaldi had certainly delivered. It took him days to scrub the blood out of his hair and from under his fingernails.

Ah Dio! He loved his work.

"And have you captured evidence of the hit, as Saga requested in his correspondence?"

Grimaldi waved his hand in the air in a flippant manner, his Italian heritage coming through. "You wanted me to take a photo of the mark's face for evidence."

One of the tendons in Darius' neck bulged. "Yes. This is what we ask of all our operatives. We need a photo to run through the facial recognition software so we can send proof of the hit to the client." He breathed heavily down his nose. "This part is rather important. Did you take the photo?"

"I do not carry a phone," he replied. "I do not like them. They are distracting."

"I see," Darius made a face, his eyes flitting to Saga. "That is a bit of an issue. You see, we also use tracking software here so our tech team can locate our operatives when out in the field."

"I understand. Get me a phone. I'll use it."

"Good. But that does put me in a bit of a predicament with the client, however," Darius added. "Plus, without the photo, I have no real proof that you carried out the assignment."

Grimaldi held his hand up. "*No, signore. We do not need a photo.*" He lowered his canvas bag to the floor before kneeling and unzipping it slowly. Reaching into the depths, he lifted out the contents and got to his feet. "I think this will satisfy both yourself and Gael Ruiz in proving that I carried out the hit as per instructions." He flung the decapitated head of Cruz Moreno onto Darius' desk. It rolled once and came to rest with the eyes looking up at the boss man. *Bello.* Grimaldi couldn't have planned it better if he'd tried.

"Bloody hell," Darius gasped, staring down at the head. "I wasn't expecting that."

Grimaldi chuckled. "This is acceptable? It's enough proof for you?"

"Yes. I suppose it is." Darius shook his head, but he was laughing now, too. He wagged a finger at Grimaldi. "You're a bloody genius and a showman to boot. I love it." He moved around the side of the desk and approached him with an outstretched hand. "If you're interested in the position, I'd love to have you join us."

Grimaldi grabbed Darius' hand, practically consuming it

within his huge palm. "Thank you. I believe we will do great work together and I would like to accept your offer to join Kancel Kulture." They shook hands vigorously but he pulled away first. "Tell me. I am interested in knowing. Who will I be working alongside?"

"All in good time, my friend," Darius replied, rubbing his hand as he took it away. "Once we have everything in place, I plan to hold a welcome party for the whole organisation. There will be drinks, canapés, entertainment. You'll love it. But before then, if you are ready to get stuck in with some work, there is something I need you to do."

"A hit?"

"Not entirely." Darius looked him up and down. "Do you have a passport and papers?"

Grimaldi sneered at the question. "Of course. I have three passports in my hotel. More secured in safe deposit boxes at airports all around the world, for emergencies."

"Excellent. Then I want you on the next flight to London. Saga will fill you in on the details. But suffice to say, this is a very important mission and I need you to follow my instructions to the letter. Don't get creative with this one. Do you hear me?"

Grimaldi bared his teeth. "*Non c'è problema.* Just tell me what you need me to do. *Boss.*"

CHAPTER 13

Spook was sitting at the kitchen table examining the raised scar that now snaked across her forearm, a bowl of half-eaten muesli in front of her, when Acid walked into the room.

"How's it looking?" Acid asked, squinting at the wound through her heavy fringe.

Spook looked up, surprised at how friendly Acid sounded after their fight a few nights ago and the subsequent tension ever since. She'd always possessed these erratic mood swings, but the last few months had seen them intensify, leaving Spook in a constant state of unease. One minute Acid could be hissing in her face, explaining how she wanted to kill her in numerous vile ways, and the next minute she'd be strutting around full of sweetness and light as if they were the best of friends. Though Spook carried a deep empathy for Acid's internal battles, the emotional whiplash was becoming increasingly difficult to bear. She was always on the back foot.

"It still hurts a bit," she replied, turning her attention to her arm and choosing to take Acid at face value. "But it's more of a weird ache or an itch."

Acid leaned down and placed her forearm beside Spook's. "It's similar to mine," she said, twisting her forearm around to present the almost identical scar that ran from below her wrist to just below her elbow. "The Dullahan gave me that, you know?"

Spook hadn't known. She smiled, not knowing how else to respond. 'Oh, cute' or 'That's cool' didn't seem to cut it.

"I know what you mean about it aching," Acid continued. "Especially in cold weather. But it looks cool. It gives you an edge you didn't have before. You've got battle scars now. Literally."

"Hmm." Spook wasn't convinced. She was less convinced by Acid's amicableness at this time of day. It was past 10 a.m. but still early for Acid. Spook rolled her sleeve down. "I've made coffee, if you want a mug."

"Thanks. I'd bloody love one, actually." She walked past Spook, heading for the machine in the corner.

In contrast, Spook had been awake for hours. She'd pushed through three sets of fifteen push-ups and a hundred sit-ups, each rep a testament to her determination. As well as that, she'd spent an hour on YouTube immersing herself in martial arts videos, eager to learn offensive techniques. If Acid refused to take on the role of trainer, Spook had no choice but to forge her own path. With the spectre of Darius Duke lurking in the shadows, she had no other option. She was sick of feeling scared. She was sick of feeling like a nerd.

Yet, something else still bothered Spook. She'd touched on it a few days earlier, but had been too fearful to pursue the matter. Now, with Acid more amiable than she had been in weeks, it felt like the perfect moment to bring it up again.

Picking up her coffee mug, Spook downed the contents, telling herself as soon as she placed the mug down on the table she'd say what was on her mind.

Three-Two-One...

"Do you want me to try to locate Darius?" She said it and froze, waiting for the inevitable blow-up or snide comment. When neither came, she twisted around on her stool to see Acid leaning against the kitchen counter with her coffee mug poised at her lips. She looked so small and ordinary huddled over her hot drink, that for a moment Spook lost her train of thought. She blinked. "What I mean is... I can do it. If you want me to. I've been on the Crypto Jones One Thousand forum and there's a lot of chatter about a new organisation. It's got to be Darius. And I've found someone who might have been recruited by him. A woman calling herself The Gorgon. She's from Hungary and is new on the scene but already making a name for herself."

Acid slurped at her coffee. "Yeah. I've heard of her. That's good work, Spook." But she sounded distant. She was staring straight ahead without blinking.

"Wait for the best bit," Spook went on. "You see, like most people who use that forum, the avatar she uses for her profile isn't of her face. But, unlike most of the people on the forum, she does use a real photo image for her profile rather than a jpeg grabbed from the internet. The photo is a blurred image of a snake. It's not great. But I downloaded it and found the metadata was linked to the same photo on an old Myspace account from two-thousand-and-four. It's the same photo. Meaning the Myspace account is her old account. It's a rookie mistake, and I imagine now she's working for someone like Darius, there'll be someone more versed in tech who will wipe the internet of any records of her. But for now it exists.

"The Gorgon's real name is Mika Galambos. She's now twenty-three and grew up in care. I also got a photo of her face from the Myspace profile. It's an old shot, but the biometric signifiers won't have changed. It means I can find her. And if I can find her, she can lead us to Darius. From what I've gathered, he's based in Europe. If it's a major city, then it'll have an extensive CCTV network. They're easy as pie to hack into for someone like me. Once I link the feeds to my facial recognition AI software, we'll find him in a heartbeat."

She sat back, sensing her cheeks burning a little as she waited for Acid to reply. And she waited. Spook wasn't expecting praise – that was too much to expect from Acid Vanilla – but some acknowledgement of her hard work and expertise would have been nice.

"Acid?" she said. "Do you want me to..."

"No. Leave it for now." She remained staring straight ahead, but her brow was creased in a sharp scowl.

"Seriously? Because I'm sorry to keep going on about this, but it feels a little like we're sitting ducks right now. We need to find Darius and we need to stop him before he can hurt either one of us. Do you not agree? *Either* one of us. I'm in danger, too. This isn't only your decision. I really think we should—"

"Please! Spook! Let me think!" Acid spat out the words and glared at her. At least it was some kind of response.

Spook held her gaze. "What the hell do you need to think about?" It shocked her how cold and angry her tone was, but it represented how she felt. "He murdered The Dullahan. He was about to murder me. Then you. Do you remember?"

"Of course I do."

"So why hesitate? What's going on?" Spook's chest tightened. "Is this about the DNA test?"

Acid's stare remained locked on Spook, but her left eye twitched – a tell-tale sign of stress. Spook couldn't blame her; discovering a potential half-brother after all these years would freak her out as well. But Darius Duke was evil and had to be stopped. Surely Acid knew that. Surely she wasn't...

No.

It wasn't worth considering. But Spook couldn't help feeling Acid was hiding something.

"Do you want to talk about it?" she asked, her tone soft now.

Acid averted her eyes. "No. Maybe later." She set her coffee mug down and moved towards the door. "I'm going to head out for a while. I need to get some air. Okay?"

"No worries. We can talk later."

"Yeah. Whatever."

Spook watched as Acid grabbed her leather jacket from the back of the kitchen door and slipped it on. "Be careful, yeah?"

Acid smiled, but it was hollow, devoid of joy or even her usual playful defiance. It was the kind of smile you gave someone to whom you were about to deliver devastating news. "You know me, Spook," she said. "I'm always careful."

CHAPTER 14

Acid had walked the length of Wardour Street and was heading down Sheraton Street towards Soho Square when she became aware of footsteps behind her. It being a Sunday, the streets around Soho at this time of morning were quiet and the footsteps distinct. Hard leather soles slapped against concrete pavement, the sound reverberating through the crisp spring air.

With no cars in sight, Acid moved into the street, tracing the white line as if she was about to cross over and turn right onto Carlisle Street. At the last second, she jumped back onto the pavement and ducked down a narrow side street between two shopfronts. Her pulse pounded in her ears as she walked, but she was already questioning herself. Had she imagined the footsteps? At times like this, when she was unable to properly get a handle on her mania, she was prone to intense paranoia. But then she heard the footsteps again, echoing down the empty street. She was correct. She was being followed. Head down, she pressed on, not stopping for a moment or looking back to see whoever was behind her. That wouldn't be helpful. Not yet. Presently, this person still believed they had the element of surprise, the upper hand. As long as they underestimated her, the opposite was true.

Up ahead she saw a passageway in between the rear entrances of two restaurants. Quickening her pace, she veered behind a large industrial waste bin and, once hidden from view, stopped to peer around the side of it. This passageway led down to another back street, which would provide her with an easy escape route to the main road if it came to it. She slid the push dagger out of her belt and gripped it tight. Whoever this prick was, they'd rue the day they took this assignment. The same way that pathetic no-mark the other night did—

Shitting pissing hell.

Her breath caught in her throat as her pursuer appeared at the end of the passageway. To say he was huge would be an understatement. He was also ugly and mean-looking and so wide he practically filled the narrow lane. His shoulders brushed against the wall on either side of him as he slowed his pace and moved down the alley. His black hair was receding at the temples and on the crown, but that hadn't stopped him from growing it long and wearing it in a greasy ponytail. Acid would have placed his age anywhere between late thirties and early fifties. His large ears were mangled and swollen like a seasoned rugby player's and he had a bulbous nose which, like his cheeks and chin, was pitted with acne scars. He glanced up the alley, seeing her straight away. His eyes were dark and piercing.

"Acid Vanilla," he growled in a deep Italian accent, going in heavy on the final consonants in each of her names. "What a treat it is to meet you."

She raised her head, sticking out her chest as she came out from around the back of the industrial waste bin. "That's what they all say."

He chuckled. "I bet they do." His smile dropped away, making his large features even more grotesque.

Acid's muscles tensed, her mind racing as she weighed her options. There was no way she could take out this man blow for blow, but she could easily outrun him. Yet something was stopping her. It could have been the bats, gnawing relentlessly at the fringes of her sanity, their shrill cries demanding vengeance. It could have been the searing wave of indignation – at the audacity of yet another arrogant prick seeking to annihilate her. Or perhaps, deep down, she really did harbour a craving for oblivion.

Spook had always accused Acid of having a death wish, but mostly she'd played down the idea. Yet in moments like these, the possibility was hard to ignore. More than fear, anger, or her self-destructive tendencies, however, it was an insatiable curiosity that kept her here. Her instincts told her this man had the answers she needed.

"I take it Darius sent you."

The man threw his head back, revealing rows of yellowing teeth. "Is that what you think?"

"Who else? Why else would you be here if not?" She tightened her grip on the dagger and shifted her weight onto her thighs. "Or do you want to tell me different?"

"Why don't you come here and find out." His eyes fell on the blade in her hand, but he didn't flinch. In fact, his beady eyes seemed to grow more lustful.

Acid pulled in a slow breath and held it in her lungs. The bats were deafening, their screeches filling her soul.

Kill him!

You can take this prick!

And maybe she could. Despite the man's huge frame, he looked sturdy; but everyone could be toppled if you knew where to hit them. A well-placed swipe across the femoral artery in his upper thigh with the push dagger and he'd bleed out within minutes.

No.

Staying and fighting was foolish, bordering on suicide. She might have had a death wish, but she wasn't ready to throw her life away in a backstreet brawl.

She stepped back, making to turn and flee into the next street.

"What's wrong, dear?" the man called out. "Is the great Acid Vanilla scared? Oh *merda*. Whatever next."

She stopped. "I'm not scared of you."

"No? Come then. Let's dance. I am unarmed. You have a dagger, I see. The advantage is all yours. Why don't you show me how brave you are? You see, I have heard many things about you, my dear. They say you were special. They say you were the best. But me, I don't see it. All I see is a washed-up bitch with bad style and a worse attitude."

Acid didn't move. She knew what he was doing. She knew she should walk away. Yet a part of her, the part that was already chaotic and manic – and now confused as hell since Darius' unceremonious reveal – told her to stay, to face this foul brute.

But she had to get close to him first.

The thought of sending another of Darius' flunkies to the morgue spurred her on as she readied herself for an attack.

The man in front of her still hadn't moved. Their eyes met and he bared his teeth some more as he smiled.

That was all it took.

With the push dagger raised to her chest, Acid launched herself forward, seeing her trajectory mapped out in front of her. A thunderous cacophony of chaos filled her head as the brick walls and debris-ridden streets merged into the heavens above. All that existed was the man – her prey, her sole purpose for being. She locked her sights on his upper thigh, raising the blade to shoulder height, ready for her attack. The man crouched in anticipation, hands splayed and defenceless. He hadn't lied. He had no weapon.

He was finished.

In these situations, primal instincts and ingrained muscle memory reigned over logic or contemplation. As Acid closed the distance, she trusted her senses, unleashing the dagger in a vicious arc. It was done. She had the prick. The blade gleamed, a ribbon of metallic light dancing through the air. Acid readied herself to leap back, to remove herself from the playing field once the lethal blow had been administered. But something was wrong – there was no resistance. It felt as if the blade had cut through nothing but air. Had the prick evaded her in time? She righted herself, slamming her shoulder against him to create space and assess the situation.

She didn't get a chance.

Her face collided with a brutal, unyielding force that sent her spinning like a drunken ballerina in a macabre pirouette. It felt like her cheekbone shattered with the impact. The walls morphed into the sky, into unforgiving concrete. As she struggled to discern up from down, a crushing boot collided with her ribcage, sending a shockwave of pain through her torso. Gasping for air, she felt as though her lung had been punctured. And he was coming for her again, grabbing for her ankle. She managed to clamber away from him and put her back to the wall, hands groping the dusty ground for the push dagger that had slipped from her grasp.

She gritted her teeth, struggling to focus as the man loomed down on her. Her vision was blurred, but the bats were now in charge. She kicked out wildly, her boot colliding with the man's knee and bending it back against the joint. At the same time, she used the momentum the force of the attack provided to scramble away and get to her feet. The man staggered over onto his other leg, grunting through the pain. Acid lunged at him, putting all her weight into her right shoulder as she drove it into his solar plexus. She knew from experience, size difference or not, if she got him on his back it would be all over.

But the bastard wouldn't go down.

She shoved against him, grabbing the material of his jacket and kneeing him in the balls with as much force as she could muster. He cried out, the cry of a wounded animal. As Acid stepped back, her eyes fell on her push dagger lying against the wall a few feet away. Perfect. She deftly manoeuvred around the staggering man, his groans amplifying, and reached for the weapon. Her fingers grazed the handle, dragging it into her grasp, when her ankles buckled and the world upended once more. She landed with a thud on her back and for a moment was unsure who she was and what had happened. The second her clarity returned, she sprang to her feet, only to be slammed against the wall by a massive, sweaty hand gripped around her throat.

"*Smettila!*" the man snarled. "Stop this, you crazy bitch. It's over." He pushed her head against the wall, grinding the back of her skull against the hard brick. "Done!"

The two of them stared at each other, their faces only inches apart. "Go on, then," she gasped. "Do it. Get it over with."

The man laughed. His hot, meaty breath made her want to vomit. "Get what over with? I am not here to kill you. Far from it. I am here to deliver a message." Yet as he spoke, his grip tightened around her throat. If the message he wanted to convey was that he could kill her with one swift constriction of his huge hand, then she was getting it, loud and clear.

"What message?"

He leaned in closer. "You were right before. Darius Duke sent me. But not as your killer. I am here to display to you the power of his new organisation. The organisation he hopes you will soon join." His grin widened and his eyes seemed to double in size. "Think about it. Soon we could be working together. It will be fun. No?"

He loosened his grip on her so she could respond. But only a little. "What if I say no?"

"I don't think Duke knows the meaning of this word," he replied, tilting his head to one side. "He asks that you come to see him. To discuss what he can offer you. If you choose to dismiss his wishes... then more like me will come for you. And they won't be as polite or as friendly." He stepped back and adjusted her leather jacket, flattening down the collar like a tailor might do. "You should do as he requests, Acid. You were good today. You fought hard. I can see why Duke wants you on board."

"Tell him he can go to hell."

He laughed again, in the resigned way one might laugh at an old joke. "You can tell him yourself when you meet with him. You have three days, Acid Vanilla. Then he loses his patience with you. You and Spook and anyone else you care about will be wiped off the face of the earth. Do you understand?" He slapped her gently on the upper arm. "But see, it doesn't have to come to that. We will be friends, you and I. Allies. It will be *glorioso,* yes?"

He moved away and reached down for the push dagger, handing it to her as he straightened up. She glared at it for a moment, but took it from him.

"Good. Now I must go." He pointed a fat finger at her. "Three days, Acid. Then we stop playing nice and you and I are no longer friends. *Capisci?*"

With that, he turned and walked back the way he'd come. Acid rubbed at her neck as she watched him go.

"Wait," she called after him. "If I do decide to meet with Darius, how do I find him?"

The big man stopped but didn't turn around. "That's for you to work out," he called back. "Think of it as a test of your mettle. I'm sure you and your little friend can find him if you put your minds to it."

"But three days, that doesn't give us much time."

Now he turned around and she saw he was giggling, almost girlishly. "No. It really doesn't. But there you go." His face fell into a stern scowl. "Three days. Then you both die. *Arrivederci,* Acid Vanilla."

CHAPTER 15

I t took Acid thirty minutes to make what should have been a ten-minute journey back to her apartment. She'd stuck mainly to back streets and alleyways, zigzagging her way through Soho and the theatre district and steering clear of the eyes of the world. Her ribs hurt like hell, and she could feel her face swelling up on one side. Her ego and pride had taken just as much of a beating.

Upon entering the apartment, she found Spook standing in the hallway, a sandwich-laden plate in one hand and her phone in the other. "Whoa. What happened to you?" she asked, concern raising her voice as she took in Acid's dishevelled appearance.

"I'm fine. It probably looks worse than it is." But she leaned against the wall all the same. "I was followed. A big ugly guy with a ponytail. He was Italian, I think."

"Shit!" Spook placed the plate and her phone on the side table under the hallway mirror and rushed over to her. "Let me look." She placed her hand under Acid's chin, tilting her head to one side so she could examine the damage. "What happened to the guy? Did you...?"

Acid moved away, freeing herself from Spook's hand. "No." She stumbled into the kitchen and took a seat at the table. "He overpowered me. But he wasn't after killing me. He had a message. From Darius." She'd been in two minds whether to share this information with Spook, but now she was here in front of her, she realised it was the fair thing to do. Spook's life was in danger as well.

"What message?" Spook hurried over and pulled a chair out to sit. "Did he tell you where Darius was?"

Acid shook her head, realised it hurt, and stopped. She grimaced. "Do we have any painkillers?"

"In the drawer next to the fridge. Here, let me." Spook got up and grabbed them out of the drawer. Returning to the table, she slid the box across to her. "Tell me what happened. Tell me everything."

Tell her everything...

Acid puffed out a sigh. "Darius wants me to join his organisation," she said. "That's what this is about. The message is, if I don't join he'll kill us. Both of us."

"But you can't join him. He's an evil bastard. You were there that day. You saw. He's insane."

Acid opened the box of painkillers and liberated two of the caplets from their foil casing. After tossing them into her mouth, she swallowed them dry. Not easy when you had no saliva and you could still feel the phantom grip of your attacker's hand around your throat.

Spook was staring at her. Acid shrugged. "Yes, you're right."

And she was. Probably. Darius was insane, as well as

selfish, egotistical and dangerously unpredictable. But wasn't Caesar all of those things? Wasn't Acid herself?

Darius was also smart, innovative, and diligent. He was building an empire from the ground up and appeared to be succeeding where so many had failed. From what people were saying about him, he was fast becoming a contender for Caesar's crown.

But this wasn't the only thing that intrigued Acid. It wasn't what had consumed her thoughts for the past month, chipping away at her confidence and sense of reason. There was still one question that needed answering. A single resounding question that haunted her days and invaded her dreams.

Was Darius Duke her brother?

She needed to find out. But at the same time it was the not knowing that was keeping her going. Presently, she found herself in a Schrödinger's cat-style paradox. Darius was simultaneously her brother and he also wasn't. Until she opened the box she'd never know. But she also knew this was no ordinary box or one that she could simply close if she didn't like the answer inside. It was a Pandora's box brimming with unimaginable consequences.

"For heaven's sake!" She was confusing herself with these mangled analogies. Yet, wasn't that the point? Everything about this damn situation was confusing.

Did she want Darius to be her brother?

A part of her did. She had no family. Her mother was dead; Caesar, too. Even Acid, with her icy demeanour and cynical, insular nature, yearned for connection now and again. The vulnerable and lonely Alice Vandella – still inside her head somewhere – yearned for it even more. She had

Spook, of course, but their relationship had been more strained than ever lately and, despite Spook's insistence that Acid teach her the lethal arts, her American friend couldn't truly understand her. She never would.

"Shit," Spook gasped, sitting back. "You're wavering, aren't you?"

Acid bit her upper lip as she considered the question. "I don't know," was the only response she could come up with.

"Did the guy who attacked you say anything else?"

"Like what?"

"I don't know. Did he hint at where Darius might be? Where we could find him? Because if you don't join, we need to strike first. And soon." She slapped her hand on the table. "Come on, Acid, snap out of it! This is serious. We're going to die unless we take action. We have to find him. Once he's dead, all this uncertainty, all the speculation, it ends. We both get to carry on with our lives without this dark, existential threat hanging over our heads."

Acid sniffed. "Yes. I know."

"Oh? Do you? Great." Spook was angrier than Acid had ever seen her. "You know what, Acid. Maybe you should join him. Get out of here. Get lost. Go be an assassin and work for that evil prick. It's what you want, isn't it? It's what all this has been leading up to. So, yeah. Go. Do us both a favour. If that's what it takes to stop him, you join his fucking organisation."

Every word hit Acid harder than any punch or kick she'd endured in the alleyway earlier. "It's not as easy as that, Spook."

"Why?"

"Because of everything else you've said."

Spook averted her gaze, staring out the window. At that

moment she reminded Acid of her mother, Louisa, who would do the same when she was chastising the pre-teen Alice and had become too exasperated to even look at her.

Acid opened her mouth, ready to reveal the man's ultimatum – that she had only three days to decide and to find Darius. But something held her back.

Tell her everything...

No, not everything.

"I'll work through it," she muttered. "I'll sort this out, I promise."

"Whatever." Spook got up and was about to leave the room when she turned back. She walked over and placed both hands palms down on the table. Now she reminded Acid of every bitchy teacher or warden at Crest Hill; everyone who'd ever got in her face about something she had or hadn't done. "I don't know how you can even consider joining that man's ranks. You should hate him for what he did."

"I do," she replied. "But it's complicated."

"Is it? How?"

"Because... all's fair in love and war and the killing business. The Dullahan knew that as much as anyone. He understood, more than most, the world he was a part of. He probably suspected he'd die from a bullet or at the sharp end of a blade eventually. When you work in this industry you get yourself into a certain mindset. You make a friend of death. You accept that it's lurking for you around every corner." She stood, mirroring Spook as she leaned over the table at the opposite end. They looked like a pair of hardened army generals, scrutinising a map of war. Perhaps because they were. "I know you think I've got a death wish, but I've been hearing that since I started in this game, and it's not true. I made a choice early on to embrace the samurai way. I read about it in a book at Honeysuckle House, where Caesar trained me. Before entering battle, a samurai will undergo a mental transformation where they accept that they're going to die. They call it dying before dying. This way they can fight unencumbered by doubt or fear. It's the only way you survive in this world."

She straightened her back. "I do hate Darius for what he did, Spook. But I understand why he did it, as well. I need to think about a few things, okay? But I swear to you I'm going to sort this out. Give me a few days." With determined strides, she navigated around the table and made her way to the door. She needed a shower and to deal with her injuries. An ice pack for her bruised cheek would be a good start.

"Acid?" She was in the hallway when Spook called after her.

She stopped. "Yes?"

"What if we don't survive?"

It was another good question, and one that hit her as hard as the previous ones. She paused for a moment, working out how best to respond. The atmosphere felt still and oppressive. She knew Spook was waiting for an answer, but rather than reply, she continued down the hallway and into her room, shutting the door behind her. Some questions couldn't be answered in a few choice words or a pithy soundbite. What Spook wanted was reassurance and Acid couldn't give her that. Not yet. Maybe not ever.

Three days.

She had a lot to consider.

CHAPTER 16

t was thirty-two hours later (plus one more to allow for the time difference between London and Rome) and Darius Duke was standing in the centre of the main hall at Kancel Kulture headquarters. The impressive ancient building had now been christened *Casa di Cicero* – The House of Cicero – named after Marcus Tullius Cicero, the first-century BC scholar, philosopher and writer. Darius had always had a strong affiliation with the classics, but Cicero's famous defiance of Caesar, his refusal to partake in the First Triumvirate assembly and his efforts to undermine Caesar's reign, resonated deeply with him. The fact that Cicero was also somewhat of a dandy goth for his time, growing his hair long and wearing only mourning dress, added to his renegade charm.

Darius held up the heavy leather-bound book he'd been reading from, regarding the people arranged in a semi-circular formation before him. No one spoke. All eyes were on him. Perfect. That's how he wanted it. He was their leader. He should command respect.

He cleared his throat and continued reading, a passage from the epic poem *Annales* by Ennius.

"*All men were anxious over which would be their ruler. They wait, as when the consul prepares to give the signal, everyone eagerly looking to the starting gates for how soon he sends the painted chariots from the barrier: so the people were waiting, visible on each face a concern for their affairs, to which the victory of supreme rule is given.*" He glanced up, noticing The Gorgon, merely a few feet away, seemed to be lavishing him with an intensely provocative gaze. And why shouldn't she? He was standing on the precipice of greatness. He was Darius Duke, the mastermind behind Kancel Kulture, the agitator, trailblazer, king. He returned her his most devilish grin and returned to the passage. "*Meanwhile the sun had set into the depth of night. Then struck by rays the shining light showed itself openly and at once on high from far away a beautifully winged leftward flight advanced. Just as the golden sun arises, there comes descending from the sky a dozen blessed bodies of birds, settling themselves on fine and favourable seats. Thus Romulus sees that given to himself alone, approved by auspices, were the base and bulwark of a kingdom.*"

With a decisive snap, he closed the book, allowing the words to sink in before addressing his new team. "Hear those words again. *A kingdom. Our* kingdom. For I have created a kingdom here and soon you will all reap the glorious benefits of my supreme reign of power. This industry will not know what has hit it. With our advanced network and elite eradication tactics, we will conquer the world. In due time, Kancel Kulture will be the only organisation anyone will ever need. The competition will crumble under our superior and collective might."

He flashed his eyes at his people, eliciting the fervent applause he'd anticipated.

"You have all been handpicked, not only for your skillsets and capabilities, but for the way you conduct yourselves in the field. Each of you brings something different to the table and, as a whole, we will ensure Kancel Kulture remains a pioneering, lethal and impenetrable organisation. So... welcome. All of you. I am so happy to have you here."

He spread his arms wide, basking in the thunderous applause, his eyes surveying each of his new recruits. Alongside Saga, Grimaldi, and The Gorgon, stood Nokizaru, the lethal and enigmatic assassin hailing from Japan's Iga Province and versed in the ancient ways of the shinobi-no-mono. He didn't speak any English – in fact, he didn't speak at all, with all communication occurring via the dark web – but he was known to be an intelligent and elegant craftsman. Although merely twenty-three, his impressive tally of kills (twenty-nine men, eleven women, two Ussuri brown bears) spoke volumes.

Rounding out the formidable yet eclectic team, at least for the time being, were Frederik and Freek Kriel, the South African 'Blood Diamond Twins'. The most experienced of the bunch, with a decade in the industry under their belts, the brothers had earned their status as two of the most vicious and brutal killers the world had ever seen. If you wanted to send your enemies a stark message, it was the Blood Diamond Twins you sent. Legend had it that Freek murdered his mother and father at the tender age of seven, and the brothers dismembered their parents' bodies using a hand axe before feeding them to the family dog. Darius had wondered whether the tale was apocryphal, but it was too a good story to question. Besides, the Kriel Brothers unnerved him to the point that he would never dare question the veracity of their origin story aloud. The way they looked at people, as if neither party were human or deserving of humanity, gave him the creeps. However, as long as he paid them the big bucks, their loyalty would be assured. As he regarded them, they grinned at him in unison, revealing their infamous metal teeth. Freek's were gold, while Frederik's were white gold. Being identical twins, it was the only way to tell them apart. Both had blood diamonds embedded in their upper canines.

"Okay then, everyone," Darius went on, widening his attention and taking in the whole group. "That's enough from me. I know most of you are strangers, so I suggest we spend a few hours getting to know one another better. Behind you, as you can see, we have provided an extensive buffet with food from all over the world. Amongst the delicacies on offer, we have New Zealand Bluff oysters, artisanal goose foie gras and Iranian Pearl caviar. Only the best, most luxurious food for my people. We also have an entire Wagyu beef rib on its way, as well as some rare Cemani chickens that we've had flown in from Indonesia." He nodded proudly at the excited murmurs going around the room, led by Grimaldi. "Please, eat as much as you like. As you can also see, there is a well-stocked bar. We have covered all tastes. The finest wines from all over the world, Grey Goose vodka, Bollinger, plus a rather cheeky thirty-five-year-old Hibiki whisky, which I'm told is to die for. All I ask is that you leave me a couple of glasses of the Collina Rionda Barolo, which I am rather partial to."

He clapped his hands together, his eyes fixated on the dispersing group as they gravitated towards the grand mahogany dining table against the back wall. It was funny to him. Even expert killers acted awkwardly around new people. It was also reassuring. Because Darius might have fast been making a name for himself as the new king of the murder-for-hire industry, but he still had the same doubts he'd always had. He was still crippled by indecision and nerves on occasion.

This was precisely why he needed *her*. Although he'd been masquerading as Freddie Pearce when they first met, he had managed to get to know her. Her fiery spirit and jaded outlook on both the industry and life itself would serve as the perfect counterbalance to his zeal and tenacity. Together, they might just be able to silence the relentless inner conflict that continued to haunt him.

He caught Saga's eye and beckoned him over with a flick of his head.

"Great speech," Saga said as he walked over.

"Do you think so? I felt as if I lost Nokizaru towards the end."

The Swede turned his mouth down. "It was the energy and feeling you gave it that was important. You showed yourself to be a leader. Someone to be listened to. You have done well here. These people will ensure our organisation reaches its full capabilities." He turned so they were standing shoulder to shoulder and they watched, in silent reverence, as the five assassins stuffed some of the most expensive food on the planet into their beautiful murderous faces and guzzled Champagne from cut-crystal flutes.

"Is there any word from you know who?" Darius asked.

"Nothing new." Saga lifted his arm and flicked out his cuff, revealing a Cartier watch. It was a new purchase, bought using the finder's fee Darius had paid him for securing the Kriel Brothers' contracts. "She has less than forty-eight hours."

Darius sucked in a deep breath. "Yes, I am aware. Don't worry. I still have a strong sense that she'll turn. I'm not saying it's a sibling's intuition, but... maybe it is. Right now she's on the fence. We need to give her a push."

Saga nodded. "What do you suggest?"

"I think, my friend, it's time for us to instigate the next phase of our plan." He placed his arm around Saga's shoulders, feeling the stoic Swede stiffen as he did so. "If my big sister won't listen to reason. Then maybe she'll listen to force."

CHAPTER 17

Eman Aziz reclined against the hood of his rental car, absentmindedly rolling the toothpick he'd been chewing between his lips. A cold, damp day unfolded around him. It was miserable, even here under the shelter of the disused railway tunnel outside of Hounslow. This was the sort of English weather that Aziz loathed the most – not quite rain, but more like the air was just... wet.

Aziz had been living in London for less than a year, but he was already weary of the city's perpetual greyness. Nostalgia for his homeland consumed him, particularly for his cherished city of Tripoli, with its sweltering, arid climate that persisted throughout the year. If he hadn't had to flee to the UK after Omar Shebani, one of Libya Dawn's most formidable leaders, had taken offence to Aziz supplying arms to a competing militia, he would still be basking in the familiar warmth of his home city. The ache of longing stirred within him, a constant reminder of the life he'd left behind.

He pulled out his phone. It was now 7.15 p.m., and the man he was supposed to be meeting was fifteen minutes late.

He'd give him another five minutes and then he would leave. Flicking through the messages on his phone, he grinned to himself as he opened up the thread from Anneke – a sprightly young Dutch girl he'd met the previous week at The Gaslighter Club in Farringdon. The fact she was working as a lap dancer and was paid to be nice to the guests didn't bother him. Everyone had a price in this world. It was only the truly honest souls who could admit this to themselves. Initially, Anneke had been somewhat standoffish toward him. After all, Aziz was a short, hairy man who seemed to have a problem with sweat, even on damp, miserable days like this one. However, her attitude had shifted dramatically once she'd seen how much money he had on his person.

Yes, everyone had a price.

He typed out a new message, telling Anneke he was looking forward to seeing her later and for her to wear the same red underwear she'd been wearing in the club. As he stuffed his phone in his pocket, he looked up to see a lone figure, a man, standing at the mouth of the tunnel. Aziz raised his head in recognition as the figure walked towards him. As he got closer, Aziz could see the man was tall, slim and very pale, and was carrying a briefcase in his left hand. From the way he was walking and the cut of his clothes, he didn't appear to be carrying a weapon. Good; that was the arrangement. The man was dressed in a smart cream-coloured suit with thin grey pinstripes. Underneath the jacket, he wore a light blue shirt, open at the collar to reveal a V of almost translucent white skin. His clothes looked expensive, and he had an elegant way about him. His white-blond hair was cut short and neat, and his razor-sharp cheekbones and fine chin, along with his pallid complexion, gave the impression his face was carved from pure alabaster. He certainly didn't look like the sort of people Aziz usually met under railway bridges.

"You're late," he told the man. "We said seven."

The man stopped a few feet in front of Aziz and looked him up and down. His nostrils flared. "I told you I'd be here. And here I am. Do you have the merchandise?"

"Of course." Aziz removed the toothpick from his mouth and pointed it at the man. "Do you have the money? Show me."

There was usually a bit of to-ing and fro-ing at the start of meetings such as this, neither party wanting to show their hand too early lest one of them was wearing a wire or was an undercover cop. But Aziz was already impatient. He wanted to get back to the city and meet with Anneke.

The man walked around the back of him and set himself up at the side of the car. He placed the briefcase on the bonnet and clicked open the clasps.

"Here." He lifted the lid and spun the briefcase around so Aziz could view the contents – three piles of banknotes, each stacked an inch high. "Five thousand euros. This is what was agreed, yes?"

Aziz sucked his teeth. He had half a mind to tell the guy the price had gone up – it would serve him right for making him wait. But he thought better of it. He'd never met this individual before, and there was every possibility he could become a recurring customer. He could also be a total psycho who'd take offence and do something they'd both regret. It was hard to tell with some of the European ones.

Aziz reached into the case and lifted out one of the piles, fanning it out to check the notes were legit all the way down.

"Okay. All good. Come." He gestured for the man to follow him. They walked around to the rear of the car and he popped the boot, glancing down the length of moss-covered train tracks in case they were being watched. There was no one in sight. He lifted the boot lid to reveal a long canvas bag. "Here you go. Check it if you want. Everything you need is in there."

He stepped aside so the man could lean into the boot. Slipping the toothpick back between his lips, he watched as the blond man unzipped the bag and examined the contents before zipping it up again. Seemingly satisfied, he lifted the bag out of the boot and hung the strap over one shoulder, smiling at Aziz as he did. It was the sort of smile that made you feel worse after seeing it.

"Are you sure you want this thing?" Aziz asked him, frowning. "It's pretty heavy duty."

"I wouldn't be here if I didn't."

Aziz slammed the boot shut. "Fair enough. You just don't seem the type, that's all. What does a guy like you want with an RPG-7 rocket launcher?"

"I don't think that's any of your concern. Do you?" He turned his head to look down on Aziz, craning his already slender neck at least half an inch.

Aziz held his hands up, laughing through the tension. "Forgive me. I should be less curious, huh?" He lowered one hand and made a pointing gesture with the other, waving it in the man's face. "While I'm apologising... I know the price this time was pretty steep. But what with it being such short notice and with the war going on over in Ukraine, these things are hard to get hold of. Next time we do business, I'll make sure the goods come at a more reasonable price."

The man snorted. "Don't worry about the cost. We've not paid for this weapon."

"Huh? What do you mean?"

"My organisation. *We* have not had to use our own resources to acquire this merchandise. The money was given to us. You could call it a gift. You could also call it payment." Aziz stepped back as the man slipped a hand into his jacket and brought out a small black handgun. Even with the fear response twisting at his guts, he recognised it as a Bersa 9mm. Small and compact; made in Argentina. He could get hold of them for under fifty-thousand pesos and sold them for more than triple that.

"Please, friend. You do not need to..." The toothpick dropped from his lips as he stuttered to speak. He raised his hands. "This is a secure trade. I am a businessman. I am legit."

"I don't doubt that," the blond man said, aiming the gun at his head. "But this is *my* business, and Omar Shebani sends his regards."

"No!" Aziz raised his hands, wracking his brain for anything he might say to make this pale, sinister figure see reason. But before he had a chance, the man pulled the trigger and his brain stopped functioning altogether. A fraction of a second later, Eman Aziz was no more.

CHAPTER 18

I t was late. Past midnight. Acid knew this because she'd been checking her phone every ten minutes for the last few hours. She'd wanted to get a decent night's rest, but sleep was proving elusive. When the bats were in flight, in the middle of one of her manic episodes, she rarely needed much sleep. It was one aspect of her condition she once considered a superpower. Being able to stay awake and alert for days on end was a valuable trait for an assassin in the field. But now, confined to her apartment with only Spook for company, her ceaseless wakefulness got rather tedious rather quickly.

Tonight, however, Acid's insomnia was fuelled by more than just her usual frenetic energy. If it was past midnight, that meant she was running out of time. Fast. The man who'd attacked her had said she had three days. Which meant she now had only one day left to find Darius before her time was up. The problem was she still had no idea what to say to him, or how to approach his request.

And it wasn't for lack of consideration.

Over the past forty-eight hours, all she'd done was wrestle

with the weight of Darius' proposition. She had ventured out for a couple of runs in a desperate bid to clear her head – sticking to daylight and well-populated areas for a change. But, ultimately, she found herself back in her bedroom, pacing relentlessly, drowning out the cacophony of bat screeches with loud music. She was waiting for a lightbulb moment. A flash of realisation that would inform her what to do.

She was still waiting.

Could she join Darius' organisation? That was the big question. It was the *only* question, really. She despised him for killing The Dullahan and still wanted vengeance. Yet, at the same time, she knew this was against her best interests. Caesar had killed her mother and somehow, in the end, she'd been able to forgive him. Could she do the same with Darius?

The turmoil within her threatened to rip her apart.

But then, what else was new?

Before she'd learned of Darius' true identity – before he'd done what he did – she had felt inexplicably close to him. Admittedly, he had been masquerading as a man named Freddie Pearce to infiltrate her life, but there had been an undeniable connection between them that seemed to transcend words or artifice. She hadn't experienced such a bond since her first encounter with Beowulf Caesar over two decades earlier. A lifetime ago. She wasn't getting any younger.

I know you miss it!

The words of Darius' message seared through her mind. It was undeniable. She did miss it. Spook might struggle to understand how Acid could even consider joining forces with such a man after what he'd done, what he'd tried to do, but she didn't understand this world. Not really. She might claim otherwise, and after all these years working together Acid should give the kid her dues more than she did, but there were facets of a killer's psyche that remained elusive to those who hadn't crossed that line.

Becoming a contract killer changed a person. It was why Acid had been so reticent to train Spook. No matter how insistent Spook was about her readiness to learn and her eagerness to be a more formidable foe, she didn't know what she was letting herself in for. To succeed as a killer you had to close up your heart, learn to devalue life – your own and everyone else's. Acid didn't want that for Spook. She was too innocent. She was good.

But Acid did miss it. She missed everything about her old life. And with time pressing on, there was another aspect to consider. Something else Darius had said in his message that plagued her every waking hour since she'd read it.

Think of how powerful we could be. Brother and sister. A true family business...

We.

Think how powerful WE could be.

She knew there was a place for her at the big table if she joined. She liked that idea. A lot. And maybe she liked the idea that she had a brother just as much. After having no one but her mother for so long – and later, Caesar, Ratty, and even Spitfire as a sort of surrogate family (albeit a fucked up, dysfunctional one that she had lost within days of Spook crossing her path) – the idea of a long-lost relation was appealing.

However, the revelation came with a heavy price. If Darius was her brother, it meant Oscar Duke was her father.

That vicious thug of a man had battered her mother relentlessly until the young Alice Vandella took fate into her own hands and brutally ended his life. She felt cold thinking about him and her and their possible link, but the more she thought about it, the more she sensed it was true. That one violent act, all those years ago, started a chain of events that led her to become who she was today. If Oscar Duke was indeed her biological father, then in a twisted sense he'd given life to her twice – first as Alice, and later as Acid.

"No. Screw this."

She flung off the bed covers and climbed out of bed, walking over to her bureau to retrieve the laptop. Time was ticking away and she had to act. She'd reply to Darius' message, tell him she needed more time. Hopefully then she could figure out once and for all what to do – kill the bastard or become his ally.

She opened the drawer and had her hand on the computer when an unsettling noise shattered the silence – a splintering crack and then a bang and then a deep rumble that rattled the building to its core. She crept to the door, every one of her senses on red alert, every nerve fired up, evaluating the danger. Should she move? Should she stay? Seconds ticked away like minutes. Another whizz, a deafening boom, and the building convulsed once more. The floor shifted beneath her. It felt as if she was in the middle of an earthquake. She grabbed the door handle. She had to wake Spook.

She called out, but her voice lost beneath a thunderous groan of wrenching metal and splintering concrete. Her stomach turned over as the ground fell away. Grasping for purchase, she found only empty air.

Plummeting, she slammed against something hard. It felt as if she'd been ripped in two. Dust filled her airwaves. Pain consumed her.

And then, stillness.

And then, nothing.

CHAPTER 19

Acid's eyes snapped open. Where the hell was she? What was going on? Struggling to make sense of her surroundings, she attempted to sit up, only to be met with a searing pain in her side that forced her back down. She was lying in a bed. But it wasn't her bed. The room smelled weird. Of chemicals. She blinked a few times to try to focus her mind and fully regain consciousness.

The ceiling loomed above her, a patchwork of dull, greying polystyrene tiles interwoven with panels of mottled glass, arranged in a disorienting checkerboard pattern. Feeble, low-wattage light strips glowed behind these panels, providing a dim illumination, but the main light came from an open doorway over in the corner. The way Acid's bed was positioned, she couldn't see what was on the other side of the door and there was some sort of curtain blocking most of her view.

The room was quiet except for a beeping noise, which as soon as she noticed it, became incessant. Was it this that had woken her? Searching for the source, her gaze fell upon the ECG machine stationed beside her bed.

Shitting hell.

The explosion. The earthquake.

She was in a hospital. Or course. Now fully alert, she could hear snoring and the creak of bed springs as other people on the ward shifted in their sleep. It was unclear how many other beds or patients were in the room with her. Faintly, coming through the open doorway, was the low hum of a radio, its melodies distorted and distant.

Gritting her teeth against the pain, she cautiously sat up and lifted the covers. She was naked except for a flimsy hospital gown made from papery material. As she lifted the gown, she discovered electrodes attached to her skin – one on each side of her sternum and four more across her side, near her heart. The fact the machine was beeping steadily was a good sign, at least. It showed her heart was working okay. It proved she had one. A large bandage on her other side displayed a blood-stained Rorschach pattern – either a captivating butterfly or a snarling devil, it was hard to say.

"Oh. You're awake. Be careful there, won't you?"

Acid dropped the covers and looked up to see a young nurse standing by the door. She was curvy and red-cheeked, with dark auburn hair scraped back into a bun. She hurried over to the bedside. "How are you feeling, Alice?"

Acid narrowed her eyes at the nurse. How did she know her name? For a heart-stopping moment, she wondered if this woman was not a nurse at all, but another of Darius' people come to finish the job. But then she recalled listing her name as Alice Vandella on the apartment's rental agreement. It had happened back when she was still toying with the idea of returning to her old persona.

"I'm okay. I think," she said, shuffling up the bed to sit upright and not really managing it. "Can you tell me what happened?"

The nurse cleared her throat. She looked troubled. "I'm not sure what I can say. Sorry. I've not been working here long – in fact, this is my first night shift – and I don't know if I'm supposed to talk to patients about their injuries before the doctor has seen them."

Acid adjusted herself on the pillow. Now the shock had dispersed, the pain in her side was a numb ache; she was aware of it, but it was nothing she couldn't handle. The young nurse looked as if she wanted to help her get comfortable. But she didn't touch her. The name on her badge said Samantha.

"Look, Sam, I get it," Acid said, laying on her sweetest smile. "The last thing I want to do is get you into trouble. But you've got to give me something. You don't have to go into detail. I take it my condition isn't critical?"

The young nurse smiled. "No. You've been very lucky. No broken bones. Just bruises and a few cuts. An old wound on your side did open up, but the doctor has sutured the area and you'll be fine."

Acid nodded, her mind already racing ahead. "Are the stiches absorbable?"

Samantha scrunched her face in uncertainty. "Sorry. I'm not sure."

"No worries. And that's all?"

The young nurse's expression remained troubled. She leaned in and lowered her voice. "Is everything okay, Alice? I mean obviously it's not, you've just been in a gas leak explosion. But when the doctor was stitching you up, we did notice a lot of old wounds and scars on your body. And I mean *a lot*. If you need to talk to someone about... anything, then I can arrange it. It would be in strictest—"

"No! It's fine." Acid cut in. "I'm just rather accident-prone, that's all. But, sorry, did you say it was a gas leak? That's what they think?"

Samantha nodded. But Acid wasn't convinced. They might be calling it a gas leak for now, as it was probably the most likely scenario. But as soon as they investigated the explosion more thoroughly, she'd put money on them finding remnants of grenade shell casings. She had to disappear before that happened. The last thing she needed right now was the police sniffing around and asking questions. Then another thought hit her.

"Shit. My flatmate? My friend? She was there, too. Is she—?"

Samantha held up her hands. "Hey, hey, don't get worked up. She's fine. She's asleep, two beds down. She was lucky as well. You both were. I only know vague details from what the first responders told us, but it sounds like when the explosion happened, your building caved in on itself." She steepled her hands together, interlocking her chubby fingers. "But because it was an old building, the metal structure sort of crumpled together and formed a barrier that protected you from most of the rubble."

"Right. Yes. Thank you. And Spook, my friend, she's definitely okay? No broken bones?"

"Nope. You should be allowed to go home in a few days— Oh. No. I'm so sorry, I didn't think."

"It's fine," Acid told her. She'd already realised she no longer had a home to go to. Everything she owned was in that building, including her beloved leather jacket. "We'll make arrangements. We've got people we can stay with for now."

That wasn't entirely true. But regardless of where home would be in the future, there was no way she or Spook could lie around in hospital for a few more days. They had to get out of here. Now. They were sitting ducks.

"Well, thank you, Sam," Acid said, feigning a yawn. "I think I need to get back to sleep. I'm exhausted."

"I bet you are," the nurse replied. "I'll leave you to your rest. Rita and I are the only ones on your ward this evening, but we're here if you need anything. Just press the red button on the side of your bed, and one of us will come to see you."

"Excellent. And where are you?"

"In the room at the end of the corridor. In front of the main doors."

"Perfect. Goodnight, then."

She closed her eyes and settled back, listening as the soft plastic soles of Samantha's Crocs flip-flopped out of the room and faded away down the corridor. Then she opened her eyes and flung the bedsheets off her. It was time to move.

CHAPTER 20

Acid knew that removing the electrodes from her skin would cause the beeping to intensify, alerting the medical staff that something was wrong. Leaning over on one side, she got a hand down the back of the machine and felt around for the plug socket. Holding her breath, uncertain if turning off the ECG machine would also trigger an alarm, she flicked the switch.

Thank God.

Nothing happened.

She sat up, swung her legs onto the floor, and yanked the electrodes off her chest. As she stood, the pain seared into her side and dizziness momentarily overwhelmed her.

Come on, keep it together.

She shook her head and clenched her teeth, pushing through the discomfort. She was barefoot and the hospital gown they'd put her in was one of those that was more like an artist's smock. It gaped open at the rear, exposing her bare arse to the world. Scanning the area, she saw no sign of her clothes – they must have cut her t-shirt and leggings off her when she was brought in.

Leaving the confinement of her curtained enclosure, she tiptoed a few meters down the room and peered through the gap in the curtains two beds down. There was Spook Horowitz, asleep but with a deep furrow creasing her brow. Her thick-rimmed glasses rested on the table beside her bed. Without them she looked older and far less nerdy.

Acid left Spook sleeping and cautiously made her way toward the door at the far end of the room. Peering around the corner, she found herself in a wide corridor illuminated by a series of fluorescent tube lights dangling from the ceiling. On her left, four doors were evenly spaced, leading to a set of double doors at the far end. Glancing in the opposite direction, she noticed two additional closed doors marked *Staff Only*. Along the wall in front of her, a row of windows stretched from waist height to the ceiling.

Outside, London was waking up, the deep black of night transitioning into a charcoal-blue sky, with the faintest hint of a fuchsia glow along the horizon. Acid estimated it was around 4 a.m., meaning they hadn't been at the hospital for long. If Darius was responsible for the explosion, he or one of his operatives would have been keeping tabs on the situation – perhaps even tailing the ambulance that brought them here.

Stepping into the corridor, Acid decided against heading toward the double doors that led out of the ward. Instead, she approached the first of the doors marked *Staff Only* and tried the handle. Finding it unlocked, she pushed the door open and was immediately hit in the sinuses by an overpowering smell of bleach. As her senses recalibrated, she saw it was a small storage cupboard with shelves lining three walls, filled with cleaning supplies, face masks, and protective gloves. This wasn't what she needed.

Closing the door, she threw her attention down to the far end of the ward. She could hear laughter coming from the nurse's station. It could have been Samantha; it was hard to tell.

Side-stepping over to the final door, she grabbed the handle and gave it a tug.

Shitting buggering shit.

It was locked. She glanced around, her chest muscles tightening as her plan of escape began to slip through her fingers. She tried the handle again, giving the door a shake. It didn't look like a complex lock. If only she had her professional lock-picking kit, she'd be inside in no time. But she had nothing. Not even a bleeding back piece on her hospital gown.

Continuing down the corridor, she came across a noticeboard displaying typical hospital information – posters on how to spot a stroke, or a heart attack, or bowel cancer, each with a useful acronym to help you remember the symptoms. There was also a poster advertising a charity ball for breast cancer awareness that caught her eye. This one had been laminated, its glossy surface reflecting the light.

Acid pulled it down and returned to the locked door, bending it in half as she went. Positioning the stiff plastic between the lock and the frame, she jimmied it up and down, sliding it in and out of the narrow gap in an attempt to force the lock back into the door casing. She'd done this many times over her life using a credit card, and her hope was the stiff laminate would be as effective.

"Come on," she whispered at the lock. "Give me a break."

Scrunching her face up in concentration she kept going, jiggling the door as much as she could without making too much noise. Then, finally, she felt something give way. As she twisted the handle, the lock released and the door opened.

Yes!

She still had it.

Getting to her feet, Acid opened the door into a large room with a row of lockers along one wall, and a line of coat hooks and a narrow wooden bench opposite. Bingo – the nurse's cloakroom and changing area. Just what she needed. In the corner of the room was a metal bin with a pile of blue clothes stuffed inside.

Acid smiled to herself as she walked over for a better look. They were all medical scrubs. Old and damaged, from the looks of it; probably placed in the bin to be disposed of or repaired. Sifting through the pile, she found two pairs of trousers and two tops about the right size for her and Spook that weren't too damaged. They were certainly better than their current attire, and wearing them would mean they would avoid suspicion as they left the hospital.

Next she checked under the bench, then the lockers for any that had been left unlocked. Inside one, she discovered a pair of black slip-on pumps. She pulled them out and checked the size: a five. Too small for her, but they'd fit Spook. She'd have to go without and hope no one noticed her bare feet.

Clutching the clothes and shoes to her chest, she left the room and returned to the storage cupboard, grabbing two face masks from one of the boxes before heading back down the ward to the room where Spook was sleeping.

"Hey, kid, wake up," she whispered, as she slipped around the curtain into Spook's section. "It's me. Acid."

Spook didn't stir. Acid moved over to her bedside, dropping the scrubs on the end of the bed and using both hands to shake her by the shoulders.

"Humphgoaway..." she mumbled. "Mmmasleep..."

"Spook! Wake up!" Acid hissed in her ear. "We have to get out of here. We're in danger."

Another hard shake and Spook's eyes flickered open. She glared at Acid as if she couldn't make out what she was looking at. Was she that blind?

"What happened?" she asked.

"Someone tried to blow us up."

Spook's eyes sprang fully open. "Shit. Yeah. I remember. I was in bed... and then I wasn't..."

"Here, put your glasses on." Acid reached over and grabbed them from off the side table. One of the arms was bent, but otherwise they'd survived the blast. "Wait a minute. How are they here?"

Spook scrunched up her face. "I think I fell asleep wearing them," she said. "It happens more than you'd think."

"Well, small mercies," Acid replied. "At least I don't have to lead you around physically as well." After sliding them onto Spook's face, she stood back so she could focus better.

"Where are we? Hospital?" Spook asked, then grimaced. "Argh, shit. My head is killing me. Am I hurt?"

Acid assessed the damage but saw no visible bruises or wounds. She moved down to the foot of the bed and checked Spook's medical notes. She'd had an MRI and was considered stable. She may have had a mild concussion, but nothing serious. Either way, they had to move. Acid returned to the head of the bed and switched off the ECG machine, removing the electrodes from Spook's chest as she sat up and glanced around. She was making a lot of weird whimpering noises, like a small animal who'd lost its mother.

Acid bit her lip, instructing herself to stay calm. "Listen to me, Spook. I know this is a lot to take in and you've just woken up. But I really need you to get a grip. We're in danger the longer we stay here."

She pulled back the covers and held her hand out to Spook, who stared at it as if she were being handed a severed penis. "What happened? Was it...?"

"Yes. I think so. And if it was, he'll also know we're in hospital. Which is why we need to get out of here. So get up and put these clothes on."

Spook started to mumble something else. Acid paid no attention as she helped her out of bed and stood her upright. Twisting her around, Acid unfastened the back of Spook's gown and yanked it to the floor. "Hey. Shit. I'm naked."

"Not for long. See?" She nodded at the pile of blue scrubs as she reached back and undid her own gown. Spook gawped at her as she slid out of it and chucked it to the floor. "Get dressed, Spook. We haven't got time for this."

She flung a pair of trousers and a top at Spook and put on the remaining set. The top fitted okay, but the waistband on the trousers had lost most of its elasticity and was rather baggy. They'd be fine if they were walking out of here, but could be a problem if they had to run.

Once they were both dressed, Acid knelt and helped Spook on with the pumps. "Now follow me and don't make a sound," she told her. "There are two nurses in the room at the far end of the ward near the double doors. Once we're past them, we should be fine."

Acid slipped out of the room with Spook following close behind. They moved quickly down the hallway until they reached the doorway to the nurse's station and stopped. From inside, Acid could hear chatter and the sound of music playing through a crackly old speaker. It was some anodyne modern pop song she didn't recognise. Crouching, she angled her head around the side of the doorframe until she had enough of an eyeline to scope out the room.

Directly in front of the door was a desk, with a large open ledger and a plastic box on top. Further back in the room was a U-shaped plinth, presumably there to give the nurses who were on a break some privacy. Acid could see the top of Samantha's head on the other side and a mop of curly grey hair. Both nurses appeared to be facing away from the door and looking down at something, perhaps a television set or their phones. Acid glanced back at Spook, raised her eyebrows and nodded. *Good to go.*

Spook, now alert and on the same page, nodded back. Acid stepped out, covering the distance between the doorway and the double doors at the end of the ward in three strides. Once there, she waited for Spook to join her and then leaned back against the closest door, opening it enough that Spook could slip through before following her into the corridor and letting the door close without a sound.

"Where now?" Spook whispered.

There was a sign on the wall for the lifts and an emergency stairwell. Acid set off in the direction it was pointing. "We get out of here," she said. "Before those nurses realise we're gone and sound the alarm."

"But where then?" Spook asked, as they got to another set of double doors and Acid barged her way through. "We can't go back to the apartment."

"Don't worry," Acid told her. "I've got an idea."

CHAPTER 21

Nate Winters was exhausted and his head spun from the paint fumes that filled the air. He'd been tirelessly painting all night long, and now, save for a tiny section of one wall, his work was nearly complete. This was the first time in his thirty-five years he'd ever turned his hands to any 'do-it-yourself' endeavours and he was surprisingly pleased with the results. He'd even found the process quite enjoyable. It helped that he was creating something he'd been dreaming about for the better part of five years. A headquarters. A training camp. A foundation upon which he hoped to one day establish an empire. If Beowulf Caesar could do it – if that shadowy ponce running Kancel Kulture could do it – then why not him?

Over the past twelve years, Winters had carved out a reputation for himself, not only as a sought-after assassin but someone who was intelligent, industry savvy, and what stuffy corporate types might call a 'blue-sky thinker'. The organisation he envisioned would revolutionise the murder-for-hire industry. It would be a co-operative, managed by its members yet overseen by him, where operatives collaborated on jobs, supporting each other in the field and in the background to ensure every mission, every hit, was executed to the utmost potential of not only the individual operatives but the organisation as a collective force. There was safety in numbers. There was also real power.

But he wasn't there yet, and sometimes the weight of his aspirations bore down on his shoulders. It was going to take time and patience – as well as some very clever marketing on his part – to amass the class of people he hoped to work alongside.

The colour he'd chosen for this room was 'Natural Slate', a subdued mid-grey with a matte finish. Nate had initially been drawn to the shade that was one darker, but the name of that paint, 'Urban Obsession', struck him as inappropriate for an assassins' training camp nestled within a sprawling farm in rural Wales. So, 'Natural Slate' it was. And it was a good choice. Now covering all four walls and the ceiling, the colour seemed to suck all the light and atmosphere out of the windowless room. That was a good thing. It was important.

He envisioned this small square room inside one of the three separate outhouses standing in a row on the eastern edge of the vast eight-hundred-acre farm, serving as a sensory deprivation training pod. The plan was to confine trainees inside the room for hours on end, subjecting them to relentless noise that would prevent sleep and inhibit coherent thought. Once suitably disorientated, they would be taken from the room and thrust into different challenges – target practice or knife skills – and would have to learn how to adjust to their change in environment fast or they would fail. The grey room would also prepare his new band of would-be assassins for a world where patience and composure were of the utmost importance, even when dealing with intense, high-pressure situations.

As well as the grey room, Winters had also painted the entire ground floor in the main farmhouse building, which was going to be used primarily as a training ground for sparring and knife skills, as well as a gym. For that room, the red room, he'd opted for 'Ruby Starlet'; which, again, wasn't that appealing as a moniker, but the closest shade he could find to fresh blood. It seemed apt.

Because as well as honing his own skills and abilities over the last twelve years or more, Winters had kept a watchful eye on the industry. He saw how the world was changing. Fewer people were joining the ranks of elite assassins than ever before, and he knew if he was to attract and cultivate a fresh generation of supremely skilled killers, then the need for savvy marketing and captivating showmanship was more crucial than ever.

Nate's ambition was to create an organisation that was innovative and forward-thinking, appealing to the values of both Millennials and Generation Xers. To do this, he had to cater to the Millennials' desire for purpose-driven motivation, distaste for hierarchy, and task-centric focus, as well as Generation X's entrepreneurial and financially driven mindset. By resonating with both generations and their shared enthusiasm for learning, creativity, adaptability, and receptiveness to emerging technology, Winters hoped to assemble a team of highly innovative and sought-after operatives. Consequently, in addition to providing training in the traditional aspects of assassin work, the emphasis here would also be on technology – staying ahead of the curve in terms of AI and drone warfare. Soon, someone behind a computer would be able to hit a mark on the other side of the world with an invisible laser deployed by a tiny drone that they never saw coming. Though the idea sounded like science fiction to some, and provoked unease and resentment among the industry's older generation, Winters knew that embracing these advancements was essential if he was to create the sort of organisation he dreamed of.

That was how you became the best.

That's how you won.

All he needed now was the right name. But up to now it had eluded him.

He placed the lid on the paint he'd been using and wiped his hands on his overalls. The room looked good. Two down, another thirty-six to go. It was a daunting task, but would be worth it in the end.

He stretched, feeling a twinge of pain in his right trapezius muscle. It was an old injury from his early days in the industry. Back then, he had been brash and arrogant, far from the calculating professional he was today. A rival assassin – a half-Korean, half-American woman calling herself Reptilia – had taken a swipe at him with a katana blade as he slept in his hotel room in Croatia. He'd got cocky that night and allowed himself a few cocktails at the hotel bar. He'd woken up from his slumber in time to see the flash of the blade, and his lightning reactions had him jumping out of the way in time. He'd overpowered Reptilia and snapped her neck in the process, but it taught him a valuable lesson. Never let your guard down. Don't get cocky. The local Croatian woman who'd shared his bed hadn't been so fortunate.

Leaving the grey room, he walked down the corridor past the other two rooms in this outhouse and through the old wooden door to the outside. He was in the process of replacing all the original doors with ones made of reinforced steel, but it was a big job, and even with three million euros saved to put into the project, the budget was tight. He already suspected he might have to start his recruitment drive earlier than planned and get some client money coming in before the farmhouse renovations were complete. But that was life. It was a juggling act.

The cool morning air revived him as he stepped outside and stretched his arms wide. He'd been at it all night, but having become mostly nocturnal over the last decade, that wasn't an issue. Like any good assassin, he'd trained himself to grab sleep when he could rather than at the times prescribed by polite society. He estimated it to be around 5 a.m. The early morning sky was a calming shade of light blue – although, paint charts might have described it as 'Nordic Lake' or 'Stonewashed Reflection'. An orange glow from the new day's sun was just visible over the orchard on the south side of the plot.

Nate was walking over to the main building when his smartwatch vibrated to inform him he'd received a direct message on the Crypto Jones One Thousand forum. The grey room, like the others, had been lined with a conductive metal mesh, making it a modern-day Faraday cage. Thus, he only picked up alerts in certain areas. It was probably about a job; or maybe even one of the operatives he'd reached out to recently, getting in touch regarding their involvement in his organisation.

Motivated by this thought, he locked the front door

behind him and went through into the large room at the back of the property. He'd done little renovation in this room, so it was still an open-plan kitchen-dining area, with classic shaker-style kitchen units, an oiled wooden worktop and a huge cast-iron Aga cooker. A large eight-seater oak dining table occupied the other half of the room. Floor-to-ceiling patio doors lined the external wall, granting a breathtaking view of the farm's expansive grounds. Nate knew they'd eventually have to be replaced with something more secure, but for now he savoured the scenery. On the table his laptop sat open, already logged into the cryptocurrency trading forum that doubled as a front for the covert world of professional contract killers. He opened up his direct messages, finding a new one from user *ACiD_V4NiLL4*. A smirk crept across his face as he clicked it open.

He'd hoped she'd be interested.

But as he read her message his grin faded. It was both brief and vague. She said she was in trouble and needed his help. Said she was on her way to Wales and to ring her on a number she'd provided so he could provide directions to the farm.

"Acid Vanilla. Coming to see me," Winters muttered to himself. "She must be in trouble."

He lifted his phone from his pocket and tapped in the number. The timestamp and metadata on the message told him it had been sent at 4.28 a.m. from somewhere in West London. It was now almost 6.15 a.m. Even if Acid had set off by car straight after sending the message, it would still take her a few more hours to reach the farm. Relieved at the prospect of squeezing in some sleep before her arrival, he closed the laptop. The ringing tone echoed in his ears as he stood.

He had no idea what Acid was doing in Wales, or why she needed his help, but he had a bad feeling in the pit of his stomach. He knew her well enough to know she was a maverick and a loose cannon with the potential to leave chaos in her wake. Something told him life on the farm was about to get very interesting very quickly.

CHAPTER 22

Spook eyed Nate Winters with suspicion as he waved them out of the taxi and led them across the courtyard to the large farmhouse. Sure, it was commendable of him to offer them shelter on such short notice, but she couldn't help wondering about his intentions. What was he getting out of this arrangement? She'd seen him talking to Acid at The Dullahan's wake and he appeared nice enough – his smile seemed genuine – but if he was at the funeral, and a contact of Acid's, the likelihood was he was also a killer.

Contrasting with Spook's wariness, Acid seemed unusually upbeat, flirtatious even, considering recent events. It irked Spook, but she knew Nate was doing them a massive favour and Acid was probably acting that way to keep him sweet. Spook had never been a particularly sexually charged being, not like Acid, but she acknowledged the strategic value of one's sexuality in the right circumstances. And it was *sort of* empowering and feminist if you squinted at it from the right angle. Plus, Nate was handsome, she supposed. If you liked that sort of thing. He was tall and toned, with tousled dirty-blond hair and the sort of eyes one could get lost in.

If you liked that sort of thing.

But Spook didn't. Even if she did, she was too distraught to consider such trivialities. As Nate gave her and Acid a tour of his farmhouse-come-headquarters-come-training-camp, she found her mind wandering, thinking about all the things she'd lost in the explosion. Her cherished collection of graphic novels, her Blu-ray discs, her complete series of 1/8 scale Sailor Moon 'cutie' model figurines. They were all gone. Along with her laptop, too. Her beloved trusty laptop. Her heart ached as she mourned the loss, its outer casing adorned with stickers, its hard drive brimming with her ideas and innovations – including the facial recognition AI she had been perfecting. It hurt. Not only had she narrowly escaped death, but she'd also been robbed of her home and every possession she held dear. Then she'd had to escape from the hospital whilst still groggy and unsure what the hell was going on.

She'd burst into tears when faced with the pile of bricks, metal and plasterboard that was once their apartment. But of course Acid had offered no comfort. She was too preoccupied with rummaging through the wreckage for her own belongings. Fortunately, the small metal safe housing their essential documents had withstood the blast and they were able to salvage passports, credit cards, some burner phones and a little go-money to pay for the taxi. It was a small consolation amidst the chaos. Spook's indignation had threatened to bubble over when Acid recklessly scaled a precarious wooden beam to salvage her cherished leather jacket from what was left of their kitchen. But Spook knew how much the jacket meant to Acid, so she didn't say anything.

And there were more pressing matters to worry about right now.

In the past, Spook would instinctively dissociate to shield herself from the crushing weight of high-pressure situations. But she recognised now that such a defence mechanism was not only unproductive but dangerous, and she was striving to remain anchored in the present moment at times such as this.

But it was hard.

Anyone would feel discombobulated after enduring what she had. It was also more than likely that Darius Duke was behind the explosion, a clear indicator that he still wanted them dead. As his attempt had failed, chances were his next move would be even more calculated and ruthless.

But Spook got it now. There was nothing like being targeted by a malevolent genius to focus the mind. What truly unsettled her, however, was Acid's reaction. Had this transpired at any other juncture in their shared past, Acid would have been incandescent with rage, chomping at the bit to find Duke and eliminate him before he had a chance to strike again. It would have been her leading the charge with Spook trying to hold her back, pleading for a more measured approach rather than diving headlong into danger.

But not this time.

After locating an all-night internet café and messaging Nate, they'd hailed a black cab and Acid had waved a wad of hundreds at the driver as an incentive for him to take them to Wales. In the taxi, though, she'd been quiet. Brooding. Hard to read. The journey had taken almost five hours from London and would have allowed them ample time to talk (albeit in a stunted and heavily coded way, given the driver's presence) about the recent events and their subsequent course of action. Unfortunately, the driver, a middle-aged cockney, had been one of those over-friendly ones who never seemed to stop talking. A few choice words from Acid would have cut him down, but she'd just smirked in a bemused way and with a distant look in her eyes. And then had fallen asleep.

All Spook could surmise was that Acid had a lot on her mind. The problem was, Spook had a good idea what notions her friend was so consumed by presently, and if correct... well, she didn't want to think too deeply about what that meant.

"And through here I've got a few rooms already set up," Nate said, snapping Spook's attention back to the present. She sucked her stomach in as he shimmied past, his sizeable chest almost rubbing against her less sizeable one. He led them along the upstairs landing towards the back of the building. "I've got three singles and a double room. It's up to you guys which you take."

"Two singles are good," Acid told him curtly, before Spook could answer.

"No worries. This is the first one." Nate opened the next door they came to and stepped back as Acid approached. She disappeared into the room and Nate gestured for Spook to follow him to the second room. "This can be yours," he said with a smile.

"Thank you," she told him. "So much."

"Yes, we're very grateful for you putting us up," Acid added, reappearing and following Spook into the room.

Probably, she was assessing the size of the two rooms, wanting to know if she had the better of the two.

Spook glanced around the place. It was a basic bedroom with a single bed, an unremarkable wooden desk, a chair, and a large five-drawer bureau. She caught Acid's eye and smiled, but Acid didn't reciprocate.

"I know the rooms aren't up to much," Nate said. "But this accommodation will be used by new recruits going forward and I don't want it to be too comfortable. I also plan on making the basement into bedroom suites, which will be used by working operatives and will be a lot more luxurious. But I've yet to complete the full renovation."

"The rooms are fine," Spook said. "Thank you so much. I don't know what we'd have done without you. It's been a real whirlwind these last few hours."

"It's cool," Nate said. He smiled at her, and she turned away and pretended to examine the desk, feeling her cheeks burning. "Like I told you, the place isn't ready yet. But it's got bags of potential, and I've got a real vision for the place and this new organisation. Give me eighteen months and I reckon it'll be a real force to be reckoned with. People will be saying Annihilation Pest Control who? Kancel Kulture what?"

"Hmm. Yes, I'm sure," Acid said. But her tone was stern and when Spook spun around to look at her, she was staring at the floor.

"Shit," Nate said. "My big mouth. Sorry."

Acid snapped her head up and glared at him. "What are you sorry for?"

"I wondered if I spoke out of turn just now. Mentioning Caesar that way. Or the new guys. You said on the phone it could have been them behind the explosion."

"That's what I think," Spook chimed in. "It has to be. Darius Duke is an evil psycho. He won't be happy until we're both dead."

Spook noticed a sharp glance pass between Acid and Nate before Acid cleared her throat. "Yes, well, we'll discuss it later, once we've properly settled in. Oh, Nate, while I think about it – Spook and I both require access to a laptop while we're here. Do you have any spare we could use?"

"Sure. I'm setting up a fully equipped tech room at the moment and just bought ten new computers and the best intelligence-grade server money can buy. I'll grab you a couple."

"Preferably with encrypted hard drives, VPNs and password protection on the input-output system," Spook added. When Nate looked her way, she shrugged. "I mean, if you have all that. If not, I can sort it for you easily enough."

Nate stuck his lip out as if impressed. "You're a bit of a wiz, are you?"

"You could say that. I wrote my first piece of code aged six. When I was thirteen I hacked into the mainframe at the Pentagon, undetected. Just to prove to myself I could."

"Awesome," Nate said. "I could use someone like you around here."

Spook giggled. "Really?"

"Definitely. I've got big ideas for how we're going to use technology going forward and I really think if we can—"

"All right, you two," Acid cut in. "Can we stay focused? Nate, if you wouldn't mind getting us those laptops."

He coughed. "Sure. Give me a few minutes." He gave them both a nod, then left the room. Spook waited until his heavy footsteps had faded away and then turned to Acid.

"Hey! That was rude. He's helping us out here."

"Oh, for heaven's sake." Acid sighed and rolled her eyes. "I know he is. But he wants something in return."

"Oh? What's that?"

"Never mind."

Spook narrowed her eyes. "What's going on, Acid? More than ever before we need to be working together. Exhibiting a united front. We might be safe for now, here in the middle of nowhere, but we can't hide out forever. That's not what either of us wants."

Acid sat on the edge of the bed and stuck her chin out at her. "What would you have us do then, little Spooky?"

She wrinkled her nose, choosing to ignore the disparaging name-calling. She was used to it by now. "You need to train me. Properly. Show me how to fight so we can take on Darius. Together. Like I keep saying to you, we need to get him before he gets us. We were fortunate last night, but next time—"

"Yes, and like I keep saying to you – you're not ready."

"I am! I'm more than ready. What is this really about? It's like you don't want to take Darius out. Why is that? Because he might be your brother?"

"Piss off."

"He killed The Dullahan. He was going to kill me. Then you."

Acid stood. "I'm sick of having this conversation, Spook. You have no idea what you're talking about."

"Don't I?"

Acid lurched forward as if she was going to hit her, but Spook tensed and stood her ground. Acid stopped an inch away, fixing her with a piercing stare that, in the early days of their relationship, would have crippled Spook. Today, however, she didn't flinch. She didn't even blink. Her insides were churning and the voice in her head, like always, was screaming at her to back down. But she didn't. She was done backing down.

It felt for a moment as if the world had stopped turning.

Then Acid shook her head and moved away. "Screw this," she muttered, as she left the room. "You're a bloody idiot."

Spook remained standing in the centre of the room. She was shaking, but for once, adrenaline was the reason rather than nerves. Something monumental had shifted between the two of them just now. She'd felt it. She knew Acid had felt it too. Spook was no longer scared of the enigmatic assassin, and crucially, she didn't need her as much as she once had.

That changed things between them.

It could potentially change everything.

CHAPTER 23

Acid sat back on the chair and stared at the laptop, shaking her head at the message on her screen. She'd read it and reread it three times and each time she'd felt the same prickle of nervous energy run down her back. It was intense and not unpleasant, but she couldn't figure out if it was trepidation or excitement that triggered it. Although, if she was honest with herself, she knew it was a bit of both.

And that right there was the problem.

She'd been sitting in her room with the door closed for the past twenty minutes, ever since Winters had returned with the laptops. She'd expressed her gratitude sincerely this time, telling him she would discuss the new organisation, and his offer to join, once she possessed the mental bandwidth to consider it properly.

It did burn a little that Spook's scolding had clearly affected her, but she dismissed it as the kid getting too big for her boots. All this talk of Acid training her up and the two of them taking on Darius together was ludicrous. Spook would never be her equal. Thinking that way was ridiculous at best and downright bloody irritating at worst.

As was the speed of the Wi-Fi at Winters' place. She appreciated it was only early days and they were nestled deep within the rural Welsh countryside, but for Winters to even entertain the notion of rivalling Caesar's organisation at its peak, his technological infrastructure would have to function far more efficiently.

"Come on, what's taking so long?"

At last the page loaded, granting her access to the Crypto Jones forum. Upon logging in, she discovered two new messages awaiting her attention. The first was from Winters, inquiring about her ETA, sent after they'd spoken on the phone. She sniffed. He ought to have known she wouldn't be able to access the secure dark website from the back of a taxi. Either he was so eager to have her here he'd forgotten himself, or he was a lot greener than he made out. If so, that was a shame. Based on her initial impression of the farm and the little Winters had shared regarding his vision, he seemed to have the right idea about what the industry needed and what it would take to grow the organisation into something powerful. But Acid wasn't confident he'd ever achieve his lofty ambitions. Perhaps with her experience and guidance, he could build something great here. But that would demand an immense investment of time and energy. Neither of which she had in abundance presently.

Which brought her to the second message. Another one from Darius. He'd sent it at 2 a.m. local time. That was two hours after the explosion. Meaning if he was behind the blast (which he definitely was; why was she still only considering it as an option?), then he knew she'd survived.

She clicked open the message, leaning closer to the screen and breathing heavily as she read.

Hey Sis! Sorry about the mess we made of your place! It was a bit run down, though, from what I could gather. You deserve to live somewhere better. Somewhere more fitting of who you are. And don't worry. I made sure my man was clever about it and took out the bottom level of the building strategically. From what I was told, taking into account the structure of those old Victorian buildings, and with you being on the first floor, you had a 60% to 70% chance of survival. And if you're reading this – yay! You did survive! Good for you!

That malicious bastard.

The smiley emoji alone made Acid want to smash the laptop against the wall.

Prick. Fucking wanker.

He was playing with her. Like he'd been doing from the start. And it was one hell of a dangerous game. Sixty to seventy percent were good odds. But they weren't a certainty. She took a deep breath and carried on reading.

Believe me, Alice, when I say to you, I have complete control of this situation. I only sent Alexis and the great Grimaldi as warning shots. A taster of what I can do. What I will do. But their assignments never involved killing you. Likewise, tonight. You were not meant to die. I am simply showing you my capabilities. Proving to you that I have not only the

manpower and strategy to be the best, but also the
finesse. It would have been easier to kill you, but I
didn't want that. I DON'T want it. Not anymore. Not
since I realised we have much in common and that
you are more valuable to me alive.

I want you on my team. I want you to join me. As Acid
Vanilla, you were once the best assassin in the world.
You can be that again. I can make you the best. I know
you want it. I want it too.

She rubbed at her eyes, reading the last part again. *I can
make you the best.* She'd liked being the best. She'd loved it, in
fact. And if she was given full range to run things how she
wanted, then—
No! Stop this!
He has to die.
He has to...
She screwed up her face, battling the tempest raging in
her mind. A torment of conflicting thoughts fought for
dominance amidst the relentless screech of the bats.
She read on.

But now, Sis, the ball is in your court and the fun stops here. I imagine if you're reading this you've already gone underground. I'll give you some time to lick your wounds and consider my proposal. How does two weeks sound? I think that's more than enough time for you to get your affairs in order and join me in Kancel Kulture's wonderful new headquarters in Rome.

And one last thing, Alice, dear sister. If I do not hear from you, if I have to send another of my new operatives to see you, then this time the outcome will be very different for both yourself and Spook Horowitz. You have two weeks. The clock is ticking...

Darius Duke.

"I fucking knew it!"

Acid spun around to see Spook standing behind her.

Shitting pissing hell.

Her bedroom door had been closed. How the hell had Spook managed to slip inside without her noticing? Either Acid was more engrossed in Darius' message than she realised, or Spook's stealth had improved significantly. Acid glanced her up and down. Her round face was distorted in an angry snarl.

"So is this it?" she said, pushing her glasses up her nose and leaning over Acid's shoulder to look at the screen. "You're going to join him? This is why you've been so secretive and self-absorbed recently? I thought – I *hoped* – you were considering how best we strike back. But no. You were thinking about being with the bastard. Not how to kill him."

"Calm yourself, Spook," Acid hit back, getting to her feet. "You don't understand. It's not like that."

"What is it like, Alice? Dear sister? Please, do tell. All I ever hear from you is that I don't understand. That I'm not like you. That I don't get your world. Well fuck you, I do get it. Maybe for a long time I fought against it, but no longer. I'm a part of this world. You made me a part of it."

"*You* made *yourself* a part of it."

"I'd say that's debatable. It's also not the point. Answer my question. Are you considering what Darius is suggesting? Are you going to join him?"

"No! Of course not!"

"And don't you want him dead? After everything he did, everything he put us through?"

"For the last time – yes!"

"Prove it."

"Get lost. I don't need to prove anything to you."

Spook stepped closer. "What's going to happen now? Because it sounds like we're fast running out of time. Were you going to keep the fact that we've got a ticking clock hanging over our heads a secret from me, as well? Because that would have been good to know."

Acid again looked her up and down. Who the hell was this person? She'd never encountered Spook so angry, or intense. "I'll tell you what's going to happen," she replied. "I'm going to go to Rome. I'm going to find Darius. And I'm going to kill him. Okay? Is that good for you? I'll take him out and end this ridiculous farce."

"Alone?"

"Yes."

"No. I'm coming with you."

162

"Because you're worried that I might join his little gang?"

"Because you need me."

Acid spluttered out a laugh. "No. I really don't. You'll get yourself killed. Or me."

"Then train me up. I can be ready in two weeks. We'll go to Rome together and take the bastard out." Acid made to reply but Spook held a finger up in her face. "I know two weeks isn't long, but I've been working on myself for a while, getting myself into the right mindset. I'm a fast learner, I always have been, and all I need is some practical application and a bit of confidence. Maybe some weapon practice, too. But I can do this, Acid. I'm ready. My life is at risk as much as yours and I need to be proactive. We both do. Show me you're on my side, Acid. Show me how I survive."

Acid looked away and crossed her arms. "You want me to train you, so you can kill Darius?"

"Yes. You have to."

She didn't. She didn't have to do anything this foolish, bombastic woman said. But she was also bored of having this conversation.

"Fine," she replied. "If that's what you want, I'll train you. But don't say I didn't warn you."

CHAPTER 24

Nate Winters had hoped having Acid Vanilla and her friend hiding out at the farm would give him time to convince the fierce ex-assassin to move away from being an ex- and join his organisation. He was risking a lot having them stay, especially now he knew who they were hiding from. Yet the farm's basic defence structure was complete, and it would be a good measure of how well those staying here could remain hidden whilst being actively searched for.

He hadn't expected his training camp to be put through its paces quite so soon, but life came at you fast in this industry. As he leaned against one of his freshly painted blood-coloured walls, he watched Acid and Spook circle each other in the centre of the red room, both clutching a brushed-metal sparring knife.

When Acid had explained her plan, to spend the next two weeks training Spook in the way of the assassin, he'd been rather unsettled by the idea; though her intense stare, the rigidness of her jaw, and the way she seemed to be almost vibrating with energy as she spoke, might have had something to do with that. However, her determination had ignited something within him and once he'd got his head around the idea, it had spurred him into action. This main room now had a fully padded floor and was fitted with a large industrial air-conditioning unit on one of the external walls. He was pleased. The place looked good.

Along one side were three long shelves on which he'd meticulously arranged an array of weapons from around the globe – knives, swords, staffs, nunchakus – alongside an assortment of sparring knives similar to those Acid and Spook now brandished. Crafted from cast iron, these blunt instruments were hefty and could still do some damage, but were not as lethal as their gleaming, razor-sharp counterparts.

"Make a damn move, kid," Acid snarled at her opponent, as Nate turned his attention back to the fight. "We can't dance around here forever."

Spook remained silent, her expression hard with concentration. She launched herself at Acid, her blade carving an arc through the air. The older woman stepped back, bending her torso as she evaded each slash of the blade.

"Is that the best you can do?" Acid taunted, when Spook jumped back to reassess. "I thought you said you were in the right mindset these days, killer?"

It was clear Spook was becoming riled by Acid's trash talk. Clenching her teeth, she sprang forward again, before deftly side-stepping around her opponent and catching Acid off guard. Spook's dagger found its mark, striking her on the top of her arm.

Nate winced. Not because the blow looked painful, although it did, but because of the ferocious retaliation that was sure to follow.

Sure enough, Spook's lucky strike appeared to ignite a new level of fury inside of Acid.

She hurled herself at Spook, crashing into her with the full weight of her rage, and slammed the solid base of her sparring dagger's handle into the vulnerable point between Spook's shoulder blades. Spook let out a cry of agony as she reflexively contorted her body, dropping her guard and leaving herself exposed.

Acid seized the opportunity like a predator closing in for the kill. She grabbed Spook's wrist, the one clutching the dagger, and forced it upwards, digging her thumb and forefinger into the sensitive pressure points. Spook yelped and dropped the knife. As she did, Acid whirled around and snaked her arm across Spook's neck. Her other hand, still gripping the sparring dagger, braced against Spook's forehead, tightening the embrace.

"We're done," she snarled in Spook's ear. "Say it."

"Piss off."

"Say it. I only have to apply a bit more pressure and it'll be goodnight Vienna. Is that what you want?"

"Fine. I'm out."

Acid remained in position for another second – maybe so Spook would get the message – and then released her, pushing her away as she did.

Spook bent over, gasping back air. "You were lucky," she told Acid, straightening up and putting her hands on her hips. "I knew you were going to try that move. I just lacked the muscle memory and speed to counter it."

Acid cast a sidelong glance at Nate, a wry smile twitching at her lips. "Oh, is that so?"

Nate didn't reciprocate the smile. This was the third training session he'd observed, and he couldn't shake the feeling that there was more at stake here than just honing Spook's fighting skills. Both women seemed to be driven by a relentless need to assert dominance over the other, and he was determined to stay as neutral as possible. He'd already expressed his desire for Acid to join his new organisation, but the more he knew of Spook, the more he believed she too would be an invaluable asset.

Her unyielding determination and passion were undeniable, as were her exceptional technical skills. She was also proving herself to be far more resourceful and resilient than he'd initially given her credit for, a revelation he suspected Acid was discovering as well. Despite what had just happened in the middle of the room, Spook was no pushover, and from what he'd witnessed, was giving Acid a run for her money. Rather than a simple teacher-student relationship, they were putting each other through their paces.

He leaned off the wall and stepped forward as the women approached him. Sweat shimmered on their faces and, he presumed, on their bare arms as well. They were wearing the form-fitting black spandex jumpsuits he'd had commissioned from a company in China and he knew better than to let his eyes drift any lower.

"You're doing good," he said, addressing Spook. "I'm impressed."

She squinted up at him. "You think? I'm still adjusting to these contact lenses."

He liked Spook in her glasses, but on the first day, Acid

had insisted they go to the opticians in the nearby village and order a set of lenses. Easier for training. They'd arrived that morning.

She blinked. "I'll be better once I'm less conscious of them. I won't make mistakes like just now."

"Excuses... excuses..." Acid muttered.

"Regardless," Nate told Spook, "if you ask me, your commitment knows no bounds. You get up at dawn every day to exercise, do everything Acid asks of you. You even stay up late to study technique videos, reinforcing what you've learned. I hope all my new recruits display such dedication."

Acid scoffed. "Easy there, Winters. It's only the second day. Let's see how she fares by the end of the week."

"Bring it on," Spook replied. "I'm ready for whatever you can throw at me."

Acid arched one eyebrow. "Are you sure about that?" She caught Winters' eye and smirked. She was pushing Spook hard, but he knew why. He also knew that taking on Kancel Kulture was a suicide mission, but he wasn't going to say that out loud. Not yet, at least. Not until he had a clearer understanding of Acid's intentions. He had only gleaned fragments of information from her and Spook's conversations between training sessions, but they both seemed resolute in their decision to face off against the new organisation. And he knew Acid Vanilla well enough not to argue with her once she'd made her mind up.

"So, sweetie, do you need a breather after that?" Acid asked, resting her hand on Spook's shoulder. "Or shall we keep going?"

"Whatever you think," Spook replied. "I can handle it.

And I feel my confidence growing more and more with every session. You'll make a badass out of me yet."

Acid stuck out her bottom lip. "If you say so. But how about we break for lunch?"

"Yeah. Sounds good," Spook agreed, glancing at Winters.

"UH-URGH!" Acid blared, imitating a game show buzzer to indicate Spook's incorrect answer. "Sorry, kid. No lunch for you yet. First, shooting practice, then a fifteen-kilometre run, then lunch. Ready?"

Spook's eyebrows rose to meet over her button nose for a moment before she adjusted herself to her full height and jutted her chin. "Yeah. Cool. Bring it on."

Acid grinned. "That's what I thought you'd say."

Winters smiled sympathetically at Spook and winked. Yes, Acid was pushing her hard. But she needed to. If the pair of them were to stand a chance against Kancel Kulture, she really needed to.

CHAPTER 25

Acid was impressed. Very impressed. Surprised, too. Something had most definitely shifted inside Spook over the last few months. The once nervy, awkward girl – prone to lack of focus and sticking her head in the sand at times of stress – had vanished, and in her place was a woman single-minded in her desire to learn and better herself.

After their first few days of training, Acid had been certain Spook would throw in the towel. But she hadn't. No matter how brutally Acid had designed the sessions – hand-to-hand combat, sleep deprivation, sensory overload drills, firearms practice, knife skills – Spook had faced them head-on, absorbing the lessons with a fierce determination and unwavering focus. What she lacked in strength, she more than made up for in speed, agility and spirit. She was also a naturally good shot, particularly when handling smaller handguns such as the Glock 19 and Springfield Hellcat. She was less confident with larger firearms and rifles, but that wasn't too much of an issue. Acid had faced similar challenges when she'd first started in the industry.

Yet regardless of how impressed she was with Spook's progress and the tenacious embrace of her newfound 'badass' persona (as she kept rather annoyingly describing it), Acid refused to ease up the pressure. If anything, things were going to get a whole lot worse for Spook Horowitz before their two weeks were up.

"Wakey, wakey, soldier," Acid called out, banging the base of her fist on the door to Spook's quarters.

It was Sunday morning, 5 a.m. After completing such a successful and accomplished first week, Acid had told Spook that she could have a lie-in today.

She'd lied.

But this was what happened out in the field. The shit hit the fan more often than not and one had to learn to deal with the unexpected. To expect it, even.

"Spook! Get up!" She opened the door to find the American sitting up in bed rubbing at her eyes.

"What time is it?" she mumbled. "I thought you said—"

"You thought I said what? I didn't say anything. It's 5 a.m. We've got work to do. Knife skills training. Get dressed and meet me in the main room in five minutes." She clapped her hands together. "Come on, kid. Let's have you!"

"Yes. Yes. I'll be there."

She flung back her bedsheets and swung her feet onto the floor. Acid watched her as she reached for the bottle of water on her bedside table. She was awake now. She'd be ready. Leaving her to get dressed, Acid wandered along the corridor and down the stairs to the red room. As she got to the door she took a deep breath, already detecting the musky smell of fresh meat in the air.

On entering, she saw Winters had carried out her wishes to the letter. In the middle of the room, hanging from one of the support beams that spanned the width of the ceiling, was a fully grown dead pig. Suspended by its hind legs, the creature's sizeable head hung low, its vacant, lifeless eyes fixated on nothing. It was a bigger beast than Acid had imagined, but that was good; its size would only enhance the training. Winters had maintained a small collection of animals on the farm for potential cover, and had slaughtered and prepared this particular pig for her just half an hour ago.

Acid approached the suspended animal and slapped its side. It was still warm.

"Sorry about this, Peppa," she told it. "But it's all for the greater good. I'm sure you understand."

While she waited for Spook, she paced around the room, stretching her arms across her chest as she went. It was a great space, well-equipped and perfect for their needs. Winters had done a good job. Though whether he'd be able to follow through on the grandiose claims he'd made over dinner last night regarding his new organisation was another matter. But he was a decent guy and she wished him well. Up against Darius, he'd need all the luck he could get. Which is why she didn't feel too bad about imposing on him currently. His success hinged on whether Darius Duke would survive long enough to propel Kancel Kulture to the lofty heights predicted by industry insiders. And whether Darius did survive was down to her – and Spook as well, perhaps. That was the reason they were all here: her, Spook, and Peppa.

"Whoa. What the hell is that?"

Acid turned around to see Spook standing in the doorway, her eyes wide at the sight of the immense pig hanging from the ceiling.

"Good morning, sunshine," Acid said. "Today you're going to be practising your knife skills on our friend Peppa here."

Spook's face paled slightly, but she nodded. "O-kay."

They walked over to the table in the corner of the room, where Winters had left an array of knives for them to choose from. Acid picked up a small nimble blade and handed it to Spook.

The kid's hands were shaking as she took the knife from her and examined the sharp edge. It was the first time she'd properly held a sharp blade designed for combat rather than to cut up a steak, and they both seemed to get the gravitas of the situation. This was one of those no-turning-back moments. Acid could see the caution in Spook's eyes, but also the determination to push through her fears. There was that plucky resilience on show again, but Spook needed to be pushed even further if she was going to make it in this world.

"All right, Spook. We're going to start with some basic incisions. This will help you understand how much pressure needs to be applied when faced with an enemy. To fully incapacitate someone, you need to pierce skin and muscle – and also bone when it comes to it." She slapped the pig's heavy cranium for emphasis. "Do you think you can handle it?"

Spook frowned. "Is pig skin the same as human skin?"

"I could go and find some kid from the next village if you'd prefer." She laughed. Spook didn't.

"Fine," she said. "Let's get on with it."

Acid nodded, surprised once more at Spook's assured

response. She walked over to the pig and gestured for Spook to join her. "We'll begin with the belly," she said. "It's the softest area and a good place to start."

Spook nodded and took a deep breath. She positioned herself next to Acid and raised the knife. Acid watched her closely, noting the tension in her muscles and the focus in her eyes. She had potential. Whether that was enough to get them through an encounter with Darius and his new team of deadly assassins was another matter.

"Okay," Acid said. "I want you to stab poor old Peppa right here – as hard as you can." She pointed to a spot on the pig's belly.

Spook raised her knife and, with a grunt, stabbed the knife into the pig's guts. The blade only went in a little way, but enough to send blood spurting out over Spook's hands and onto the floor.

"Ah. Gross."

She stepped back, waving her wet hand in the air.

"Oh, were you not expecting any blood?" Acid asked, unable to disguise the delight in her voice. "Animals bleed, Spooky. Freshly killed ones do, at least. Humans certainly do."

Spook scowled at her. "It was a shock. That's all."

Acid dropped her smirk into a stern look. "Yes. And you have to learn to deal with shocks. Because there'll be plenty if you're serious about coming with me to Rome. Mark my words."

"Yes! I get it!" Spook snapped. "It won't happen again."

She turned back to the pig, eyes blazing.

"Let's try again," Acid said. "Except this time, push the knife in like you actually want to do some damage. As far as it will go. To the hilt if you can manage it. If Peppa here were an assailant, we'd want to be doing damage to internal organs rather than flesh and muscle. Reckon you can manage that?"

Spook nodded and readjusted her stance. Hefting the knife up, she gulped back a deep breath and thrust forward with the blade, stabbing it into an area above the pig's flank. This time there was no blood, the blade had penetrated further than it had the first time, past veins and capillaries and deep into the pig's body. Spook stepped back, leaving the knife sticking out of the animal's flesh and wiping her hand on her thigh.

"Done."

"Good work." Acid walked over and yanked out the knife to examine the wound. It was deep. It had almost reached the spine. "That's not bad. I'd say poor Peppa would be well and truly weakened by that attack. She'd be severely pissed off, at the very least. Well done." Spook beamed. Acid turned to her, wagging a finger in her face. "But I want to see more conviction next time. Less holding back. That means feeling the blade's power. Not worrying about the pain you're inflicting. If you hesitate at any point in the field, you're finished. Dead. Do you understand, Spook?"

"Yes. I do. You've been telling me the same thing for the last five years. Don't hesitate. I get it." She pointed her own finger, glistening with pig's blood at Acid, her voice lowering an octave as she did. "I know I've been flighty and unfocused for a lot of that time, but that's the old Spook. I'm not that person anymore. Just like Alice Vandella changed, so can I. And I'd appreciate it if you stopped patronising me and trying to convince me that I'm not capable of helping you take down Darius Duke. Because I damn well am!"

As Spook spoke, her eyes darted over Acid's shoulder. Acid followed her gaze to see Winters had appeared and was leaning against the doorframe watching them.

Ahaaa.

So that was what Spook's impassioned speech was all about – impressing Winters. She must like him. How pathetic of her. After everything she'd just said, here she was letting her feelings dictate her behaviour. There was no room for emotion here; not anymore. Acid had been correct all along. Spook wasn't ready.

"I tell you what," Acid told her, stepping around the other side of her so Spook had to tear her gaze away from Winters. "Why don't you go again? This time, aim for this spot – the tough skin around the back of the pig's neck. See if you can penetrate it as easily."

Acid traced her finger over the general area on the pig's neck before stepping back. At the same time, Spook adjusted herself into the guarded attack stance that she'd learnt the previous week – arms up and protecting her vital organs, the knife held close to her body, ready to strike. Acid glanced at Winters, but his expression remained inscrutable. He was watching Spook.

"Imagine this pathetic porcine is Darius," Acid whispered in Spook's ear. "Go get him. Show him what you're made of. Finish him!"

Spook nodded eagerly, her eyes wide with concentration. Acid jumped back as she lurched forward, swiping the blade through the air and stabbing it into the pig's throat with a heavy grunt of effort.

"Ah. Shit. Fuck!"

A jet of crimson pig's blood spurted out from Peppa's

throat, hitting Spook in the eyes and mouth, covering her face, hair, and most of her top. For one, maybe two seconds, it was relentless (it probably seemed a hell of a lot longer for the one in the firing line), before it drained down to a trickle.

Acid stepped forward and slapped Spook on the back. "Oh shit. I think you might have nicked the poor sow's carotid artery." She glanced over at Winters and grinned. "Think yourself lucky it was already dead. That was just from bottled-up pressure in its system. If its heart was still beating, a beast like this would spurt blood for thirty seconds at least. You'd be drenched."

"I am drenched!" Spook growled, dropping the knife and wiping the blood from her eyes. She stepped up to Acid and lowered her voice. "You knew that was going to happen, didn't you? You planned it to make me look stupid."

Acid pressed her hand to her chest. "*Moi?* How can you say such a thing?" She laughed and looked over at Winters. Finally he reciprocated and she winked at him.

"Screw you," Spook shouted, as she spun around and sprinted towards the exit.

"Where are you going?" Acid called after her.

"To take a shower!"

As the kid's footsteps faded away up the stairs, Acid shook her head. "Dear, oh dear." She walked over to Winters, meeting him halfway as he crossed to her.

"That was harsh," he said. "You did plan that, didn't you?"

Acid's lip curled into a sarcastic smile as she shook her head. "This industry is messy and bloody and it does not give two shits about your feelings or your pride." She tilted her head to one side. "It's only ever about the survival of the fittest, Nate. Spook needs to realise that. I think we all need a reminder of it now and again."

The truth was that Acid dreaded what lay ahead. Darius was still playing on her mind, but an even greater fear lurked beneath the surface. A fear of herself, of what she might do, given half the chance.

"Hey, everything all right with you?" Winters asked. She noticed his hand twitch as if he wanted to reach out to her.

"Why wouldn't it be?" she asked.

"With everything that's going on. You seem a bit, I don't know... strange."

Acid nodded. "Yes, well, Winters. There's a good reason for that."

"Oh?"

"It's because I am strange." She gave him a manic grin and punched him on the arm. "Now come on, Farmer Winters. Let's get this place cleaned up."

CHAPTER 26

Spook knew she'd been putting on a good show – excelling in whatever medium or skillset Acid was throwing her way – but as the days went by, the training was taking its toll on her. And not just physically. Every muscle in her body burned and the skin on her hands and feet was raw from handling weaponry or going on long treks in the countryside, but it was more than that. Her mental health was also being pushed to the hilt.

Every night for the past eleven days she'd had vivid nightmares. Demons and ghouls came at her from out of the darkness; ghastly apparitions of past victims and near-death experiences tormented her. Blood-soaked visions and faces of death haunted her like cackling harpies. And always there each time, Darius Duke's malicious grin hanging in the sky like an evil Cheshire Cat, reducing her heart to ash.

That was at night. In the day it was worse. Spook found she was growing numb to what was happening around her. Whether this was due to the four sensory overload sessions she'd experienced in the grey room, or her ego's desperate attempt to shield itself from the crushing pressure it was under, she wasn't sure. With each passing day, the world seemed colder and more indifferent and her connection to it more distant and brittle. She felt herself closing off, barricading her emotions behind impenetrable walls. Perhaps this emotional detachment was necessary for the tasks ahead – it certainly appeared to be how Acid dealt with life – but it was daunting and strange and Spook worried her entire personality was slipping away. However, this didn't mean she was going to put a stop to her training or even slow down. Darius was still out there. Bastards were still running the world. As long as those things were true, she had to be prepared for any danger, ready to confront whatever came her way.

Despite the turmoil raging within Spook, she couldn't deny that she was relishing certain aspects of her training. She had discovered an innate talent for firearms, and her knife and hand-to-hand combat skills, although shaky initially, were improving all the time. Following the humiliating pig incident, she'd even forgiven Acid for making her appear foolish in front of Nate. After all, there was no place for humiliation or conceit when you were a badass. Although, the kudos she'd received after completing a gruelling thirty-mile trek over the hills and mountains of South Wales after a forty-eight-hour stint in the grey room, had bolstered her spirits. Besides, Nate hadn't mentioned the pig incident and remained as charming and amenable as ever whenever they spoke.

Spending extended periods in the sensory overload room was intense and challenging, but after a while Spook had learnt to quieten her mind and was able to retreat from the ear-shattering noise and blinding lights to a sanctuary deep within herself. In that introspective space, she considered her life, her desire for revenge, and what path she should take. She thought of Darius, of The Dullahan, of Acid Vanilla. She thought of Nate Winters, too. But it was Acid who occupied her thoughts the most. For Spook, it was imperative that her often capricious and perplexing friend was fully on board with their mission. Right now she still wasn't one hundred percent confident that was the case. She couldn't shake the feeling that Acid had been wavering lately, and that the possible familial link between her and their chief antagonist had shaken her resolve. But Acid would do the right thing. She had to. In the end, with Spook's influence, she always did.

"Come on, Spook, concentrate."

Nate's firm instruction carried her back to the moment. It was day twelve, a few minutes after ten in the morning, and they'd been in the red room since eight running rote combat practice.

Spook raised her hands, both strapped up inside a pair of shiny black sparring gloves. Nate raised the pads attached to his.

"Right, let's see what you've got."

"No problem." With a yell, Spook launched herself at him, fists thumping heavily into the pads, utilising the powerful muscles in her shoulders as she rained down each blow. In turn, Nate defended himself skilfully, blocking and dodging her attacks. Spook gritted her teeth, fascinated by his speed but determined to break through his defences. She kicked at his stomach, but he caught her foot in mid-air and shoved it to one side, causing her to stumble. He laughed.

That annoyed her. She regained her balance and attacked, her movements now faster and more fluid.

After focusing Nate's attention with another flurry of punches, she side-stepped him and ducked under the pads, delivering a blow to his solar plexus that knocked him back.

"Whoa!" he said, coughing through the shock. "You're supposed to aim for the pads."

Spook raised her eyebrows. "Oh yeah. Sorry about that. Did I wind you?"

He shook his head, but he was smiling, obviously pleased with her progress. "That was sneaky, Spook. But I like it. You're applying yourself, thinking a few steps in advance. It's good."

"Thank you." She wiped the sweat from her forehead with her wrist. She was finally starting to feel as if she belonged in this lethal world of assassins. It was thrilling and terrifying in equal measure. "How long have you been... you know... how long have you worked in the industry?"

"As an assassin? A hit man? A hired killer? Come on, Spook, you can say it. You've been hanging out with Acid for long enough. If you're going to be the badass that you want to be, you'll have to make peace with what we are. Maybe what you'll be one day."

Spook scoffed. "No way. This is about stopping Darius. Not learning how to kill people for money."

"Okay. It is good money, though. Very good. Especially if you build on the level of skill you're already displaying. As well as your sneakiness." He grinned. So did she. "I've been in the industry since I was twenty-three," he went on. "Long enough to know what I'm doing, but not long enough to have lost my humanity. Or so I hope."

Spook nodded, taking in his words. It was a relief to know that not everyone in this industry was a heartless killer. "And Acid? Do you think she's still got some humanity left?"

Winters' expression shifted and he appeared solemn. "Acid's been doing this for a long time. Longer than me. She's seen things and done things that would be too much for most people. I think she's strong and she acts as if nothing fazes her, but beneath all that she's still human. She cares about you, you know."

Spook let out a short laugh. "I used to believe that."

"But not now?"

"I don't know. Our relationship has been strained lately. Almost to breaking point. I used to be able to get through to her. We were a good team. But not anymore."

Winters gave her a sympathetic look. "This cut-throat world of ours is a hard world to exist in when you don't have a friend. I know that much. Yet it's loners who thrive. Those without ties, or family."

Spook squinted up at him. "You sound like you're speaking from experience."

"A little," he replied. "I don't talk about my past. It's against every rule in the book in terms of what I do. But let's just say lately I've been missing human contact. It's good to have people around. I suppose that's one reason why I want to build an organisation around me. I want to be a part of something bigger than myself. A team. A family, even." He laughed and looked away. If Spook hadn't known better, she would have sworn his cheeks were flushed. It made her like him a whole lot more. She'd been wrong about Nate Winters. He was a decent man. Deep. Interesting. She found herself wanting to know more about him.

"Where are you from?" she asked. "Sorry, I know, but—"

"It's fine. I'm actually from Wales, originally. A town called Blackwood, further south than here."

"You don't sound Welsh."

"No. I lost my accent over the years. It's best to in this game. Keep it neutral. I haven't been back to Blackwood for years now. Even being back in Wales, I can't bring myself to go."

"No family there?"

"No family anywhere. Not anymore. Once, it was me, my parents and three brothers. I was the youngest." He raised his head, peering off into the middle distance. Spook was compelled to grab him and squeeze him tight. But she didn't. She remained where she was and Nate shook away the memory capturing his attention with a flick of his head. "Anyway. Onwards and upwards. But, yes, I get where you're coming from. It's tough. It really is. But you have to remember why you're doing this." He stepped back and held up his pads. "Speaking of which, do you want to get back to it?"

"Sure. Let's give it five more minutes, though, yeah? I could do with a rest."

A voice rang out behind her. "Five minutes' rest? Bloody rest? I thought you were serious about this training, sweetie?"

Spook spun around to see Acid marching towards them. She'd just returned from a run and her skin was flushed and shiny. Her hair was scraped back from her face, highlighting her cheekbones and wide jawline. She was wearing a pair of black jogging bottoms that Nate had provided, along with a black t-shirt with the sleeves cut off. Her running shoes and her calves were caked in mud. As she got closer, Spook detected a hint of body odour, mixed with a fresher scent she could only describe as 'the outside'.

"We've been training all morning," Spook told her. "It's going well. Isn't it, Nate?"

Winters nodded. "She almost took me out just now. You need to watch this one, Acid; she's pretty sn—"

"Yes, well, there's still plenty to do. I've got a new challenge for you. Maybe the most important one yet. Wait there."

As Acid exited the room, Spook peered up at Nate for an answer, but he just shrugged. "Don't look at me."

Suddenly a high-pitched scream, or perhaps a squeal, resonated throughout the farmhouse. Spook tensed as the noise grew closer and she realised the source of it. A second later Acid reappeared carrying a pig in her arms – a piglet, really, judging by its proportions. She walked over to Spook and held it up. It was about the size of a small child. Its eyes were bright and full of life, and someone – Acid most likely – had attached a small pink bow around one of its ears. It snaffled and squealed as Spook stared at it.

"Spook, meet George."

Spook swallowed. "What am I supposed to do with him?"

"Oh, come now, Spook." Acid smirked, shoving the piglet at her. "I think you know."

CHAPTER 27

Spook glared at Acid, feeling the piglet's warm, soft body squirming in her arms. She had never held a pig before. "No, Acid. Please. I can't. You don't seriously want me to...?"

"Yes," Acid replied, eyes widening with intensity. "I want you to kill little George here."

A shiver of dread ran down Spook's arms. "No! I can't kill a pig!"

"Can't, or won't?"

"I won't. I can't do it."

Acid's face hardened. "I see. I thought as much. Well, you know what this means?"

"What?"

"You're not cut out for this world. You don't have what it takes."

Spook felt a surge of anger. "I do have what it takes. I just can't kill an innocent animal."

Acid shrugged. "It's not an innocent animal. It's your next test. And a bloody important one, I'd say, sweetie. If you can't do this, the most basic of acts, then I can't trust you to be any sort of help out in the field."

Spook looked down at George, who was still wiggling in her arms. "Piss off, Acid. You know I've killed people. You were there."

"You reacted in a moment. You were full of adrenaline and rage and you acted accordingly. Great. But there have been plenty of other moments when you've frozen. When you couldn't do what was needed. I need to know that whatever Darius throws at us, you're able to deal with it. Because, like I say, the second you freeze, you die." She walked over to the side of the room and took down a large knife that was hanging on the wall. Holding it up to the light, making a show of examining the shiny steel blade, she walked back to Spook and flipped it over, clutching the blade and presenting the handle to her. "So here we are."

Taking a deep breath, Spook set George down on the floor and took the knife from Acid. "You're sick. Do you know that?"

Acid pulled a face like she was considering this comment deeply. "Yes. I think I do know that." She glanced down at George, standing between the two of them. Spook caught the piglet's gaze. He looked so trusting. So cute.

"Fine. I'll do it." Spook knelt beside the pig, her hand gripping the warm flesh on its back as she raised the knife. Tears streamed down her face. She paused, the knife raised and ready.

No.

She couldn't go through with it.

She lowered the knife, unable to look at Acid.

"Come on, Spook." Acid's voice was low and menacing. "If

you can't do this, what's the point of being here? We're not running a charity."

Spook glanced up at Nate. "Is he one of yours? Are you okay with this?"

"We'll sort out any compensation later," Acid cut in, before he could answer. "I'm sure Winters appreciates the importance of this element of your training. Right?"

Nate cleared his throat. "Yes. Sure," he said, giving Spook a reassuring nod. "I get it."

"Okay, I'll do it." Spook gritted her teeth and raised the knife again, trying to steady herself. Closing her eyes, she took a deep breath and brought the knife down. The blade sliced through the air and landed with a thud as it hit the thickly padded floor. Her eyes snapped open and she looked down. The blade had narrowly missed George's head. The pig snorted and shuffled his feet, sensing something was wrong. He peered up at Spook with big, trusting eyes and let out a soft oink.

Jesus.

This was torture. But she had to do it. She knew what was at stake.

"Do it!" Acid snarled.

"I can't."

"You will."

With a cry, Spook brought the knife down again, but at the last second she hesitated and ended up stabbing it into the fleshy part of the pig's back. It wasn't a fatal blow. George squealed with pain and skittered away, leaving a line of blood in his wake. Ricocheting off the walls, the wounded animal found the far corner and tucked himself into a ball, letting out a high-pitched whimper as his curly tail flicked back and forth.

"Shit!" Spook whispered as she viewed the blood. It was everywhere. She got up and hurried over to the piglet. She had to finish the job.

"I'll hold it down," Acid said, following her. "Don't let it bolt again." She knelt beside the pitiful little animal and placed a hand on her back.

Spook held the knife in front of her. This was now as much about mercy as it was brutality. She stared at her distorted reflection in the steel blade as she mustered the courage. She hated the person looking back at her.

Acid reached forward and stroked the scared pig's wet nose. "It'll all be over soon," she said in a quiet voice. "You'll be fine."

It wasn't clear to Spook if she was talking to George or her. She raised the knife again, and this time brought it down into the middle of the pig's skull. She felt resistance, then heard a cracking sound as something gave way. George let out a shrill squeal and a warm, wet sensation splashed onto Spook's hands and up her bare arms. Gritting her teeth, she leaned forward, pressing down on the hilt of the knife with all her strength. The knife went in deeper. The pig ceased squirming. The squealing stopped.

Spook looked up.

The whole room was silent. Acid's face was an unreadable mask. Nate's was expressionless. Spook let go of the knife and stood. The dead pig was lying in a pooling circle of blood. She stepped back before it reached her feet.

"Good work, kid," Acid said, placing a hand on her

shoulder. "I wasn't sure you were going to go through with it. How do you feel?"

Spook glared at her. "Fuck you!"

"Excuse me?" Acid stepped away and held her hands up, palms facing Spook. "I had nothing to do with this. It was your idea, sweetie. You wanted me to train you. You wanted to learn how to kill. Remember? And now you have done. How does it feel?"

Spook didn't answer. She was so angry and upset she had no words. Turning on her heels she marched to the door, moving fast but not too fast. The last thing she wanted was for Acid to think she was running away.

"Where are you going?" she called after her.

"To my room. To get changed," Spook replied, slowing as she got to the door. She turned back. "I did what you asked of me. I passed your little test. Let's move on, shall we?" Her voice was shaking with emotion, but she had no control over it.

Acid nodded. "Fine with me. But, seriously, good job today, Spook. Why don't you get cleaned up and we can have lunch?" She slapped her hands together and grinned, one eye on Nate. "Bacon sandwiches all round, I'd say."

CHAPTER 28 ·

Thankfully, Spook was able to make it through the main farmhouse, up the stairs, and back into her quarters before she burst into tears. When they came, it felt like they brought with them huge waves of emotion and pain she didn't even realise she'd been carrying with her. She flung herself onto the bed and buried her face in the pillow, allowing the deep sobs to flow freely. She understood what Acid had been doing, but it didn't stop her from feeling wretched and stupidly naïve.

Had she got too cocky, too quickly?

Maybe. But up to this point she'd been doing so well. Acid wasn't one to administer praise, but Spook had seen it in her face – she'd been both shocked and delighted with her competence.

But today felt different. It wasn't merely the guilt from taking an innocent beast's life. Spook felt betrayed, as if Acid had tried to shatter her spirit. And yes, that might be what was required to make someone into an effective killer, but coming from her, someone Spook had looked up to and cared about for so long (sometimes too much), it hurt. It was crushing.

But screw her.

Screw the whole damn world.

Acid hadn't succeeded in breaking her. Far from it. She felt more resolute than ever that she would prove how much of a badass she could be and eliminate Darius fucking Duke.

She might have wobbled today. But she was ready. She was more than ready. The two weeks were almost up and she couldn't hide away in rural Wales forever. Didn't they say you learnt more out in the real world than you ever could in a classroom or a training camp?

Spook wiped her tears and sat up, her mind focusing on her next move. There was no point in wallowing in self-pity, action was what was needed. With that, she rose from the bed, her mind already racing with possibilities. Moving over to the desk, she opened her laptop and sat down.

She might have excelled at the challenges Acid had thrown at her so far, but her true talent – her secret weapon – was her mastery of technology. And she had an idea.

Leaning over the keyboard, she logged into the VPN she'd already set up, and opened the Tor browser she'd downloaded the previous week. From there she accessed the dark web and the cloud version of Epsilon – her IDE of choice – and began to type. Her fingers danced across the keyboard as she tapped out lines of code, only stopping momentarily to switch to a new browser window and instigating a deep search of Rome's CCTV networks and any active security feeds in the city.

She felt a rumble in her stomach but she ignored it. There was no way she was eating with Acid and Nate. She leaned over and grabbed a couple of energy bars and a bottle of water from out of her drawer – classic sustenance for a hacker consumed by her task. As she chewed down the first carob and nut bar, she used her free hand to tap out more lines of code. The events of the day faded into the background as she typed, her focus razor-sharp. She was determined to make progress and gain any advantage she could to take down Darius. Being able to show off her expert skills to Acid and Nate wouldn't hurt, either.

It didn't take long for her to find a way in; a back door into the ancient CCTV network that she could exploit. A sense of excitement rushed through her veins as she delved deeper into the system and found live feeds from all over Rome. Her heart beat in time with the click-clack of the keyboard as she found other security feeds – buildings with poor levels of security, whose networks she could hack into with her eyes closed.

This was what she really excelled at, manipulating complex systems and finding vulnerabilities. Her eyes scanned through the feeds, looking for any sign of Duke or his henchmen. She knew it was a pointless exercise, but that was what the code was for, a basic version of the facial recognition AI she'd been developing over the past two years. With her own laptop lost in the explosion, she'd have to start all over again. But with the advancements in AI technology, it could write a lot of the peripheral code itself.

The program she was writing today would be a short-term fix, but she only needed it to carry out one task. It only had to search for one likeness. Someone she knew was part of Darius' crew and whose photo was already available to her via an old Myspace account – Mika Galambos. The Gorgon.

A smile spread across Spook's face as she grabbed the URL of the photo and fed it into her rudimentary program.

"There. Let's see how well you can hide with every camera in the city looking for you. Bitch."

Chuckling to herself at her apparent change in mood (and perhaps even personality), she got to her feet. Leaving the algorithm to do its job, she grabbed a towel and went into the bathroom for a long overdue shower.

———

STEPPING out of the shower ten minutes later, she wrapped the towel around herself as she walked over to the mirror. She barely recognised the woman staring back at her. Her black hair was slicked to her face, and her eyes were red and puffy from the tears she had shed earlier. But there was something new in her eyes now, too. A fierce determination that both frightened and exhilarated her.

Returning to her laptop she scanned the screen, scrutinizing the various feeds she'd accessed, before turning her attention to the rudimentary facial recognition software.

Well, shit.

Her heart skipped a beat. She had a hit. No, two hits.

She opened the folder she'd set up for collecting automated screengrabs and clicked on the two image files inside. Her breath caught in her throat as the grainy black-and-white photos popped up on the monitor. Mika Galambos – The Gorgon – was clear in both shots.

"Come to momma," Spook muttered, as she zoomed in on the first photo. The Gorgon was walking down a wide avenue flanked by high-end boutiques. It was a solid capture and proved she was in Rome, but it wasn't enough.

The next image, however, was different. This one showed the Hungarian assassin approaching a large neoclassical building with a bustling piazza in front of it. Huge stone pillars rose up on either side of the wide entrance and a man was standing in the doorway, arms open, seemingly welcoming The Gorgon. His jet-black hair was slicked back. He wore a long black overcoat and a wicked smile on his face. Despite the grainy quality of the CCTV capture, Spook recognised him instantly.

Darius Duke.

"Got you," she snarled at the photo. "And now we're coming for you."

CHAPTER 29

The sun was setting over the Welsh hillside as Acid left the farmhouse and strolled across the courtyard linking the main building to the animal sheds and the nearest outbuilding. The air was cool, but still carried the warm floral scent of a summer's evening. Birds cheeped and chirruped as they roosted down for the night, lone bees buzzed while drifting from flower to flower in search of the last of the day's pollen. You might say it was an idyllic setting.

If you liked that sort of thing.

Acid preferred dark basement bars and music so loud it drowned out the screeching bat chorus in her head and stopped the intrusive thoughts from taking hold. She couldn't deny, however, the impressive nature of Winters' operation. Once complete, the farm would be bigger and better equipped than Honeysuckle House, Caesar's training camp, where she'd learnt her deadly trade. Although, Acid knew mastering techniques was only part of the equation. You couldn't call yourself an assassin until you'd stared into the cold, dead eyes of your first hit.

This harsh reality was what she'd been trying to convey to Spook earlier. Their world was cruel and unforgiving. It tore families apart and left a trail of destruction in its wake. It was true, most of the people Acid had killed had deserved it in some way, but beyond their nefarious endeavours, they were human beings with lives and families and dreams. Death was the main currency in this industry. The only currency. You had to face it head-on without backing down for a second.

And, yes, her tactics today had been rather heavy-handed and perhaps even a little cruel. But if Spook was serious about becoming an effective killer, she'd need to get over herself. She said she didn't want to kill for money (God she'd certainly said that – over and over and over again and at any opportunity), but Acid found that rather hypocritical. For her, there was no grey area. You were prepared to kill, or you weren't.

One thing was certain, however, Spook wanted revenge. She wanted to hit Darius with as much force as she could muster. Acid did as well, of course. He'd killed The Dullahan, for Christ's sake. It cut deep. The fact that the last thing her old friend had been privy to was her being tricked and humiliated by Darius cut almost as deep.

She wandered past the animal sheds and over to the first paddock, looking out across the sprawling field where a sea of tall shoots, some kind of grain, swayed gently in the evening breeze.

She puffed out a long sigh. "What the fuck am I playing at?" She shook her head.

And, who the hell was she talking to?

Yet it was a valid question and one she still didn't have a concrete answer to. Her thoughts circled back to Darius' last message. He'd called her 'Sis'. More than once. Did that mean it was true? Or was it just him messing with her, trying to get into her head?

She had to find out. This possibility he might be her brother was consuming her. She had no choice but to confront him, if only to find out the truth.

Then she'd kill the fucker.

"Penny for your thoughts?"

"Excuse me?"

Acid turned to see Winters standing behind her. It had been hours since she'd last seen him, and the sight of his muscular form in dirty jeans and a plaid shirt hit her like a punch in the guts. Maybe a little lower. His hair was more tousled than usual, like he'd just crawled out of bed. But it was the two bottles of beer he was carrying that really caught her attention.

"You look like you've got a lot on your mind," he said, holding one of the beers out for her. "I thought you might appreciate a little lubrication."

"You're a bloody lifesaver," she told him, taking the beer and gulping down the first third of it in one gulp. It was ice cold and malty, and on her parched throat tasted like ambrosia.

Winters leaned against the wall beside her, taking a swig from his own bottle. They stood in silence for a while, staring out at the field as the sun dipped lower on the horizon.

"Did Spook resurface?" Acid asked, breaking the silence.

He stuck out his lip. "Not yet. She's in her room. I think she's struggling a bit with... everything."

Acid took another sip of her beer. "She'll get over it. Or she won't."

Winters frowned. "You're still as cold as ice, aren't you? Assassin or not."

"It's not about being cold. It's about being realistic."

"I know that, but... it doesn't have to consume you. We can still be human beings. We can still feel things."

Acid turned and looked him straight in the eye. "Don't you be getting shmaltzy on me, Nitro. I'm not in the mood."

"Fair enough." He drank. "Do you miss it?"

"Being an assassin?" She had a pithy retort lined up, but she stopped herself and changed tack. "I guess I do. I miss being part of something greater than me. An organisation. A team. I suppose I miss Caesar, is what I'm saying."

"Right, yeah. It's just... Didn't I hear that you were the one that..."

"Technically," she said, waving the beer bottle in the air. "But the poor old fucker had Huntington's disease. He didn't have long to go. It was his idea for me to take him out in the end. Sort of. It's a long story." She gulped back more beer, her shoulders suddenly tense. She glanced at Winters, defying him to continue this line of questioning. Lucky for him he got the message.

"He was a great man," was all he said.

Acid nodded. "Damn right. And a great mentor." She laughed. "Now I suppose I'm a mentor to Little Miss Sulky Pants in there. Weird that. I never asked for it." She held her beer bottle to her mouth, sensing she was about to divulge something she shouldn't. Lowering it, she let out a sigh. "Do you know what, Nate? I've no fucking clue what I'm going to do."

He turned to look at her. "I think it's okay not to know. You've been through a lot. It's natural to feel lost sometimes.

But you'll figure it out. I mean, I could tell you what I think..."

"Oh yeah, what's that? Give up everything and partner up with you in your new project?"

"Hey, it's more than a project. And you could do a lot worse." He raised his head, eyes scanning the field in front of him. "Think about it. That's all I ask."

"I will."

"Great."

They clinked their beer bottles together in a silent toast. Acid was about to say more. She wanted to. But she heard a voice coming from the farmhouse. As she turned, Spook was walking towards them. She'd changed into a set of the black jogging pants and sweatshirt Winters had provided. Her hair looked freshly washed and she was wearing her glasses.

"I've found him," she said, as she got up to them.

"Who?" Winters asked.

"Darius Duke. But not just that, I think I've located his organisation's new headquarters. I created a basic facial recognition AI using parts of code I'd already written and saved on the Epsilon portal, and then I hacked into Rome's CCTV network and—"

"Yes, yes. We get it," Acid butted in, pointing the neck of her beer bottle at Spook. "You're a genius. But can you cut to the chase?"

Spook's eyes flittered to Winters before she looked down at her feet. "I was just explaining how..." She shook her head. "Forget it. They're in an old government building that was once used as a book depository. On the south side of the Piazza San Giovanni in Laterano, Rome. It looks heavily fortified, but now I know what we're dealing with I can hack into their systems and disable some of their security before we get there."

"Before we get there? You want to hit them at their HQ? So...what? We waltz over there, just the two of us, and take on the entire organisation? Come on, Spook, I thought you were supposed to be smart."

Spook scowled. "I was speaking in loose terms. Obviously we'll come up with a better strategy now we know where they are."

Acid puffed out her cheeks. "Obviously." She drained her beer bottle.

"Hey, I've been working hard on this," Spook snapped. "All day. And I did this." She brought a phone out of the pocket of her jogging bottoms and shoved it at Acid.

"What's this? My phone?"

"I've put tracking software on both our phones, linking them up, and the same software is on the laptop I've been using. We can stay in contact if we get split up, and Nate can track our whereabouts while we're over there."

Acid shoved the phone into her pocket without looking at it. "You've thought of everything, haven't you?"

"Why aren't you taking this seriously?" Spook hissed. "This is it! We've got them!"

Acid held up her hands. "Relax, will you? I am taking it seriously. But we don't want to rush in and get ourselves killed." She faced Spook head-on, fixing her with a hard stare. One she hoped would convey the right message. "We need more intel before we make a move. We can't just go in blind."

Spook looked over her shoulder and then back. "I just... I want to do something. I don't want to wait around anymore.

The waiting is killing me. And might I remind you there have been three attempts on our lives in the last three weeks."

"Yes," Acid said. "*Attempts*. They weren't successful. He wasn't trying to kill us. You saw the messages."

"How do you know that wasn't just him covering his shortcomings?"

"How do you know it was?"

"Jesus, Acid," Spook gasped. "What the hell is going on in your head right now?"

"I don't think you're ready," she said. "You need more training. We need more time."

"Time's up!" Spook cried. "Two weeks, he said. We've had two weeks. Now we need to make a move. We need to hit him first. Or are you still considering his other option?" She glared at Winters. "Has she told you what Darius has offered her?"

The guy looked confused. "Hey, listen. I don't want to get involved in this right now."

Good man.

That showed class. He knew when to keep his head down and his mouth shut.

"I am ready," Spook went on. "I'm more than ready. Physically and up here." She tapped two fingers on her temple.

"No. You'll get yourself killed if we go now," Acid hit back. "Me too, most likely."

"I won't. You're just making excuses." Spook stepped towards her. "Do you want Darius dead?"

"Excuse me?"

"It's a simple question, Acid. Darius Duke. Do you want him dead?"

Acid scoffed. She rolled her eyes. It was an instinctive response, but even she knew a pause now didn't look good. "Yes. Of course I do!"

"Hmm." Spook stared deep into her eyes, and it was as if all the sounds of the countryside were suddenly muted. No birds. No breeze. No buzzing insects. Spook shook her head. "I don't understand you anymore. I'm going to bed."

Acid watched as she turned on her heels and stormed off towards the farmhouse. She wanted to call after her, but what was the point? Instead, she took a deep breath and looked at Winters.

"Pathetic bloody child," she said, her voice barely above a whisper. "She has no idea what she's saying."

Winters set his beer bottle down on the wall. He looked at her, his face full of concern. "Are you okay?"

Acid shrugged it off. "I'm always okay."

He didn't say anything, but she could feel his eyes studying her. She got the feeling he was trying to read her mind, to figure out what was going on in her head. Well, that made two of them.

"Do you want to go talk to her?" Nate asked.

"No," she replied, setting off back to the farmhouse. "I want another beer."

CHAPTER 30

The training gym in the east wing of Kancel Kulture headquarters was hot and stuffy, and Darius regretted not having a decent air-conditioning system installed sooner. It was on his list of things that required attention, but not high up. After today's session, it would need bumping to the top.

He turned towards Saga, who seemed unfazed by the sweltering heat, the man maintaining a steely expression as he bounced effortlessly around the ring. "You want a break?" Saga asked.

"No. Let's go again," Darius said, smacking his sparring gloves together. "I need to keep my motivation up."

Saga grinned and assumed a fighting stance. Darius took a deep breath and stepped forward, fists raised and ready. The two men circled each other warily, like alpha wolves fighting for control of the pack.

Suddenly Saga lunged forward, his fist hurtling towards Darius' face. Darius dodged to the side and countered with a swift punch to Saga's ribs. Saga grunted and stumbled away, but quickly regained his footing and launched another attack. He feigned a punch towards Darius' face, and as he drew his arm to block, caught him with a low blow to his exposed stomach instead. Darius grunted in pain, dragging his guard down.

"All right, all right," Darius gasped, as he retreated. "Let's take that break."

"No problem," Saga replied, his hands dropping to his sides. "But you're improving. I can see it. You're fast now and your punches are finding their targets."

Darius regarded his number two as he bounced from foot to foot. How was he so full of energy? They'd been sparring for over an hour, yet not a single bead of sweat was visible on Saga's brow.

"Five minutes," Darius said. "Then we go again." He walked over to the side of the boxing ring and lifted the top rope. After clambering underneath, he jumped down onto the hard floor.

Five minutes.

Maybe ten.

But despite his weariness, Darius understood the importance of training as hard as his team. He'd made the decision early on that he wouldn't be operating out in the field (he wouldn't be the one getting his hands dirty, or bloody), but it was important he stay fit and active. Ready, for whatever challenges lay ahead. He was relatively new to the assassin industry, but he knew enough about cold-blooded killers to know his survival hinged on constant vigilance and adaptability. He was ruthless and cunning, but his goal was to grow stronger and more tactical in his outlook. To truly take over this world, he had to set himself up as the same triple threat Beowulf Caesar had been. Not only a master strategist and businessman, but someone capable of doing the brutal hands-on work if necessary.

As Darius paced, he felt his heart rate gradually slowing. He inhaled deeply, wiping sweat from his brow with his forearm. He needed to focus, clear his mind and consider his next course of action. Closing his eyes, he attempted to block out the sound of Saga's quick footsteps and the creak of the punching bag's chain as it swung back and forth, but he couldn't shake the feeling something was off. It was a nagging sensation in the back of his mind, a sense of unease he couldn't quite put his finger on. Was it the heat in the gym, or something else? Was it her?

Shit.

A bitter laugh escaped him.

Who was he kidding?

Of course it was her. She'd been on his mind for the past two years. Maybe even his entire life. She was his obsession. His muse. He had to have her.

Opening his eyes he turned towards the door, hearing the approach of footsteps, slow and steady. He tensed, his fists clenching involuntarily. While his fortified headquarters provided physical safety, paranoia and unease were fast becoming his default settings. It was to be expected, perhaps. Someone in his position, standing on the edge of greatness, with his foot on the industry's throat – he was going to have his enemies.

But this is why he needed her. She'd be a valuable asset and... yes, a partner in crime. He hated it (no, despised it) whenever gushing, loved-up couples referred to their sappy mates as their 'partner in crime', but in this case it rang true.

Alice would be his equal, his sister in arms. She could fill in the gaps in his skillset. Guard against his blind spots. Her reputation and prowess still commanded respect and fear within the assassin world, especially amongst the older, more experienced operatives. Darius' dreams for Kancel Kulture were being realised, the organisation taking shape just as he'd envisioned. He had the best headquarters, a team of elite assassins. He had the best hair in the city, the finest Italian shoes money could buy. All that remained was securing that one final piece: Alice Vandella. Acid Vanilla. It didn't matter what she called herself. Being here, working alongside him, it was her destiny. She was perfect.

Just like him.

The gym door slammed open, jolting him from his thoughts. Frederik Kriel marched into the room.

"You don't believe in knocking?" Darius asked, feeling a prickle of nervous energy run down his back. "Is this important?"

The wiry South African approached. He was wearing a pair of loose-fitting maroon canvas trousers and a matching shirt. His greying hair was wild and spiralled out at all angles, like a crown of thorns. His skin was brown and leathery, like it had been embalmed. He stopped in front of Darius and looked him up and down, a maniacal white-gold grin creasing his face.

"Oh, I'd say so, boss," he said, his thick South African accent twisting and bending his vowels. "Your plan worked. I have to admit I was a bit dubious at first. But it worked like an absolute bloody masterpiece. Last night, someone hacked into Rome's security network, and the malware program you purchased from China allowed us to see what they did next.

They were searching for a facial likeness of The Gorgon. They found her. Like you said they would."

The news pleased Darius more than he could express. He'd sensed the scepticism when he'd first presented his plan to Frederik and Saga – in fact, it had gone down like Led Zeppelin on a groupie (to confuse one's metaphors) – and it was true, the trail of breadcrumbs left around the web, in the guise of an old Myspace profile and a matching avatar on the Crypto Jones site, had been a long shot. But one that had paid off.

Another gold star for good old Darius Duke!

"I told you it'd work." He winked at Saga as the Swede walked over. "See?"

Saga nodded as he unstrapped the bindings on his sparring gloves. "Impressive. I'm pleased my limited coding knowledge was able to deliver."

Darius forced a smile. Saga was a loyal number two, but he could be a real sarcastic bastard when he wanted to be. So maybe Acid Vanilla wasn't the only missing piece in his grand plan. Despite the impressive set-up at Casa di Cicero and the vast resources he'd poured into their server unit, they lacked a dedicated tech team. For now, Frederik, Saga, and some powerful AI software acquired from the Far East filled the gap, but it was far from ideal.

"Were you able to find out where the hacker was located?" Darius asked Frederik.

The man's grin grew wider, the fluorescent light above them glinted off his teeth. "Better than that, boss," he said. "We were able to hack into their system and trace their location. They're in Wales, in the UK. Do you want my brother and me to go over and pay them a visit?" His eyes gleamed with greed.

"No," said Darius." That's not how this is going to work."

Frederik's grin faltered. "Boss?"

"Don't worry. Everything is going exactly as I want it. They know where we are." He glanced at Saga. "That's enough."

"So, what do we do?" Frederik asked.

Darius smiled. "We do nothing, my friend. Except wait."

CHAPTER 31

A sliver of sunlight pierced through a gap in the wooden slats of the window blinds, its scorching heat searing Acid's cheek like a branding iron. She groaned and rolled over in bed, turning away from the bright morning's rays. A dream struggled to stay alive in her memory, though quickly faded away as she opened her eyes. She'd hoped to sleep longer, but the bats were already awake. A flurry of troubling thoughts spiralled around in her consciousness.

Damn it.

Might as well get up and do something constructive.

Peeling her head off the pillow, she surveyed her surroundings, attempting to piece together the events of the previous evening. She'd gone to bed late, around 1 a.m., after drinking ten – or maybe fifteen – bottles of beer. But before that, she'd been up talking with Winters...

Ah, shit.

What had she said?

What had she done?

She screwed her eyes shut, striving to recall their conversation. Nate had been telling her about his ideas for the organisation, growing more animated and excitable as the conversation unfolded and the empty beer bottles grew in number. He'd mentioned his contacts all over the globe and his intention to recruit not only the most skilled operatives, but also those he trusted and respected. People like her. Their clientele would hail from the top echelons of society, he'd told her. Which also meant their marks would largely consist of total and utter bastards. There'd be no disgruntled work colleagues or unfaithful spouses on their kill lists. Only evil pricks; those who deserved a bullet in the head or to be shoved into the path of a speeding truck.

They'd be doing the world a favour, he'd said.

Yeah. That old chestnut.

But it was a cliché for a reason – because it was true. Most of the time. Acid hadn't been convinced initially, but as the night went on and their conversation progressed, she found herself increasingly captivated by Winters' vision. He seemed to have a firm grasp on what was needed to make his goal a reality and she liked his determination. He was a good guy, charming and charismatic with it, but...

"Ah, shit. You idiot."

She let out a deep sigh, massaging her temples as the memories flooded back. They'd kissed.

Had they kissed?

Yeah, they'd kissed. She flung the bed covers off her, realising she was naked. Shit. Had they...?

No. No way.

She would have remembered that immediately. She closed her eyes, replaying the scene in her mind. She'd pulled away the moment their lips had touched and had excused herself to bed. Hopefully it wouldn't be too much of an issue, but it was seriously uncool. After Spitfire, she'd vowed never to get involved with anyone in the industry. Acid was as wild and frivolous as they came, but she had rules. She had standards. Such entanglements were dangerous, given their line of work. Yet she couldn't deny there was a spark between them. Winters was handsome and thoughtful and good to talk with, and she respected his vision for his organisation.

She forced herself out of bed and stumbled to the bathroom, her head pounding from the beer. Once there, she splashed water on her face and stared at her reflection in the mirror. Her eyes were bloodshot, her face pale and drawn. Nothing new there. What she needed now was a shower, a strong cup of coffee, and a clear head.

Stretching her arms above her, feeling the stiffness in her muscles, she stepped into the shower cubicle and twisted on the water. The hot shards cascaded over her head and body, washing away the grime and shame from the previous night but not her inner turmoil. As she lathered shampoo into her tangled hair, her thoughts drifted to Darius – as they usually did in moments of solitude.

Spook wanted her and Acid to storm into Rome like they were a barbarian hoard and take him out. Only there were just two of them and it seemed to her more like a suicide mission than a strategic attack. Spook had done well locating Kancel Kulture's headquarters, but had it been too easy? They'd been down this road once before with Darius. He was a tricksy bastard and cunning with it. It could very well be a trap.

Yet she had to face him. Sooner or later. It was unavoidable.

She had to know the truth.

She rinsed her hair and turned off the shower, wrapping herself in a towel and stepping into the bedroom. As she dried off, her gaze fell upon the closed laptop on the desk. She hesitated for a moment before walking over and opening it up. The two weeks were now all but up.

Might he have sent her another message?

As she sat down, the laptop screen flickered to life. She logged in and opened up a new browser window, heading to the Crypto Jones One Thousand forum on automatic pilot. Muscle memory. As she navigated the three verification screens that led to the secure section of the site, thoughts of what *could be* weighed heavily on her mind. Darius was offering her the keys to a ready-made and already powerful assassin organisation. It would be a new career for her, a new life doing what she was good at. Doing the only thing she was good at.

Yes, Winters was offering her the same thing, but his project was nowhere near complete. Whereas Kancel Kulture was already a going concern. If she took up Darius' offer, she could be in South America or Eastern Europe in a week's time. She smiled to herself as memories of her past life flooded her recall. The thrill of the chase. The overriding feeling of power she always felt whilst closing in on a mark. Plus, being an elite assassin was the perfect outlet for her condition.

The bats had already made up their mind.

They wanted in.

There was always the possibility this could be a set-up.

Darius' way of drawing her close so he could finish her off. But she didn't think so. That big ugly bastard could have destroyed her with a carefully placed boot in that alleyway, and whoever launched an anti-personnel grenade into their apartment was either a lousy shot or had been shrewd in where they positioned the blast. From what she knew of the people Darius had surrounded himself with, they weren't going to miss their target if they'd been instructed to eliminate her. If he'd wanted her dead, she would be already. Which meant his offer was genuine.

She leaned back in her chair, staring at the laptop screen. As she kept drumming into Spook, it was the indecision that killed you. Now, she was the one caught in its deadly grip. Darius' proposition was tempting. It would give her a chance to start afresh, to leave behind the pain of her past and embrace a new identity. But it would also mean working for the man who killed her mentor and who was very possibly insane. Could she do it? Could she work alongside him, knowing what he had done?

Could she ever trust him?

Her thoughts were interrupted as the main page of the forum flashed up on the screen. The small envelope icon at the top right was grey rather than red. No new messages. The thread had gone dark. But why would he message again? He'd issued a stark ultimatum. Now, with the two-week grace period almost up, the moment of reckoning was upon her. She shut the lid of the laptop and got dressed, opting for a fresh pair of joggers and a t-shirt. The first thing she would do after this was all over – go on a big shopping spree and get some new clothes. Nate's all-black training kits suited her, but donning the same outfit every day made her feel like she was in uniform. It conjured up bad memories of Crest Hill.

She left her room and walked down the corridor, knocking on Spook's door as she passed. "Hey, you up?"

When there was no answer she knocked again, louder. "Spook. I'm heading downstairs. See you there. Don't be long." She continued to the end of the corridor and down the stairs that led to the main part of the house.

It wasn't just Spook who'd been training hard. The past two weeks had seen her push her body to the limit by lifting weights and going on gruelling twenty-kilometre hill runs each day. It was a welcome break to exert herself physically rather than mentally and helped keep the bats at bay, but there was only so much exercise one could do.

The red room was empty, so she walked over to admire the impressive array of weapons Nate had arranged on the far wall. There were guns, swords, knives of all shapes and sizes, and a few exotic weapons even she couldn't quite identify. She reached out and caressed the handle of a particularly impressive-looking dagger, before picking up a trusty Glock from off the next shelf. Holding it out in front of her, she took a deep breath and closed her eyes, picturing Darius in her mind's eye. She squeezed the trigger, but the hollow click as she dry-fired was unsatisfying. The bats nibbled at her nerve endings. They wanted chaos. They wanted noise and bloodshed and death.

A sound from behind startled her. She spun around, flipping the gun barrel into her palm and wielding the pistol handle as a blunt instrument.

Winters was standing in the doorway. "Whoa. Sorry." He held up his hands. "I didn't mean to startle you."

Acid relaxed her grip on the gun and straightened up. "It's fine. I was just... I don't know what I was doing." She put the Glock back on the shelf and rubbed her hand on the front of her t-shirt.

"What's on your mind?" Winters asked, walking towards her. "You seem tense."

Acid raised an eyebrow.

"All right," he added. "Tenser than usual."

She sighed. "It's hard to explain. I don't even know where to start." She rolled her head back and released a deep groan into the ceiling. "I'll be fine. I'm a big girl. I can sort it."

"I don't doubt that. Listen, Acid, about last night..."

"Hey, no. Let's not go there. It was a mistake. We both know that. It won't happen again."

"Sure. Yeah." Winters smiled, but the look in his eyes told her he'd been hoping for more. Hoping for something she couldn't give.

She shook herself out and sniffed. "What time is it?"

"A few minutes after ten."

"Where the hell is Spook? The lazy cow. She's probably still sulking."

Winters tilted his head to one side. "I thought she was up? I was mucking out the pigs earlier and I saw her walking across the courtyard. I assumed she was heading out on a run. But that was over two hours ago. She should be back by now."

"Yes," Acid said, as a horrible thought hit her. "She should be."

Her mind raced with the possibilities as she left Nate standing there and ran for the stairs. Spook hadn't been herself recently, but she wouldn't be so stupid. Would she?

Acid raced up to the second floor and down the corridor to Spook's quarters, banging her fist on the door. There was no answer.

Grasping the handle, she barrelled into the room. It was empty and the bed looked neatly made, but there was still no sign of Spook. The laptop Nate had given her sat open on the desk. Acid went over to it and ran her finger over the trackpad to wake up the screen. Waves of dread and rage washed over her in equal measure as she viewed the website Spook had last visited.

"Oh, Spook. You bloody fool."

"What is it?" Winters asked, appearing in the doorway.

Acid stepped aside and tilted the laptop so he could see the monitor. The browser window showed the website for a budget airline, and this particular page displayed a confirmation message. Spook had booked herself a flight to Rome. It left Cardiff Airport in under an hour. Acid slammed the laptop shut and stormed past Winters.

What was it she'd said to herself just now? *Spook wouldn't be so stupid.*

Yes, she damn well would.

CHAPTER 32

Spook sat up in her seat, her fingers gripping the armrests as the plane banked right, readying to make its final approach into Rome's Leonardo da Vinci-Fiumicino Airport. Her journey so far – from the taxi ride to Cardiff Airport, to getting through passport control, and then the flight – had been uneventful. But now the real challenge began.

Aboard the plane, she'd eaten a tuna salad sandwich, drank a soda, toyed with the idea of having a beer but decided against it, and even managed to get a little sleep. Now, alert and ready, she was eager for the plane to land so she could get to her hotel. She had Darius' location and had found a place close (yet not dangerously so) to his headquarters. Once she was settled in her room, she'd wait. Acid had the tracking app on her phone and Spook had left the details of the flight on the laptop for her to find. If Acid wasn't already at Cardiff Airport waiting for the next flight over here, she'd be surprised.

Spook knew it was a shitty thing to do, forcing Acid's

hand in this way. But she also knew Acid needed a strong shove in the right direction. Darius Duke was a twisted, malevolent psychopath who had to be stopped before his reign of terror morphed into a sovereignty of control. Spook was done waiting around, not knowing from one day to the next whether today was the day Darius sent his henchmen to finish the job. They were sitting ducks over there. This had to end, once and for all.

Her time at Nate's farm had been valuable. She'd enjoyed the training, feeling her muscles growing stronger and her skillset developing. But more than just her body hardening, so had her resolve and her heart. She'd felt the first stirrings of this new persona the day after Darius held a knife to her throat and now her transformation was in full effect. She never wanted to feel weak or scared ever again. She was ready to face Darius. Ready to kill him, if that was on the cards. She knew she'd never become like Acid – she would never crave death or chaos the way she sometimes articulated it – but a switch had definitely been flipped inside of her. She'd always been prepared to kill to defend herself. But now she was ready to be the instigator of that action. Prepared to strike first. To do what was required of her to stop evil from flourishing.

A bell chimed and the warning lights pinged on above her head, telling the passengers to fasten their seatbelts. Spook was already wearing hers, but tightened the straps a little anyway. A woman's husky voice came over the intercom, informing her they'd be landing in Rome shortly, that the local time was 3.10 p.m., and that the weather was warm but cloudy. Spook closed her eyes, allowing herself a few minutes of respite before the madness began.

But she was ready.

She was more than ready.

————

ONCE THROUGH THE AIRPORT, Spook jumped in a taxi, sensing the hustle and bustle of Rome enveloping her as she settled into the back seat and checked her pockets once again for her phone. Along with a credit card and her passport, it was all she currently owned in the world. She wished she could have brought Nate's laptop with her, but leaving it for Acid to discover had been a vital part of her plan. Once settled, she'd have to find an electronics store and buy a cheap replacement. She told the driver the name of her hotel, relieved when he didn't seem to understand much English. The distance to the hotel was about thirty kilometres. It would give her time to think, to prepare for what was to come.

Her heart was pounding in her chest, but for once it was due to anticipation rather than pure fear. Although, fear was still a part of it. She might have been stronger and more confident in her abilities, but she was still human.

She was still Spook Horowitz.

Forty-five minutes later, the taxi pulled up in front of the hotel. Spook handed the driver some of the euros she'd withdrawn at the airport and climbed out to take in the tall, slim building. Hotel Hercules; named after the Roman demi-god famed for his amazing strength and divine abilities.

She hoped that was a good omen. It felt like it was.

She entered the lobby, casting her gaze around its antique furnishings – Roman busts stood atop marble plinths, prints of old masters adorned the walls. The website where she'd made the reservation had described the hotel as 'a hidden gem for travellers wanting to escape the hustle and bustle of Rome'. Perfect for Spook's needs. Soft, warm lighting illuminated nooks and crannies, casting a golden glow on the marble floor that amplified her footsteps as she walked to the reception desk, where a middle-aged Italian woman greeted her with a warm smile.

"*Buon pomeriggio*," the woman said, her accent heavy but warm. "Welcome to Hotel Hercules. How can I help you?"

"I have a reservation under the name Hor— Erm, under the name Shorna Meadows," Spook replied, keeping her voice steady and calm. "A double room for two people."

The receptionist tapped away at her computer and nodded. "Ah, yes. Room 209." She slid a small envelope across the counter. "Here are your key cards. And breakfast is served in the dining hall just to your left from 7 a.m. to 10 a.m. each day. Is there anything else you need?"

"No, thank you," Spook said, taking the envelope and heading towards the elevator.

As she stepped inside the metal box, she felt another ripple of trepidation run through her.

Well, this was it.

No going back now.

She took a deep breath, willing her heart rate to slow down the way Acid had shown her. She couldn't afford to be uptight or nervous. The elevator transported her to the second floor and, as the doors slid open, she stepped out into a narrow corridor with a row of doors on either side. She found room 209 at the far end around a corner. She inserted one of the key cards into the lock and waited for the green light to show the door was unlocked. Once inside, she closed and locked it behind her, giving the handle a firm shake to make sure. It felt sturdy enough.

The room was small, containing two single beds, a writing desk, a narrow wardrobe and a flatscreen TV, which was attached to the wall by an unsightly metal arm. A door in the corner led to an en suite bathroom. Spook perched on the edge of the bed, her thoughts racing, a whirlwind of emotions threatening to unsettle her. Taking another deep breath she pulled her phone from her pocket, her fingers trembling slightly as she did so. It was time to check in with Acid.

She opened up the tracking app and was pleased to see Acid's phone was currently unavailable, but the last known location was Cardiff Airport. Spook smiled to herself. Her plan had worked. Acid was on her way to Rome.

Now the real challenge began.

CHAPTER 33

Acid Vanilla was furious. Seething. She was so angry she didn't know what to do with herself. It didn't help she was now stuck in a metal tube forty-thousand feet in the air, surrounded by hoards of prattling civilians. Closing her eyes, she hummed to herself, attempting to zone out the shrill woman across the aisle who'd been talking excitedly to her travel companion since leaving Cardiff about a new range of Botox injections. Acid imagined grabbing her by the throat and squeezing until the toxic poison freezing her facial muscles seeped out through her pores.

She needed a drink. A large G and T or a double Jameson, something to take the edge off. But that was a bad idea and she was holding off from ordering anything. Whatever happened next, she had to be in top form, physically and mentally.

She gnawed on her bottom lip, her fingers turning white as she gripped her hands tightly in her lap. What a bleeding arse this was. She didn't even have any music on her to drown out the incessant screeching in her head. The bats were in full flight now, her manic condition threatening to go into overload. It needed containing. She needed a release.

That bloody woman.

Winters had been adamant about accompanying her to Rome, but Acid had refused. This was between her and Spook (it was between her and Darius, too, but she didn't tell him that part) and was something she had to do alone. She had promised him, however, that she'd keep him updated and send for him if he was needed. And he had access to both her and Spook's phones via the laptop. Even with these assurances he'd persisted, forcing her to walk out in the end. He meant well, but this wasn't his fight. To appease him, she had promised to consider his offer to join his organisation while she was away. But in truth, she hadn't given it any thought. At least, not yet.

She hoped she'd get the chance.

Resting her head against the meagre padding of her seat, she released a deep, weary sigh. As she glanced at her phone, she saw the time had automatically shunted an hour forward. Another thirty minutes and the plane would begin its descent into Rome. She just hoped she wasn't too late.

She closed her eyes, attempting to relax her mind, but a fresh incursion of dark thoughts popped up instead. Spook had been in Rome for over three hours already. It was possible that Darius' people could track her down using the same software she was using, but Acid hoped Spook had anticipated this and created some kind of contingency program to block malicious attacks. If not, it was even more vital that Acid get to her and drag her back to the UK. Kicking and screaming, if needed.

Because that was Acid's plan: not to partner Spook in a desperate takedown of Kancel Kulture, but to save her from herself. This was a rescue mission, pure and simple.

The frustrating thing was, Acid had actually started to believe Spook when she claimed to have changed. But then she goes and does this. The idiot.

The stupid, bloody idiot.

Acid's eyes snapped open. She was too angry to relax. Her body shivered with righteous fury. She wasn't even sure in which direction it was aimed. At Spook? Darius? Herself?

Knowing her, it was probably all three.

The plane hit a patch of turbulence and she was jolted from her thoughts. She clenched her fists, nails digging into her palms. She needed to calm down. She needed to focus.

Spook had also left details of the hotel she'd booked on the laptop. Acid's hope was she'd be there when she arrived and they could talk. She'd be honest with her; explain how she had been wobbling regarding joining Darius but that she now realised how selfish and treacherous that would be.

And she'd tell her she was sorry.

Acid was still damn angry at the way Spook had forced her hand in this way, but she couldn't help feeling a twinge of pride. The kid's plan was sneaky as hell but it was clever. It had worked.

She sat up as the seatbelt alerts came on and an excited hush descended over the cabin. Another twenty minutes and she'd be in Rome. Another hour and she'd be with Spook.

Maybe she should tell her how impressed she was with her. It might get her onside. Acid knew she often came across as a cold, cynical cow most of the time, but she could be charming when she had to be. You didn't survive sixteen years in the deadly world of elite assassins without being able to use words and ideas as weapons just as much as knives and guns. Everyone responded well to having their ego tickled. She also knew Spook would be more amenable to her suggestions if she demonstrated a little vulnerability. She'd explain how she'd felt lost and unsure of herself since Darius came into their lives. This was, in fact, the truth, but she also knew Spook would appreciate her candour. It might go some way to mending the bridges Acid had been wilfully burning recently.

She didn't know why she did that. But she couldn't stop herself either. It was probably a self-defence mechanism. Most behaviour was, in some way. Maybe that was something else she could tell Spook. She'd explain to her how she felt troubled and scared of who she was in a civilian world she didn't understand. That might work. For Spook, feelings were currency.

Acid shuddered.

Eugh. Sharing her feelings?

Had she already become someone she despised?

Nevertheless, she was determined to do whatever it took to get Spook back to Wales safely. After that, she'd take stock. And work out once and for all what to do about Darius.

But that was for later. Right now she needed to halt Spook's ill-advised suicide mission before it went too far.

Before it was too late.

CHAPTER 34

Spook grinned as she watched the red dot on the tracking app leave the airport and travel along the Autostrada Roma-Fiumicino towards the city. It would take Acid around thirty-five minutes to reach the hotel in a taxi, allowing Spook ample time to ready herself for the confrontation. Acid would undoubtedly be mightily pissed at her, but Spook was convinced she could talk her around and make her see how vital it was they act now, whilst they had the upper hand.

In his messages to Acid, Darius had requested she come to Rome to join his vile empire. Likely, he'd be expecting a certain amount of reticence on her part, but if Acid could make him believe she'd accepted his offer, and feign allegiance, they'd have the perfect opportunity to strike him down in the heart of his organisation. He also wasn't expecting the both of them to be here. He wasn't expecting Spook to be the skilful powerhouse she now was.

To better reinforce her newfound confidence and self-image, Spook dropped to the floor and did an initial set of twenty push-ups while she waited. The task was easy for her now and once she'd finished her prescribed set of twenty she kept going, pushing herself to fatigue and collapsing onto the carpet, her pectorals and triceps burning with satisfaction.

Rising, she walked to the window. The limited view looked out on the back of a row of shops, but if she leaned out as far as the window allowed, she could see a grand square with bustling pavement cafés and an ancient monument standing proudly in the centre. Rome – a city steeped in history and passion. And now danger. More danger than those unsuspecting citizens currently passing time in the square would ever know.

Spook closed her eyes and told herself not to worry. She told herself that everything was going to work out just the way she wanted it to. The last few weeks had been a whirlwind of training and stress. But it had been worth it. She was ready for this. Ready to take down Darius and his despicable band of assassins. Ready to prove to Acid (and herself) that she was more than just a tech nerd.

She was a fighter.

A force to be reckoned with.

She opened her eyes and took one last look out the window before turning back into the room. Her phone was on the bed with the tracking app still open. Lifting it, she was dismayed to see Acid hadn't progressed very far. She was now on Via Cristoforo-Colombo, but still more than twenty minutes away. She wondered about calling her, texting her at least, but decided against it. Whatever they said to each other next was better done face to face. Spook knew her plan was risky, but it was the only way they were going to find peace. As long as Darius was alive he would be a threat; to not only their lives, but their relationship, too. Acid Vanilla infuriated Spook more often than was comfortable sometimes, but she still cared about her a great deal. She saw the good in Acid when she didn't even see it herself. She was her friend.

But she couldn't wait around in this poky hotel room any longer. The cramped hotel room was suffocating her. She paced the room, her thoughts wheeling off into weird, unsettling places. She sat on the bed to try to settle her nerves, but her heart pounded with anticipation.

No.

It wasn't happening.

She had to do something constructive.

Gathering up her phone, wallet and key card, she checked herself in the mirror on the back of the bathroom door, before heading out of the room. She recalled spotting a second-hand computer shop on one of the corners the taxi drove past earlier. If she retraced her journey, she reckoned she'd find it easily enough. She'd have enough time to walk there, purchase a reconditioned laptop, and get back to the hotel before Acid arrived. The hotel had Wi-Fi access and it would take time to set up a VPN and the Tor browser on a new machine, along with downloading the Epsilon software she'd need for writing code. But if she could demonstrate to Acid how easy it was for her to immobilise Kancel Kulture's security system, it would strengthen her argument about the two of them becoming the aggressors.

As she walked down the narrow corridor, the elevator pinged, announcing its arrival on her floor. On turning the corner, she saw a man stepping out. He was tall and slim, with weathered, tanned skin and wavy grey hair swept back from his face. He was wearing dark glasses, which he removed upon noticing her. He stopped. So did she. There were five metres between them and, despite the man's slender frame, no way of getting past him without a tussle.

"H-Hey," Spook said, trying to keep her voice breezy. "*Come stai?*" she tried, unsure if she'd mastered the pronunciation.

The man didn't answer; he just stared at her with a strange expression on his face. Spook felt a chill run down her spine. She took a step back, glancing left and right and up the corridor, searching for a different exit. There wasn't one. Her hand went to her back pocket where she'd placed the key card for her room.

"Ah, shoot," she said, pulling it out and holding it up. "I forgot something in my room. Erm... *scusa.*" She took another step back, not taking her eyes off the man.

He carried on staring at her and then his mouth opened in a wide smile.

Whoa.

His teeth looked to be made of gold. They were both incredible and creepy as hell at the same time.

"I don't speak Italian," he said, in a deep South African drawl. "But your accent is good. Spook."

On hearing her name, she froze. The chill running down her back turned to ice. The man remained still. Formidable in his calm dispassion.

"What do you want?" she asked.

His smile dropped. His eyes flashed hungrily. "I think you know."

Spook swallowed. It felt as if her heart was about to burst out through her skin. She took a step back, and another. Then, with a cry, she turned and ran down the corridor back the way she'd come. She had the key card clutched in her hand. If she could reach her room and get the door open before he grabbed her, she might stand a chance. Once in her room she could escape out of the window, maybe even call the police for help. She took the corner, pushing off from the wall to propel herself along. She could hear the man behind her. His footsteps were broad and steady but he wasn't rushing. When she reached her room, she slammed against the door and fumbled the key card into the slot.

"Come on, come on." The LED lights flashed red. "No. Shit. Fuck!" She tried again. The man's footsteps were getting closer. She could hear him panting.

Suddenly the door clicked open and Spook pushed herself into the room. Once inside, she grabbed the edge of the door ready to slam it shut but the man burst through, knocking her away.

It was he who closed the door, regarding her with eyes full of murder as she stumbled back and sat abruptly on the bed.

"Fuck you," she yelled, pushing off the mattress and launching herself at him. All the training she'd been through these last few weeks had prepared her for this moment. She swung her fist and smashed it into the man's chest.

He didn't move.

He didn't even flinch.

Shit. No.

That wasn't how this was supposed to go. She stared up at him, her mouth hanging open, before a rough hand grabbed her around the throat. Her hands instinctively rose to meet it, scrabbling at his fingers as he walked her backwards and slammed her against the wall. She banged her head, her vision glitching as she tried to make sense of what was going on. The man released his grip and she staggered forward only for him to grab her again and smash her head once more into the punishing plasterboard. This time her vision blurred completely as she fought to stay conscious and upright. She cried out, pushing against the man's taut, wiry torso. But it was useless. She could sense herself slipping away.

A sharp pain shot up into her brain, reviving her the way ammonia does to a fainting victim. As the pain blossomed into her sinuses she staggered forward, feeling blood gushing down her face. The room spun. She felt the man's presence behind her. Then everything went dark, as something scratchy and smelling like dirt was placed over her head.

"Don't struggle," the man growled in her ear. "It's better for you if you don't." But that was fine by Spook. She had no struggle left in her. The last thing to go through her mind as the lights went out was how pathetic she was – and how Acid had been correct all along.

She wasn't cut out for this world.

She wasn't ready.

CHAPTER 35

Acid folded her arms, her foot tapping a staccato beat on the marble floor as she waited for the receptionist to finish dealing with a loud American couple who were asking for assistance with where they should eat.

The Hotel Hercules. Except for the unimaginative name, Spook had picked a relatively decent hideout. The reception area featured a mirrored wall down one side, and Acid checked herself out as she waited. She'd stopped off at a boutique around the corner and bought herself a new outfit – black jeans and a black shirt – and was feeling a little more herself. Although, in the mirror, her face looked drawn and her skin pale. She looked away, focusing instead on the back of the husband's head as he continued whining at the receptionist, imagining herself shooting a hollow point bullet into the base of his skull. Like any seasoned assassin, she'd already scoped out all the entry and exit points the second she'd entered the building. A single elevator stood on the wall opposite the entrance, while three other doors dotted the area. One led to a dining area, one had a sign on it saying *Privato*, and there was one more with no sign.

"Just pissing well get out there and find somewhere yourself," she muttered under her breath. "You're in Rome, for Christ's sake. Live a little."

The husband was now grimacing and swaying his head back and forth, telling the ever-patient receptionist he 'wasn't a big fan of pasta or pizza'.

"Bloody hell," Acid said over a sigh, her voice louder this time. She pulled out her phone, the tracking app still open since she last looked. The blue dot representing her and the red dot, Spook, blinked in unison, their locations practically overlapping. Spook was here. Acid checked the time: 6.26 p.m. There was a flight back to Cardiff at 9.30 p.m. they could make. Well, at least Spook could make it. Acid had yet to make the all-important decision whether to join her.

"*Buon pomeriggio*," the receptionist sang out, leaning around the side of the American couple as they shuffled away from the front desk. "Can I help?"

Acid put on her friendliest smile as she approached. "*Ciao. Buon pomeriggio*. And I hope you can help." She leaned on the counter, knowing she only had one shot at this. "I believe my... companion has already checked in. We're sharing a room, but I can't get in touch with her." She lifted her phone and bared her teeth. "I've tried calling her a few times, but I think her phone is on silent in her bag, or she's in the bath. If you could let me know the room number, that would be most helpful."

The receptionist didn't falter. "What is the name, please?"

"Shorna Meadows," Acid replied, giving the alias Spook had been using since they acquired new passports last year. "I believe she checked in around two hours ago," she added, as the receptionist scanned whatever was written on her computer screen.

"Yes, I can see. And you are?"

"Mary Ann Hawthorne," she replied. It was an awful name, but the forger they'd found hadn't offered choices. You got what you got.

"Ah yes." Acid relaxed her shoulders as the receptionist looked up from the screen and smiled. "She is here. Room number 209. I have already provided her with two key cards, and I have not seen her leave so I expect she is in the room. In the bathroom, perhaps, as you say."

"Yes. Great." She rubbed at her chin. "I don't suppose you can provide me with an extra key card, could you? Please? I expect that's not something you normally do, but if she is in the bath, or asleep, I don't want to disturb her."

"Oh, I am not really supposed to—"

"Yes. I know. I understand. It's just... my companion Shorna and I, we're here in Rome to scatter her father's ashes. He was Italian, you see. From Rome. Shorna has had a hard time of it lately, and if she's resting I'd prefer to let her sleep."

"Oh, I am sorry to hear this," the woman replied. "I lost my father last year also."

"Oh no! *Mi dispiaci davvero sentirlo.*" Acid tilted her head to one side. "I, too, have Italian parents. I think sometimes that's why Shorna and I get on so well. *Ma chi lo sa?*"

The woman clicked her teeth, and for a moment it looked as if she was still a no-go. But then her expression softened. "Fine. Is all fine." She rummaged around below the counter and produced a key card. "But I will need all three cards back at the end of your stay. Okay?" She handed it over.

"Of course. Thank you," Acid said, accepting the card before waving her hand around the compact foyer. "And this is the only way in and out of the hotel? And that elevator over there is the only access to the rooms?"

The woman shrugged. "Unless you take the stairs, accessed through this door beside me here. But your friend has not left. I would have noticed."

"Yes. But that's it?" Acid asked. She could sense her questions were rousing the receptionist's suspicions, but it was worth the risk so she was prepared for any eventuality. "What about staff access?"

The receptionist turned her mouth down. "*Si,* there is a stairwell on the other side of the hotel, but it is not for guests."

"Of course. Thank you. *Grazie.*" Acid bowed her head and then headed for the stairs. She preferred a little exercise over taking the elevator and it took her less than ten seconds to race up the two flights to the second floor.

As she pushed through the door to the level two landing, she was presented with a long, windowless T-shaped corridor with doors on either side, the elevator at the far end and another corridor in the middle leading to more rooms. She made her way along, checking the door numbers as she went. There was a small sign on the corner as she got to the centre that indicated rooms 205 to 209 were down this next corridor.

She located their room at the far end, and paused outside to gather her thoughts and remind herself not to be too harsh on Spook. Then she knocked.

There was no answer.

"Spook," she called through the door. "It's me. Acid. Are you in there?" She slid the key card into its slot then pulled it out, grabbing the handle as the LED turned from red to green.

The room beyond was dark as she opened the door and stepped inside. The only light came from a small window opposite, which had a curtain pulled across it. She eased the door shut behind her, wondering if perhaps Spook really was asleep, but as her eyes adjusted to the gloom, she saw two empty beds. Spook's phone was sitting atop an old chest of drawers. She switched on the light.

"Spook? Are you here?"

A door in the corner was open, revealing the sterile white tiles of a bathroom. But Acid could sense there was no one else in the room.

She ventured further, eyes scanning the space for traces of her friend. A knot tightened in her stomach as she looked down.

"Shit. No. Spook!"

There was a small red stain on the cream-coloured carpet over by the wall. Her stomach twisted as she knelt to examine it, tracing the outline of the stain with her finger. It was blood. Fresh blood.

She rose, her body tense, surveying the room with more intensity now. Nothing seemed out of place. A faint waft of body odour lingered in the air, but that could be her own. She walked over to the window and parted the curtains. There was nothing to see except a wide alley and the rear of a row of shops.

"Shitting, pissing hell," she whispered to herself.

What did she do now? Spook's phone, complete with the tracking app – the only way of locating her – was in the room. She stared at it, her mind racing. Walking into the bathroom, she checked to see if there were any signs of a struggle, but the tiles were dry and there were no marks on the walls or the door. If someone had snatched Spook, she hadn't put up much of a fight.

Acid tensed. The air in the bathroom was warm and cloying, almost stale. She stepped back out into the bedroom, memories of the big fucker who'd attacked her in London creeping into her thoughts. He could have easily crushed Spook's skull with one hand.

"No, no, no," she mumbled, running her fingers through her hair. She needed to focus. Calm down. Think.

How the hell was this happening, again?

That stupid bloody woman.

She clenched her fists, fighting the urge to smash one of them into the wall. But she couldn't blame Spook entirely for this mess. She should have seen it coming. Spook had been frustrated and angry, but rather than communicate with her properly, Acid had been her usual aloof and inconsiderate self. If she'd opened up more, maybe even asked Spook's advice on what she should do about Darius, then Spook might not have taken matters into her own hands.

But it was no use wondering what if. She had to get out of this cramped room and find Spook. She picked up Spook's phone, hoping the CCTV footage Spook had downloaded of Darius' building was on there. She recalled it being near a grand piazza, but it was difficult to think straight amongst the incessant chatter of the bats. Her mind raced with a hundred possible scenarios, none of them good.

Suddenly her phone vibrated in her pocket.

She pulled it out. The caller ID showed an unknown number. Unknown to the phone, perhaps. But Acid knew who was calling even before she pressed answer and held the phone to her ear. The laugh confirmed her suspicions, flooding her with a torrent of conflicting emotions she was too overwhelmed to deal with.

"Hello, Sis," the voice sneered. "Long time no speak."

CHAPTER 36

Darius' grin widened as he awaited Acid's response. "You've got Spook," she said. It wasn't a question.

"Indeed I do. One of my top men is with her," he replied. "They're en route to me as we speak. What happens next depends entirely on you."

Acid's breathing intensified. "I expected as much. Where are you?"

Darius chuckled, still savouring the moment. "Now, now. Let's not hurry this. It's been so long since we last spoke. I've missed hearing your voice. But I'm relieved to detect that delicious hint of sarcasm is ever present – that sense that you'd rather be doing anything else than having this conversation. You know, you should be nicer to people. It'd get you further in life."

"I've come far enough."

"Is that so?"

"What do you want from me, Darius?"

He leaned back in his chair. "You know what I want, Alice." He was sitting behind his new desk in his new office, feeling every inch the powerful leader he now was. The one in control. The one with his hands around fate's throat.

Locating Spook Horowitz hadn't been straightforward, but Darius was fast learning that in this modern world anything was possible. They'd obtained her login details by reverse-engineering her hack on the city's CCTV network, which Saga and Frederik had traced back to her phone, allowing them to extract her flight details and hotel reservation information.

Darius sighed heavily. Why was she taking so long to respond? "Have you made your decision?"

"Is there a decision to make?"

Darius leaned forward in his seat. "You're well aware there is, Alice. Join me, or both you and Spook will die." He left the words hanging, anticipating a reaction. When none came, he rubbed at his goatee. "I have something else I need to tell you. I was going to wait until we were face to face, but seeing as you're still finding your choices difficult, maybe it's best that I tell you now. The DNA analysis results are in."

That got her. He heard a sharp intake of breath. He didn't hear an out breath. "Go on..."

"Our blood has been analysed by three separate independent experts. Each time the results were the same. You're my big sister! Yay! Oscar Duke's illegitimate daughter." He paused, allowing the words to sink in. He knew this would be hard for her to take. But it had been hard for him, too. At first, at least. Now he loved the idea. "I hope you can appreciate that, more than ever, I want to keep this in the family. Join me, Alice. Stand shoulder to shoulder with me. Help me lead Kancel Kulture to the pinnacle of greatness. We could have such fun, you and I."

Acid snorted, but there was no humour in it. "If I join you, you'll let Spook go?"

"Yes, about that," Darius continued. "I was actually hoping she might join us as well. The more I know about her, the more I see what she can do, the more valuable she appears. Don't you agree? Saga and Frederik have done well, but we need a dedicated tech expert. Spook would be ideal."

"She'd never join you. Not a chance."

"Maybe. Maybe not. But, regardless, without your involvement there's no deal." He rose from his seat and walked over to the window. "The ball is in your court, dear sister. The question is, are you going to return it with a flourish or fumble it into the outfield?" A knock on the office door interrupted him. Placing his hand over the microphone on his phone, he called out, "Enter!"

"What's going on?" Acid's voice echoed out from the phone as he lowered it from his face. The door swung open and Spook Horowitz stumbled into the room. Freek Kriel followed closely behind, a pistol casually held at his waist.

"Here she is, boss," Freek announced.

"What's going on, Darius?" Acid's voice rasped.

"Your little friend has arrived," he replied, raising the phone. He walked over to Spook, who whimpered and groaned as he grabbed her chin to examine her. She had a cut on her forehead, and the side of her face was red, but she was relatively unharmed. "Don't worry, she's all in one piece. For now. Although, I am wondering if she's quite as resourceful and technologically adept as I first thought. You see, we spoon-fed her our location in the hope she'd bring you here. And blow me if it didn't work like a dream."

"Fuck you," Spook spat.

"Let me talk to her," Acid said.

Darius walked away. "Not yet. But you can do..."

"If I agree to join you."

He stopped, watching Spook as she glanced around the room. Her eyebrows knitted together in a deep scowl as she took in the Bowie artwork. "Come and see me, Alice. We need to talk."

"And you won't hurt her?"

He narrowed his eyes. "That depends." He raised his chin to Freek. "Take our new friend to the Persuasion Station and see to it she's... comfortable. She can stay there for now."

Freek nodded and grabbed Spook's arm, dragging her back the way they'd come. Darius could hear her cries echoing down the corridor as she was led away. And well she might cry. The Persuasion Station was the name he'd bestowed on those rooms in the basement with locks on their doors and restraints attached to their walls. The idea was that these rooms would eventually be occupied by individuals who could help him in some way, but who might be initially unforthcoming with their aid. Modern-day torture rooms, by any other name. But as Darius told his new team, one had to put a positive spin on things in this new 'woke' era.

"I trust I don't need to be gauche and spell out for you what will happen to Spook if you fail to pay me a visit," he told Acid, refocusing on the call. "Needless to say, if I don't see you before the night is out, you won't lay eyes on her again. Not in one piece, at least. There might be body parts left over, but I can't guarantee anything."

The line was silent, save for the sound of breathing. "Fine."

"Good girl. You know it makes sense," he said, a twisted

smile playing on his lips. "I'll send you the full address. Come alone. Unarmed. You have one hour."

He hung up before she could respond, feeling a rush of power course through his veins as he did. He didn't need to hear her barbed retorts. She'd come. He knew she would. After all, she was his sister.

He was her destiny.

CHAPTER 37

Spook sat upright as the sound of footsteps echoed through her prison cell like a volley of gunfire. Her breath quickened when she heard the click of keys and the grinding of metal against stone. The door opened and Darius Duke stepped into the room, his menacing figure draped in a sleek black shirt and leather trousers. His shiny black boots clacked off the stone floor, their inch heels and pointed toes menacing in themselves. He glanced her up and down and tutted, his eyes flashing with malice and what might have been lust. She hoped not.

"What's the matter, Ms Horowitz, not enjoying your stay?" he asked, his voice dripping with sarcasm.

Spook clenched her jaw and glared at him. "You're a sick bastard."

Darius chuckled and knelt beside her, running his fingers down the side of her face. She flinched and tried to pull away, but he grabbed her chin and forced her to look him in the eyes.

"You know, there is a way out of here," he whispered, his breath hot against her cheek.

"What's that?" she asked, terrified of the answer.

"I want you to work for me."

"What?" She pulled away, and this time he let her. "I'd never work for you."

"No? Well, that is a damn shame," he said, rising to his full height. "You see, except for my charming sister who is currently en route, you could very well be the last piece of the puzzle, as it were. The last link in the chain. The last cog in the machine." He waved his hand in the air. "You get the idea."

Spook tried to swallow the lump in her throat but her mouth was dry. So it was true. Darius was indeed Acid's brother. At least, that was what he was insinuating. Until this moment, she hadn't discerned any resemblance between the two of them. Yet, now that they were face to face, she couldn't deny there was something there. They had the same jawline, the same way of staring at you as if they were trying to unpick your sanity.

"You're good. I see that," Darius went on. "And I need a tech person, someone who can work behind the scenes, communicating with operatives in the field and sending them information in real-time. You'll be paid handsomely, of course, and you can live here at Casa di Cicero for free. It's a great offer, Spook. I mean, don't you love what I've done with the place?"

"I'm not too keen on my current accommodation."

"Oh this is just a room for naughty people," Darius told her. "The residential suites allocated to our operatives are nothing short of magnificent. Truly. You'd pay over seven grand a month for the same in central London. But I appreciate you haven't been treated very hospitably up to now and I apologise. You only have to say the word and life will get a lot better for you. Just like that." He snapped his fingers, the sound reverberating throughout the stone chamber.

"No way," Spook told him. "I'll never join you. You're a murderer."

"I'm a businessman."

"You murdered The Dullahan. You were going to murder me."

Darius pouted, acting as if her words were a mere annoyance to him. He sighed. "Yes. I know. But things have changed since then. I've had a rethink." He held his arms out, his voice rising in volume. "People are allowed to change their minds, you know, Spook. It demonstrates real growth and objectivity. And we won't be committing heinous murders. Not anymore. We've already secured contracts with two government agencies and are in discussions with eight more. We're a legitimate organisation, complete with rules and protocols and systems in place, designed to establish ourselves as the world's leading eradication solution network." He flashed a self-satisfied grin, evidently pleased with this nebulous bit of phrasing.

"You still kill people. For money."

"So does your friend Acid. So did the old Irishman you're so upset about. And the man you were staying with in Wales, from what my sources tell me." He moved in front of her, kneeling once more so he could look her in the eyes. "Tell me, Spook. What's the difference?"

She forced herself to maintain eye contact. He made a

valid point and she didn't have an answer for him. It was just a feeling she had, that was all. Perhaps she'd been around death too long and this was a manifestation of Stockholm Syndrome. Yet Acid and Nate – Nate, in particular – exuded a sense of justice and righteousness in the way they approached their work. Darius, on the other hand, struck her as a narcissist and a sociopath. And yes, she'd called Acid both those things in the past, but there was something about Darius that suggested he was beyond redemption. It was evident in the cruel twist of his grin, there in his eyes when he addressed her. He was evil. Pure and simple. She could never bring herself to work for someone like him.

"Come along now, Ms Horowitz," he told her, in a calm soft voice. "I'm waiting. What's the difference between what I'm offering you and what that drip over in Wales is setting up?"

"He didn't hold a knife to my throat and threaten to kill me."

"For heaven's sake!" He rolled his eyes at her, looking even more like Acid as he did. "Will you give that a rest, Spook!? Shit happens. Okay? People make mistakes. It won't happen again." He smirked. "Well, if you agree to join us it won't. If not, I'll be honest with you – it might."

Spook looked away. She wouldn't give him the satisfaction of seeing the fear in her eyes. "I won't work for you."

Darius stood, his leather trousers creaking as he did. "Very well. Just remember you had a chance to be on the winning team, Spook. If you won't join us, then you'll die. Maybe you'll both die today."

She looked up at him. "What do you mean?"

Darius walked over and banged his fist against the metal door. "Freek. Bring her in."

The door opened to reveal a figure framed in the doorway. A figure wearing black jeans and a black shirt. A thick hessian sack over the face.

"Acid?" she gasped.

"Hey, kid," she said, blinking in the light as the man who'd brought Spook here from the hotel yanked the sack off her head. "Fancy seeing you here."

CHAPTER 38

Acid had taken Darius' ultimatum seriously. One hour. But that hadn't prevented her from slumping down on the edge of the bed after he'd hung up, to contemplate her next move. The fact he'd ended the call so abruptly had pissed her off, but this anger was fast overshadowed by a bustling invasion of disturbing emotions which sent her spiralling into even darker places. The intrusive, ominous thoughts that had haunted the periphery of her consciousness for the past few weeks could no longer be ignored. She had to face them head-on. It was time.

And now she knew the truth.

Her gaze fixed on the phone in her hand, and the photo that had pinged through a second after the call ended. The proof in black and white.

Darius Duke was her brother. Her blood. Oscar Duke was her father.

It felt like a switch had flipped inside her. Everything she thought she knew about herself had changed forever.

Had she ever had a chance at a normal life?

Even as a young girl she'd felt as if she belonged to the darkness. Now she knew why. She was a Duke. The spawn of that odious prick who would have beaten her mother to death if she hadn't stopped him.

The thought made her sick to her stomach.

Darius wasn't his father but he was just as bad. He'd killed The Dullahan. He was going to kill Spook. Could she really work alongside him? And if not, could she kill her brother? She'd killed many people who she'd once cared about, starting with Jacqueline and ending with Caesar. But after him she'd vowed never to make it personal again. It had taken too much of her. Far too much. She was still piecing herself back together.

But if she didn't kill Darius, they'd always be looking over their shoulders. She couldn't deal with that either. It wasn't fair on her or Spook.

Sitting on the hotel bed with her head in her hands, she'd longed for Caesar's presence, or The Dullahan's – someone older and wiser who could smack her into life and point her in the right direction. More than that, though, she'd just needed a friend. A confidante. Someone who understood her and what she was going through.

After twenty minutes had gone by, she'd got to her feet, feeling the weight of the world on her shoulders. She had to do something. She couldn't just sit around and let Darius win. She had to find a way to save Spook and take him down. Brother or not. Sticking out her chest, she'd attempted to channel the inner rage threatening to consume her into a more useful emotion. Maybe that was the way to defeat Darius – she'd use her self-hate and death wish tendencies to save Spook and take out Kancel Kulture. After that, who cared what happened to her? She'd known this was a suicide mission before she'd got on the plane.

Death or glory.

She'd be doing the world a favour.

With that in mind, she'd left the room and headed down to the lobby. She'd been almost out the door when a hand grabbed her arm and a deep voice said, "Stay calm, do as I say, and everything will be fine."

After that, she'd been led down a side street by the lanky South African with terrible dress sense and then bundled into the back of a waiting car with a sack over her head.

Now she was here, standing in a small windowless room with Spook on the floor in front of her and Darius to her right, beaming like the fucking Cheshire Cat.

"So what now?" she asked, looking around to see the South African standing behind her.

"Now we have some fun," Darius replied, rubbing his hands together. "Come with me, both of you. I'm going to give you the full tour. I think you're going to love it!"

He exited the room with a flourish, his silk shirt wafting as he turned the corner and disappeared. Acid held her hand out to Spook and helped her to her feet.

"How are you holding up?" she asked her.

"I've been better."

"Did they hurt you?"

Spook shook her head as the South African beckoned them out of the room with an angry wave of his hand. "Out! Now!"

They complied, discovering Darius waiting for them in the corridor. "This way, ladies," he said, practically skipping down to the end of the corridor, then into a more spacious, well-lit area. The room was square, roughly the size of a basketball court, and featured a large circular sofa surrounding a central pillar, with small round tables dotted intermittently around its perimeter. The floor was made of black polished concrete and was mostly bare except for a striking blood-red rug stretching along the length of one wall. Glancing around, Acid counted six doors leading off from the room. Each was made of brushed steel. No doubt reinforced. Sunlight streamed in from an expansive skylight that occupied most of the ceiling, extending upward for several stories to reveal a pristine blue sky, unmarred by even a hint of cloud cover.

Darius clapped his hands together again, grinning excitedly at Acid and Spook. "Welcome to the living quarters. Here, let me show you one of the rooms." He ushered them towards the nearest door, swinging it open with a grand gesture. "Not bad, hey?"

Stepping past them, he walked backwards with arms outstretched, directing their attention to the luxurious sitting area. Plush chairs and sofas were arranged in a semi-circle around a fireplace, with a large flatscreen TV mounted on one wall and expensive-looking artwork adorning the others.

"There's a kitchen over there," he said, motioning to the other side of the room. "And the bedroom is through that door. Everything you can possibly imagine, every appliance, every gadget, every device is here. Whatever your favourite food or drink, whatever your predilection in any field, it's yours. If you make the right choice today and join us, you'll want for nothing."

"Yeah, not going to happen," Spook muttered under her breath, staring at Acid as she did.

Acid knew Spook wanted her to return the sentiment, to renounce Darius and all he stood for. She remained silent.

"Follow me," Darius said. "There's so much more for you to see."

He led them down another long corridor, eventually arriving at a small atrium with two metallic elevators on one wall. They stood in silence as Darius scanned his eyeball into a biometric reader and pressed a button to summon one of the elevators. The one on the left arrived first and he stepped aside so Acid and Spook could enter first.

"No. It's fine. You're welcome," he said pointedly, as the door closed.

"Where are we going?" Acid asked him.

Darius hunched his shoulders, pantomiming excitement. "Up to the main training arena. It's quite a sight to behold. We've taken over the entire second floor and I think you'll find it rather exhilarating. I know I certainly do."

As he spoke he nodded vigorously, staring at Acid the whole time. He reminded her of an eager puppy, but there was no denying the extent of what he'd created here. It was impressive. Very impressive.

The elevator delivered them to the second floor, where the doors opened to reveal an expansive room with soaring ceilings and a gleaming wooden floor. The far wall showcased an array of flags from various nations, each displayed to perfection. On the adjacent wall hung a large banner emblazoned with two stylised red K's against a black background –Kancel Kulture. The design evoked imagery of far-right insignias used elsewhere in Europe.

Opposite, another wall was cloaked in long, red velvet curtains embellished with intricate symbols that shimmered in the soft light cast by opulent chandeliers. The room exuded luxury while retaining functionality, modernity, and state-of-the-art equipment. In the centre stood a raised padded platform, piled high with mats and martial arts equipment. Towards the side of the room, an assortment of boxing bags dangled from the ceiling at varying heights. The scent of oil and perspiration filled the air.

"Impressive," Acid said.

"Isn't it?" Darius beamed. "Come. Have a closer look."

They exited the lift. Darius striding across the floor, Acid walking after him, and Spook dragging her heels in the rear.

"Obviously it's still a work in progress," Darius told them, side-walking as he beckoned them further into the room. "But you get the idea. This will be the primary area where our operatives will refine their skills and elevate themselves from great to the very best. My dream is to assemble a team of elite killers unrivalled in the field and feared across the globe. I want to create a world where a mark only has to find out a Kancel Kulture operative is on their tail for them to die of a heart attack right there on the spot. After they've shit their pants, of course." He let out a deep chuckle.

"Yeah, sure, it's all incredibly impressive," Spook cut in. "But why are you showing us this? We've made it clear. We aren't going to join you. You're a psychopath. You killed our friend." She moved over and stood beside Acid. "So why don't you just get it over with?"

Darius' laughter ceased. "You don't get it, do you? You think I'm some kind of mad man, some kind of evil villain. But you're wrong." He swept his arm, encompassing the entire room. "This isn't merely about killing people. It's about creating a force that will bring righteous justice to a world that has gone to hell. I'm not the evil one. I want to rid the world of evil."

He took a deep breath, gathering himself before continuing. "I'm looking for warriors. Men and women who can stand shoulder to shoulder with me in the fight against tyranny. I don't want to kill you, Spook. Not anymore. I want you by my side. Both of you. Together we could make history. I know we got off on the wrong foot and I am sorry about your friend, but I needed to show you I was serious. That I possess the edge required to make it in this world." He paused again, his gaze flitting between Acid and Spook and back to Acid. He smiled. "Now, what do you say?"

Acid stared at the floor. "What do you expect us to say, Darius?"

"I expect you to say yes! I expect you to welcome my offer with open arms."

"And if we don't?" Spook asked.

"If you don't accept my offer, I'm afraid I'll have no choice in the matter." Darius' tone was now cold, serious. "There will be no negotiation. No second chances. I need an answer right now. Acid, Spook – it's a simple decision. Join me or die."

CHAPTER 39

Although Spook had anticipated this moment, and everything up to now had been leading to this point, she couldn't help but shudder at Darius' ultimatum.

"...Join me or die."

She inhaled deeply and puffed out her chest, anything she could think of to claw back some confidence and resolve.

"Never," she hissed, but her voice was shaky. She shuffled closer to Acid, their arms touching. "You're crazy, Darius. More than I even realised."

He chuckled to himself. "I see." His eyes were fixed on Acid, sizing up her reaction. "Does she speak for the both of you?"

Spook turned to her. "Go on, Acid. Tell him. Tell him how you could never work with a delusional, power-hungry monster like him. Tell him you don't forgive him for what he did to The Dullahan and never will. Tell him he'd better kill us, because if he doesn't you'll crucify him. Come on, Acid. Say something. Please!"

"I hope you realise this is your last chance," Darius said. "What I'm offering you here is a once-in-a-lifetime opportunity. To be part of something greater than yourselves. Something that could change the world."

Spook glared at Acid, willing her to speak up. To say the right thing. Or, better still, for her to spring into action and take this prick down while his men weren't around. Perhaps she should do it herself. Darius was tall and sinewy, but she didn't think he was as tough as he made out. It wasn't just his ostentatious mannerisms. There was an air of nerviness about him, something disingenuous. With all the training she'd endured over the past few weeks, Spook reckoned she could overpower him, maybe even knock him out. But what then? Could she make it out of the Kancel Kulture headquarters alive? Would Acid follow her? Her hands clenched into fists, but the rest of her body remained immobile. She was paralysed. The fear, indecision and all-consuming rage coursing through her system had become too much to deal with.

If you hesitate in the field, you die.

Acid's words resonated in her head. Spook looked at her. So why was she hesitating? Why the hell hadn't she spoken?

"Go on, Acid," she whispered. "Tell this prick to go to hell. Damn well say something at least."

Acid turned to meet Spook's gaze. Her eyes were intense but cold, her jaw rigid. It felt like she was looking through her. In that moment, Spook didn't recognise her at all. She looked scary as hell.

"No, Acid, please," she said. "You can't actually be considering his offer."

She still didn't speak. Spook held her arms out to her, but she turned away.

"I have to," she said, her voice barely audible. She raised her head to address Darius. "I get it now."

"You get what?" Spook yelled, frustration and disbelief boiling over. "For God's sake, Acid! This can't be happening! I knew you were troubled – more than usual – but you can't mean this." Spook moved around so she was standing in front of her and grabbed the tops of her arms. She wanted to shake her, to force her to see reason. But Acid wouldn't even meet her gaze.

"I'm sorry, kid. This is the way it has to be." Her face was hard, her eyes dead.

Over Spook's shoulder, Darius was rubbing his hands together. "Excellent. I knew you'd see sense. What a day. My big sister and I united at last. This is going to be one hell of a ride. You mark my words. You and I are going to rule the world. Literally."

"Acid," Spook said, squeezing her arms. "Look at me. Please. Talk to me. Think about what you're doing."

But she wouldn't meet her eye. "I have thought about it, Spook. It's all I've thought about. I understand where you're coming from and why you can't join, but it's different for me. Very different." She rubbed at her forehead. "I've just got too much going on. The bats are incessant and I can't see any other way."

"No. Please!"

She shook Spook off. "I'm an assassin, Spook. A killer. That's what I am. That's all I've ever been." Darius' chuckles grew louder as Acid's voice dropped. "I tried it your way, Spook. But I can't do it. I know you wanted me to do something worthy with my skills, but I'm not cut out for it. Civilian life confuses and irritates me in equal measure. I know this isn't how either of us thought this would end, but this way I have a chance to spend my life doing what I'm good at. Doing the only thing I am good at."

A wave of sorrow rose within Spook. She shook her head, tensing the muscles in her neck and face. She didn't want to cry. Not now. "What about me?" she asked. "What about The Dullahan?"

Acid glanced over her shoulder. "Darius shouldn't have killed him. I wish he hadn't. But I understand why he did it. And what can I say? I've done worse. I can't blame Darius, not really. And The Dullahan knew what this life entailed. He'd made his peace with it."

"Are you fucking serious?" Spook gasped. "Why are you talking like this?"

"All right, enough!" Darius called out. "I think we all need to move on from this."

Spook spun around to see he had a phone pressed to his ear. He rolled his eyes to the ceiling as he waited for whoever it was to answer and then grinned when a muffled voice could be heard on the other end.

"Saga. It's me. Bring the team up to the second floor. Yes... Yes... It's time. Bring them up." He slid the phone into his back pocket, the smile not leaving his face as he regarded the two women. "This should be fun."

Spook turned back to Acid, staring deep into her eyes, searching for any sign that this was a clever move on her part. She was Acid Vanilla. She had to have a plan.

Please let her have a plan!?

"Acid?"

A noise from the far side of the room seized Spook's attention. She turned in time to see a group of people emerging through a set of double doors. They walked over to where she and Acid were standing and arranged themselves in a semi-circle around them. She counted five men and one woman, and was shocked to see the man who'd attacked her at the hotel had an exact double. Twins. The two men leered at her in unison, flashing their shiny metal teeth. Alongside them was a small Asian man dressed in black, an incredibly pale man with white hair and eyebrows, and the biggest, meanest-looking brute she'd ever seen. Despite the woman having her hair scraped back in a long braid, Spook recognised The Gorgon from the CCTV footage. The one who had lured her to this awful place.

"Acid, meet Kancel Kulture," Darius exclaimed, with a wave of his hand. "Your new colleagues. And I've got to say, they're all very excited to be working alongside a legend such as yourself."

The big man dipped his head and gave Acid a curt salute. "Good seeing you again."

"Hmm. You were lucky," she replied.

"I don't doubt it."

Spook's head was spinning in time with her guts. Everything felt impossibly surreal. "You can't be serious?" she whispered to Acid. "We have to do something. We have to get out of here."

"Stop this nonsense!" Darius boomed. "Acid has made her decision."

"Go to hell!" Spook cried out. "She's confused. That's all. Troubled. You're messing with her head. You've been messing with it for weeks. We came here to kill you, not to join you."

Darius let out a loud, menacing laugh. "Kill me? You – kill me? I don't think so, sweetheart. But go ahead, try it. Even if by some miracle of luck you manage it, do you really think you'd leave this room alive? Behold Stig Saga, The Gorgon, Grimaldi, Nokizaru, and the Blood Diamond Twins. Six of the deadliest killers in the world, all loyal to me. There is no escape, Spook Horowitz. So, I ask you one last time – will you join us?"

Spook pulled her shoulders back. "No. Never."

"Okay, fine," Darius replied. He walked over to the side of the room and returned holding two small daggers. She watched him, not daring to blink or take a breath, as he regarded her and Acid before tossing the daggers at their feet, the blades clattering together as they hit the ground.

No...

A sickening dread coiled in Spook's belly. She felt dizzy and nauseous and completely overwhelmed. Why the hell had she come here? And why was Acid contributing to this twisted charade?

It wasn't right. It wasn't fair.

"If you won't join us," Darius said in a low voice, "then I'm afraid there is nothing else for it. Alice, dear sister – the time has come. I want you to kill this insolent woman. Kill Spook Horowitz."

CHAPTER 40

A cid stared at the knives lying at her feet. Clip-point blades with sawtooth down one side and rust-coloured rubberised handles. They looked to be Ka-Bar knives, favoured by the US Marines.

"Take one, Alice," Darius told her. "There's one for Spook also. I thought we'd give the disappointing wretch a fighting chance. But the outcome will no doubt be the same."

She glanced at him. His eyes were blazing with eagerness.

"Do this, Alice. For me. Pick up the knife. Show me that you mean what you say. Prove your allegiance."

Acid bent down and picked up the blade, feeling its weight in her hand. Time stood still as she nodded at Spook, urging her to take up a knife.

Because this was it.

There was no other way out.

"No," Spook told her. "I won't do it. You can't make me do it." Tears were rolling down her face. "Acid, please. You have to do something. We can't let him win."

Acid gripped the knife handle. "He already has won,

Spook. But you can change your mind. Do as Darius asks. Join us. Together we'll find a way of working that you can live with. I know it's not what we had planned, but you can do this. *We* can do this. It's the only way."

Spook's gaze dropped. Her voice wavered as she spoke. "No, Acid. I can't do it. You're going to have to kill me."

"So bloody well do it!" Darius yelled. "Show us what you're made of, Acid Vanilla. Show us who you are!"

Acid tensed. A part of her was dying, but she knew it had to happen this way. She had no choice. "Pick up the knife," she told Spook.

"No."

"Pick it up!" She glared at her old friend, willing her to react.

"Kill her!" Darius growled. "Do it!"

The bats screeched in Acid's head. Deafening. Deadly. Their claws were brittle on the inside of her skull, scraping at her sanity. With a grunt she lunged at Spook, swiping the blade through the air. But Spook was too fast. She kicked her knife off into the corner of the room and scrambled after it, scooping it up into her hand.

Acid pursued her over there, eyes locked on Spook as she backed up against the wall and pushed off, raising her blade.

"Really?" Spook yelled. "This is what it's come down to? I knew we hadn't been getting on well lately, but you're actually prepared to kill me?"

Acid had never seen her so incensed. Her face was bright red. The tendons in her neck strained with the force of her rage.

"I'm sorry," Acid told her. "But it's not my decision. You did this."

"Me? Fuck you! You don't get to tell yourself that. This is on you."

They circled each other, knives outstretched, blades quivering with intensity. Acid lunged forward, thrusting her knife towards Spook's chest. But Spook dodged it and returned the attack, swinging wildly at Acid's neck. She ducked in time. The blade missed her by inches.

Shit.

Too close.

They continued their deadly dance, dodging and weaving and slashing the air with their knives as Darius and the others cheered and jeered at them. Neither woman took their eyes off the other, each aware that one wrong move could be fatal. Acid's breath came in short gasps. She didn't let her guard down for a second. Spook's agility and reaction time were impressive. She'd trained her well and the kid certainly had spirit. But she didn't have Acid's experience. She didn't have her killer instinct.

Acid took a step forward, knife raised, and Spook mirrored the movement, her own blade gleaming in the light. They lunged at each other, the chiming sound of metal on metal echoing throughout the room as their knives met.

Adrenaline surged through Acid's veins and the pressure in her head was immense. The bats filled her ears and tore at her soul.

Spook was holding her own, but Acid could sense her weakening. Her movements were becoming slower and more ungainly. Seizing the upper hand, Acid leapt forward. But once again Spook was ready for her. She side-stepped and swung her knife. A sharp pain seared through Acid's body as she felt the blade slice through the skin on her upper back.

She cried out and stumbled forward, reaching back to feel at the wound. It was a gash about the length of her finger. Deep, but not deadly. She brought her hand back around. It was covered in blood.

"Acid!" Spook was standing in front of her, an expression of shock on her face and her own knife hanging limply from her hand. "I'm sorry…"

Acid didn't give her a chance to say anything else. She charged forward, lowering her own blade as she did. Spook was too stunned to move, and Acid used this to her advantage. She barged into Spook, leading with her shoulder and knocking her into the wall. The impact forced Spook to release her grip on the knife. As it clattered to the floor, she staggered forward and Acid grabbed her arm, flipping Spook over her shoulder and onto her back. She landed with a dull thud that seemed to knock all the air out of her. As Acid stepped over her, Spook raised her eyes.

"No… Please…"

Acid knelt, pressing the cold steel of her blade against Spook's throat. The room fell silent. Acid stared into Spook's eyes seeing fear, sadness, maybe even love and hate – all the emotions rolled into one. But she herself felt nothing. She was numb. In her head the bats were insistent. They demanded blood. Her fingers tightened around the handle of the knife. Time stood still. Nobody moved.

"Please. Don't do this," Spook wheezed between gasping breaths. "This isn't you. I know it isn't."

Acid wiped at her eyes with the back of her free hand. "You're wrong, Spook," she replied. "You don't know me. You never did."

She looked up to see Darius on the other side of the

room. Their eyes met and he gave her a curt nod, raising his fist. She didn't move as his hand wavered between a thumbs-down and thumbs-up gesture, indicating death or mercy. Maybe he was taking the ancient Rome theme a little far, but his actions had the desired effect. Silence enveloped the room as his gaze swept across those assembled, ensuring everyone's attention was on him. A second went by. And another. A bead of sweat ran down Acid's face. At last, with a satisfied grin, Darius slowly tilted his thumb downwards.

"Kill her!" he commanded. "Finish her off!"

CHAPTER 41

Acid's chest tightened, her heart pounding as though trying to break free from its cage. Time slowed to a crawl while her mind raced through her options. But there was only one.

Maybe two.

She closed her eyes. Feeling the pressure of Spook's neck pushing against her knife blade.

Do it, the bats told her.

Kill her.

She drew in a breath and held it in her chest. One swift movement and it would be done. It would all be over.

No!

She opened her eyes and saw the desperation in Spook's face. Withdrawing the knife from the kid's neck, she rose to her feet and turned to face Darius.

"What the hell are you doing?" he yelled at her. "I said finish her!"

"I can't. I won't."

Darius' eyes narrowed as he glanced around the room,

gauging the reactions of his followers. Acid dropped the knife, the noise of it clattering to the floor filling the room as Darius stormed towards her. As he got closer, he crouched and picked up the knife.

"Fine. If you won't do it. Then I will." He grabbed Spook by the hair, her screaming as he dragged her into a sitting position, the knife poised to strike.

"No!" Spook yelled in defiance.

Acid was filled with something like pride as Spook's hand shot up and grabbed Darius' wrist, halting the blade before it could pierce her chest. She gritted her teeth, her face strained with effort as she held Darius off. But she was fatigued and growing weaker by the second.

"Wait!" Acid called out. "Darius!" Her voice reverberated through the room. He eased off and turned to look at her, his expression cold and inscrutable. Acid swallowed hard before she spoke. She had to make these next words count.

"Let her go," she told him. "She's nothing to us. We don't need her and you don't need her dead. If you want me to be a part of what you're building here, then let her go."

Darius stared back at her for what felt like an eternity. "Are you fucking kidding me?" he scoffed.

"No, I'm not. Free her and I'm yours. For good." She went to him and placed one hand on his shoulder and the other on the hand gripping the knife. "Think about it, Darius. This way you'll have her over me, too. Proper leverage. That's how you know you can trust me." She leaned into him, easing the knife away from Spook's chest. She sensed the hesitation in his muscles, but felt his grip loosen. "You'll always be able to get to her," she continued. "Wherever Spook is, wherever she goes, someone like you, with your capabilities and resources, can find her. I don't want Spook to die. She doesn't deserve to. She's a civilian by any other name. She's not part of this world. She never was. But I am. I want this, Darius. I want to work alongside you. And after everything that's happened between us, there may be times my loyalty is in question. I don't want that. This is how you can trust that I'm here to stay. Let Spook go. She's nothing, but together you and I can be everything."

She let go of Darius and stepped back, not taking her eyes off him.

They could have heard a pin drop in the room. The tension was almost unbearable. Darius chuckled to himself, let go of Spook's hair and lowered the blade. "Fine," he said and sighed. "She can go."

As the pressure in the room dissipated, Acid felt the weight of her decision resting heavily on her shoulders. This was it. She was now a member of Kancel Kulture. As Darius strode away, shaking his head and muttering to himself, she stepped forward and offered Spook her hand. After a moment's hesitation, Spook accepted her help and stood up on shaky legs.

"Are you expecting me to say thank you?" she asked.

Acid didn't meet her eye. "I'm not expecting anything of you, Spook. The same way you should never have expected anything of me."

Spook brushed herself down, doing a decent impression of someone with their act together. But Acid detected the tremor in her voice as she spoke. "What do I do now?"

Acid made a face. "What do you do? You get the fuck out of this place, that's what. You go and live your life. You don't need me. You never did. We weren't good together anyway."

Spook brought her hands up to her face. "But, Acid, you can't seriously—"

"I can, Spook! All right? I can. Darius is offering me a lifeline here. He's my brother. And this is my world. You don't need to understand it. You just have to accept it." She glanced over her shoulder at Darius, who nodded and waved the knife at her. She turned back to Spook. "He's offering me a new life, Spook. Doing what I know. I should never have left this life behind. I should never have disobeyed Caesar. But here we are. I'm not a good person like you. I'm not even a proper adult. You're always telling me I'm a selfish teenager. Well, that's me. Being an assassin is the only thing I've ever been good at. It's what I am. It's the only life I've ever known."

Spook glared at her, the tears running down her face belying the fierce expression. "I hate you," she hissed.

"Good. It's easier that way."

"Go to hell."

Acid looked away. She couldn't blame the kid for being this way. It was a shock for her, but the trust between them had been shattered irreparably. She had no choice. One day, maybe, she'd make things right. But for now, she was here.

"Give me your word she can go free," Acid called out to Darius.

"You have it," he replied, waving the knife at the others. "Do you hear that, everyone? No one touches the nerd. Saga, can you please escort Ms Horowitz out of the building? I'm sick of the bloody sight of her."

The tall blond man approached and grabbed Spook's arm. "Come with me," he said, leading her away. Spook held Acid's gaze as she was hustled across the room, but her face was stern and her eyes cold.

"I don't want to see or hear from you ever again," Darius called after her. "If I even get half a sense that you're becoming a nuisance for me or my organisation, I will find you and I will slice off your eyelids. Then I'll round up every single person you've ever come into contact with and make you watch as I slaughter them in front of you before skinning you alive. Do you understand?"

Spook didn't respond. But clearly she understood. The same way Acid understood. Darius Duke was a madman with immense power at his fingertips. You crossed him at your peril.

Acid didn't blink as Stig Saga dragged Spook out of view. She was still staring at the empty doorway when Darius appeared beside her and put his arm around her shoulders. "There we are, Sis. All sorted," he said. "Welcome to your new life at Kancel Kulture. You made the right choice today."

Acid didn't turn her attention from the door. "Yes," she replied. "I suppose we'll see about that."

CHAPTER 42

Spook was still in shock as the blond man led her from the Kancel Kulture headquarters and deposited her on a bench in the piazza outside. The air was warm on her face as she stared up at him.

"You were very lucky today," he said, stabbing a long, bony finger at her. "It's a good job for you Darius is a sympathetic leader. But believe what he says. If you appear on our radar again, for whatever reason at all, you will regret it. And you will regret it over and over and over for many, many days until you are begging not to feel anything at all ever again."

Spook nodded. "Okay. I get it."

"Good. Now go. And do not tell anyone what you have seen today. Be warned I will be watching you. If you do anything that gives me cause for concern, I will be there. I will come for you while you sleep. I will be your nightmares personified."

"Yes!" Spook snapped. "I get it!"

Even if she'd had the courage and means to hit back at

these evil bastards, how did she even begin? She had nothing. She had no one. It was just her now.

She was alone.

She wanted to cry. She wanted to scream. But she didn't even have the energy for that. As the man walked away, she got up from the bench and wandered across the grand piazza and crossed over the wide avenue of traffic with little care for her own safety. Cars and bikes beeped their horns at her, irate drivers leaning out of their windows and shouting expletives at her in Italian.

Spook didn't react. She didn't care.

With no idea where she was going, she kept walking regardless. The hot city was bustling with traffic and people, but she paid no attention to anyone or anything. All she could think about was Acid and the look in her friend's eyes as she'd held the knife to her throat.

She walked until her feet hurt and then she kept walking. She was in a daze, lost in her own thoughts and oblivious to the world around her. Her mind was racing and it felt like it would never stop. She'd been naïve to think she could ever change someone like Acid. To believe, even, that Acid was someone who wanted to be saved.

Eventually, she stumbled into a small park and sat beneath a tall tree. There, away from the crowds and the buzz of the city, she sat back and allowed the pain and the tears to find her. She cried for herself, for everything she'd gone through in her life. And she cried for Acid, too, who seemed more broken now than she had ever been.

Had she always known it would end like this?

At some point, Spook's heart rate slowed and the tears stopped. As they did, something shifted inside of her. Her flame of determination was refusing to be extinguished. Spook Horowitz had been a thorn in Acid Vanilla's side since the moment they'd met, but Acid needed that thorn.

Spook got to her feet as a fresh spark of hope ignited in her belly. She wasn't ready to stop believing in Acid. That woman had a dark soul and more demons than most people, but she'd saved Spook's life today. Spook wasn't going to let her throw her life away with that evil bastard. With renewed confidence she set off walking again, heading back to her hotel. She had an important phone call to make.

———

SPOOK WAS SITTING in the garden, reading her book and enjoying the last moments of the day's sun, when Nate appeared carrying a bottle of wine and two glasses.

"Mind if I join you?" he asked, sitting down before she replied.

"Sure. It's your place."

He smiled. "You've been spending almost as much time here as me lately. It's starting to feel like it's your place, too." He raised his eyebrows as he leaned in. "Like we discussed, it can be."

Ten days had passed since Spook had called Nate and had him pick her up from Cardiff Airport. Eleven days since she'd last seen Acid.

The pain was still raw and Spook was still angry as hell, but with Nate's help she'd been channelling it into her training. She was determined to get into peak physical condition. Strong and able for what came next. Each day she got up at dawn, pushing herself relentlessly. It didn't take away the fear of what was ahead, or how much Acid had meant to her, but it was a start.

"Have you thought any more about my offer?" Nate asked. The sun had almost set, casting a pink tinge over the garden as he poured them both a glass of wine. It was white wine. Spook hated white wine, but she accepted the glass from him all the same.

"Are you sure you want me on board?" she asked. "I mean, I'd be more than happy to take on the role and carry out whatever tech work you need. But I want something in return."

Nate grinned. "As well as the incredibly generous salary I'm offering?"

"Yeah. Sorry, but I need this. And I'm done being Little Miss Timid. You've got to ask for what you want in this life. People can only say no."

Nate nodded, eyeing her over his glass of wine. "And what is it you want?"

She placed her glass down without drinking from it. "You know what I want, Nate. I want you to train me. Not just for two weeks, but for as long as it takes to get me where I need to be." She sat upright, feeling her face tighten along with her resolve. "I want to be the best. I want to be deadly."

Nate smiled. He'd already been helping Spook with a few extra training sessions, but she needed more. She needed to be properly trained, so when the time came she'd be ready. Ready to hit back at those evil bastards with whatever strength and courage she could muster.

"Are you certain of this?" he asked, placing his glass down. "It's going to take a lot of work on your part. And I will be asking a lot of you in terms of the tech side of things also.

Especially as more operatives come on board. Do you think you can handle it?"

Spook fixed him with a hard stare. "Yes," she said. "I can handle it. I'll do whatever I need to."

"And later – when you think you're ready – are you prepared for that, too? It's going to be dangerous. Very dangerous."

She didn't take her eyes off his. "I know how risky it will be. But it's the only way I can get my friend back."

"And what if Acid doesn't want that?" Nate asked. "What if we've lost her to Kancel Kulture? What then?"

Spook sniffed. He made a good point and it was one she'd been struggling to deal with for the last eleven days. The truth was, she had no idea what was going on in Acid's head. All she knew was she couldn't give up on her.

"I've got to try," she whispered. "I've got to."

Nate gave her an encouraging smile and patted her arm before standing up. "All right then, Little Miss Badass. Forget about drinks on the lawn. We need to head back inside."

"Oh? What for?"

"Knife skills," he replied, offering her his hand. "Until nightfall at least. Then I was thinking we could go on a midnight run to the nearest lake and back. How does that sound?"

Spook grinned and took his hand. "It sounds good," she said. "Let's do this."

THE END

––––––

WANT MORE ACID?

GET YOUR FREE BOOK

Discover how Acid Vanilla transformed from a typical London teenager into the world's deadliest female assassin.

Get the Acid Vanilla Prequel Novel available FREE at:

www.matthewhattersley.com/mak

CAN YOU HELP?

Enjoyed this book? You can make a big difference

Honest reviews of my books help bring them to the attention of other readers. If you've enjoyed this book I would be very grateful if you could spend just five minutes leaving a review (it can be as short as you like) on the book's Amazon page.

ALSO BY MATTHEW HATTERSLEY

Have you read them all?

————

The Acid Vanilla series

Acid Vanilla

Acid Vanilla is an elite assassin, struggling with her mental health. Spook Horowitz is a mild-mannered hacker who saw something she shouldn't. Acid needs a holiday. Spook needs Acid Vanilla to NOT be coming to kill her. But life rarely works out the way we want it to.

BUY IT HERE

Seven Bullets

Acid Vanilla was the deadliest assassin at Annihilation Pest Control. That was until she was tragically betrayed by her former colleagues. Now, fuelled by an insatiable desire for vengeance, Acid travels the globe to carry out her bloody retribution. After all, a girl needs a hobby...

BUY IT HERE

Making a Killer

How it all began. Discover Acid Vanilla's past, her meeting with Caesar and how she became the deadliest female assassin in the world.

———

Stand-alone novels

Double Bad Things

All undertaker Mikey wants is a quiet life and to write his comics. But then he's conned into hiding murders in closed-casket burials by a gang who are also trafficking young girls. Can a gentle giant whose only friends are a cosplay-obsessed teen and an imaginary alien really take down the gang and avoid arrest himself?

Double Bad Things is a dark and quirky crime thriller - for fans of Dexter and Six Feet Under.

Cookies

Will Miles find love again after the worst six months of his life? The fortune cookies say yes. But they also say commit arson and murder, so maybe it's time to stop believing in them? If only he could...

"If you life Fight Club, you'll love Cookies." - TL Dyer, Author

BUY IT HERE

ABOUT THE AUTHOR

Over the last twenty years Matthew Hattersley has toured Europe in rock n roll bands, trained as a professional actor and founded a theatre and media company. He's also had a lot of dead end jobs...

Now he writes high-octane pulp action thrillers and crime fiction.

He lives with his wife and daughter in Derbyshire, UK and doesn't feel that comfortable writing about himself in the third person.

COPYRIGHT

Printed in Great Britain
by Amazon